THE ACCIDENTAL HEIRESS

MARY KENDALL

BLOODHOUND
B O O K S

First published in 2025 by Bloodhound Books.

www.bloodhoundbooks.com

Print ISBN: 978-1-917449-5-57

For Dart,
With love and eternal gratitude.

PART 1

PROLOGUE
WINTER 1931

The dog's stub of a tail thumped back and forth on the old hardwood floor until it finally got Margaret's attention. An immediate grin came over her face at the sight of Oliver, her Russell Terrier. It was time for a break and some fresh air—for both of them.

Margaret stood up and stretched her back, feeling an associated crack or two. The tall windows on the front and side of the room offered glimpses of the surrounding land. Her horse farm, Needham Forest. Squinting from where she stood, she could make out two of her horses gamboling in the day's sunshine.

She tossed a last glance at the pile of paperwork, through which she was finally making some headway. "Alright then. Let's go outside, boy." Oliver scrambled to his feet and raced out in front of her to the center hallway. Wide and generous, it spanned from front to back of her Federal-era home.

Margaret opened the door and paused at the sight. It was a thing of beauty within her view, the result of her father's blood, sweat and tears before her, and her own after him. The fields were tended to, the stables all in order. It wasn't easy and she had come too close to losing it more than once. But everything was getting back on track.

She heard a low rumble from Needham Forest's driveway and recognized it right off. Robert's roadster made its approach, eventually reaching the entrance circle in front of the two-story brick house.

A smile played at her mouth, breaking out fully as he emerged from the vehicle. Their relationship was still on the newish side and her heart still pitter-pattered at the sight of him, tall, dark and handsome, almost cliché-ishly so.

"This is a surprise." She paused at his expression, serious and grave. "What's happened?"

"Margaret, I didn't know if you had heard yet." He took his hat off and brushed his dark hair back with one hand.

"Heard what? From whom? I've been here all morning. What is it?"

He wiped a hand over his mouth as if he just couldn't get the words out. She had never seen him so nonplussed, so jarred before. Oliver began to run in circles around the two of them, demanding his walk now.

"It's Bill Miller."

Margaret conjured up Bill in her mind. A friend of old from when her father had owned the horse farm and, more recently, her new business partner. In fact, Bill had become a father figure, engaging the world in the same brash, no-holds-barred style as her father had done.

Robert knew Bill from his career as an attorney. They were in separate law practices but moved in the same circles. Bill was a well-known and respected criminal defense lawyer while Robert mostly handled civil cases. He sometimes dabbled in estate affairs, which was how he and Margaret had met over her Aunt Blanche's case.

Alarm rinsed through her at Bill's fate. "What happened? Is

it a heart attack?" Bill, in his mid-fifties, had seemed in fair shape physically when they last met. But emotionally...

"No, no. Not that. But..."

She looked at Robert full-on. His visage was more than troubled; it was tortured. "Robert, spit it out. What's happened?"

He inhaled sharply and then said, "Bill shot Dr. Michaels on G Street this morning."

CHAPTER ONE

SIX MONTHS EARLIER

As Robert's automobile sped through Maryland's horse country, Margaret felt the breeze whip through her short, bobbed hairdo. It was a perfect late summer day with her favorite companion. As she snuck a peek at Robert, an all-round contentment came over her. She was still entangled in her tattered marriage (which she was untangling in divorce proceedings), but this had not diminished the luster of their new relationship. She had not realized the lack of a Robert Brady in her life—until he was in her life.

They had both been working long hours of late—she desperately trying to keep her horse farm afloat; he on a case involving a scandalous divorce between a well-heeled D.C. couple. This was not only a much-deserved day out though. It was also the premiere happening in the upcoming fall season for the horsey set, a five-star event. It was rare for such an event to occur in Margaret's little corner of the nation's horse world and so it was a not-to-be-missed occasion.

More importantly, it gave Margaret a chance to meet and greet. With the recent economic downturns from the crash on Wall Street the previous fall, Needham Forest needed an infusion of funds. Margaret, almost out of options, was toying with the idea of opening the farm up to potential investors of a sort... a sort not yet determined.

Setting those thoughts aside, Margaret reached over and gave Robert's jawline a light caress. He turned and gave her a crooked smile in return. She felt a flush of satisfaction at how harmonious they were, so unlike the turmoil she had gone through with Keith, her soon-to-be ex. There was no strife or conflict between her and Robert, rather just an ease. She marveled how they merged into a perfect sympatico, not even having to say what they were thinking. It felt like that for her, anyway.

In the near distance, the rolling fields revealed Bailey Farm, a long-established operation. They pulled into the field that was serving as parking for the many who were attending the Montgomery Hunt Cup. Robert squeezed his vehicle into a tight spot as spaces rapidly filled in. After he placed the roadster in gear and lodged the parking brake, he leaned over to give her a kiss on her cheek. "Have I mentioned how fetching you look this morning?"

"You have not. But now I will assume that is the case." She smiled at him and he gave her a wink.

Margaret snuck a quick peek in her compact while Robert exited the car to come over to her side. She took his hand feeling a spark at the contact. Upon emerging, she smoothed down her toile dress with its whimsical design: blue ponies playing on a white backdrop. Then she placed her hat on, a white straw cloche with a big bow on the back. Robert's pinstripe blue suit hung on his form perfectly, showing off an enviable physique. A straw boater hat provided the crowning touch.

They made their way on the tamped down grasses of the farm field to the big tented area where all the action would be occurring. As they walked by people she knew, Margaret was immediately pulled into the social niceties. The horsey set was not known for shrinking violets. In fact, there were more larger-than-life characters than not. Robert waited patiently through each interchange until they could eventually move to the drinks station.

A waiter, dressed in the fanciest attire of the station, a black cummerbund covering a formal white dress shirt, spoke to Margaret. "What is your beverage of choice, madam?"

"What's the house flavor?" Margaret asked.

"It's the Bee's Knees today, ma'am."

She held up two fingers, grateful, not for the first time, that her state looked the other way at the so called "Prohibition" mandates and the drinks could flow.

"What kind of witch's brew are you forcing on me, Margaret?" Robert said.

"'Tis the season, Robert—almost anyway. The fall horse season. You'll love it. Gin, lemon and a lot of honey. The honey part will keep you sweet on me."

"Fair enough."

With drinks in hand, they worked through the crowd with Margaret stopping to chit-chat along the way. Robert kept to her side, a most suitable companion, attentive with just the right touch of interest.

In the middle of a conversation with an elderly couple who lived several farms over from Needham Forest, Robert's attention was snagged. Margaret turned to see what caught his eye. A man of some stature entered into the center of the tent with a bevy of hangers-on circling around him. His voice boomed in a stentorian style while the others laughed and hung on every word. His off-white handlebar mustache matched a similar color seersucker suit. Tucked into him on one arm was a much younger woman, blonde and buxom, gazing at him with a needy expression.

Margaret felt the jolt of recognition and, with that jolt, pleasure. It had been years since her path had crossed with Bill Miller's, a man who had been an integral part of Needham Forest during her childhood. Bill Miller had been a stable-hand but, more than that, as her father had a particular bond and comradery with him. Margaret too had been drawn to him.

Unlike the other adults in their world, Bill had always greeted Margaret and her sister, Judith, with a warmth and familiarity that put them at ease. In his pocket, he carried a roll of mints, on offer upon the sight of them. With a flick of his thumb, the circular piece of sweet would fall into Margaret's open palm. Now, she could almost taste the distinctive flavor of the candy as she gazed at him.

Judging from the group circled around him, he apparently still had that same easy way with people. She strode forward until she was within his sight. He broke off mid-sentence. "Well, if it isn't little Margaret Magruder!" A huge smile came over his face as he reached out and grabbed both of her hands to shake them effusively.

Robert's voice spoke up next to her. "Worlds collide here, I guess. Hello, Bill."

"Bobby!" Bill's large arm reached forward pulling Robert closer to him to shake his hand. "What a surprise." Margaret held in a snicker at Robert being called the diminutive nickname that in no way suited him. "Now, how do you two rascals know each other?"

A confusion of re-introductions ensued with all three of them explaining their connections. Between the three of them, they sorted it out. Margaret knew Bill from the early days of her childhood, before Bill had left to enlist during the Spanish American conflict. His journey after that meandered until he ended up in the law. Now, he was the biggest criminal defense attorney in the city according to the newspaper articles she would come upon from time to time. She and Bill were strangers really these days but the sight of him was like finding a piece of her childhood.

Robert knew Bill as a brother-lawyer. They shared the same law circles and affiliations and sometimes even the same court rooms. Margaret and Robert knew each other because...well... for other reasons.

After their triangle became straightened out, Bill beamed at them both. "Well, well, well. The famous Mrs. O'Keefe. Horsewoman extraordinaire. What a lucky man you are, Bobby."

The young woman standing next to Bill tugged on his arm. Margaret assumed she was a daughter. "Huh? Oh yes. Here is my beautiful bride, Jocelyn."

At first glance, Bill's "bride" was unassuming. She stood a petite height with a wreath of bright blonde hair above big, blue eyes. But there was a deeper pull...something about her that Margaret couldn't put a finger on. Pieces of her made the package: the hair color, the buxomness, and the batting of the big eyes with a come-hither look.

Jocelyn pasted on a bright smile and shook hands first with Robert. Then she turned to Margaret. "A pleasure to meet you."

"Indeed," Margaret said, holding in her surprise at the age difference between the couple. The phrase "gold digger" popped into mind but Margaret internally berated herself for not being fair. She tried to set aside negative prejudice about older men marrying young girls as she shook the woman's hand.

The announcer interrupted Margaret's musings. His British accent boomed out that the event would now take place and to please make due haste to the seating areas. It seemed a thing that only men with British accents, fake or real, could perform the job of announcer, Margaret always thought.

"Come sit with us. Whadda you say?" Bill Miller asked them.

Robert deferred to Margaret who nodded. They had no particular plans otherwise and she felt the pull of being in Bill's orbit just as she had felt as a child. Bill's designated seating area spilled over with a cast of many but he made the pronouncement that the others needed to move aside for Margaret and Robert to sit right beside him and his bride.

In between the different events in the backdrop, Bill Miller regaled those in his circle with stories of his younger years. It finally emerged how he ended up back in the horse business with his own horses stabled outside the town of Brookeville in the upper northeast corner of the county. It was crystal clear the man still loved horses and all related to them.

Margaret snapped her fingers. "Wait a minute. Now I'm putting it together. You're the owner of Not Guilty!" The young Arabian stud had swept the previous season's races in an upset that no one predicted.

Bill's face widened with his grin. "That's right."

Robert interjected. "Well, are you in the market for other winners?" He gestured to Margaret. "Needham Forest is still going gangbusters in that department."

Bill's eyes squinted into a shrewd expression. "Is that right? Tell me more, little Margaret."

Margaret began to detail all of Needham Forest's past winners, not only under her father's reign but under hers as well. She trailed off by saying, "With the past couple of seasons, we've lagged a bit but..."

"But?"

She drew a breath in. Now was the moment. "I'm angling for a couple of folks to...invest. Still not sure how exactly that will look but we can breed winners again. I know that. And anyone involved could have their name stamped on those winners."

Bill sat back and studied Margaret. There was a look of affection on his face and, behind it, memories of days gone by, good memories. "Well, you know, that might be something for me to consider...something for me to get involved in."

Margaret couldn't stop her huge smile. "Wouldn't that be a full circle moment?"

Bill gazed out towards the horses beyond the tent before responding. Then he said, "Yes. Yes, it certainly would be. Let's think on it."

By the end of the event, they had verbally set up a loose arrangement. Bill wanted to invest in more horses and Margaret had just the plan for him to do so as a potential partner in Needham Forest's operation. The reconnection with this beloved character from her childhood was a fortuitous boon.

As they all walked together towards the field where the cars were parked, Jocelyn wobbled, unsteady in her high heels, but also maybe from too many cocktails. While Bill and Margaret chatted away, Jocelyn giggled incessantly behind them at whatever Robert said, leaving Margaret with pinpricks of annoyance.

Once they reached a dark-colored Packard, Bill said, "This is us here."

"Well, safe travels to you, Bill. We aren't too far away from the farm here for our drive."

"I remember the location well." Bill gave her a wink that she could just make out in the dimming light of the day. "It's quite a spot, your farm. You know, I've got to ask. Did you ever find that treasure that your father was always hunting for?"

Robert and Margaret shared a look, assuming Bill was referring to her Aunt Blanche's treasure trove in her father's boyhood home in Georgetown. That was how Robert and

Margaret had met, in fact. Robert had been the receiving lawyer on the case.

"You mean down in Georgetown where my father grew up? You might have read about that case in the papers. Robert was involved in it."

Bill placed a foot on the running board next to the driver's door with Jocelyn hanging on one arm. "No, no. Your pop always waxed on whenever we threw back a couple drinks. He said treasure was hidden somewhere at Needham Forest. Always swore me to secrecy but I figured all the family knew."

Margaret was struck silent. She had never heard of this. Ever. The effect from a couple of Bee's Knees drinks lifted right away at this startling revelation. "Um...did he say what the treasure was comprised of?"

"Yes, indeedy. Gold bars. Confederate gold bars. Hidden during the Civil War."

Again, Margaret fell silent, stunned by the specificity of Bill's memory.

"Anyway, we can talk more about it when we meet next. Mix in horse talk with treasure talk. How about it?" He let out a big chuckle as he walked Jocelyn to the passenger side of the car.

"Yes. I would like to hear more. Definitely."

CHAPTER TWO

As Robert and Margaret drove away from Bailey Farm, the glow of the possible arrangement with Bill was tinged with some confusion about his revelation. Robert's voice broke into rolling thoughts taking her in all directions.

"I had no idea you knew Bill Miller, Margaret. You are a woman of many secrets. He is probably the most well-connected lawyer in town."

"Huh? Oh yes. I guess it never came up in conversation. But I hadn't seen him in years. I think it was my father's funeral..." Her words drifted off. The funeral. She thought back to that gray and awful day. There would hardly have been any discussion about a hidden Civil War cache then. If there had been, in her state of grief, she would not have been aware of it.

"And how about him wanting to invest in Needham Forest? What do you think?"

Margaret's brain switched to business mode. "What an unexpected godsend. And thank you...for steering Bill in that direction."

"Of course. I think it was good fortune overall running into Bill Miller today. In more ways than one."

"Absolutely. The only downside so far is that it's a package deal. That wife."

"Now, now. She's just young."

"Ugh, yes. Well, tell me about that marriage, Robert. How many years between the pair of them? Twenty, you think?"

"Oh, north of that I suspect. I've heard twenty-five."

"My word! That just seems preposterous."

"Well, they seem quite happy though. He is clearly besotted with her. Treats her like spun glass, doesn't he?"

"But, Robert, think how it would look if it were the other way around."

He shot her a glance. "What do you mean, the other way around?"

"Well...if she was fifty or so and he was twenty-five or thereabouts..."

"Wouldn't work, would it?"

Margaret gave an inelegant snort and Robert chuckled in an unspoken recognition of that societal double standard.

"Anyway, it's nice to see Bill happy. He was so devoted to Katie. Her death devastated him."

The name was unfamiliar to Margaret. "Katie?"

"His first wife. Oh...you didn't know he was married before?"

"No. We lost touch with him...what happened?"

Robert shrugged. "I think it was sudden. A couple years back."

"Well...how long after did he remarry?"

"Pretty soon after I think. He certainly takes delight in having Jocelyn on his arm. Kind of like he has won the spoils in a game."

Margaret shook her head and again kept silent thinking about that particular game. Especially because she had never revealed her exact age to Robert. She was older than him by about four years, give or take. It had never come up directly in conversation and she saw no real need to put too fine a point on the matter.

Many women played a bit of subterfuge when it came to their ages. She and Robert were in the right ballpark of each other's birth years as far as she was concerned. Unlike the Miller couple. And she could hardly imagine Robert to be bothered by such a minor detail.

She put it out of her head and instead thought about Jocelyn. Margaret had been ensnared into a plan to meet for lunch at Jocelyn's preferred department store in the city, Woodward & Lothrop. With Bill gazing at his wife with indulgent eyes, Margaret knew she had to say yes. Even though she did not know how she would make it through a meal with the woman.

From their limited engagement at the Hunt Cup event, it was clear the two of them didn't have much common ground aside from Bill. Jocelyn had seemed simple at best, yet, given her marital situation, maybe she was craftier than met the eye.

Margaret would go and make it happen. If nothing else, she might check out the lingerie section to spruce up her nighttime wear. On the off chance...she looked at Robert...well, on the off chance she might have a gentleman caller soon in the evenings.

After Robert had departed with some last lingering kisses, Margaret sat by her phone table to place a long overdue call to her sister, Judith, in New York City. Judith led a bohemian lifestyle as an off-Broadway actress. The vast differences between the sisters had been a source of contention but they had recently bridged the gap. Ironically, the death of their estranged aunt, Blanche, brought them together, the harsh reality making them both realize their need for connection with each other. Now, Margaret needed to tap into Judith's memory to see if she had ever heard anything about this supposed treasure.

As the call whipped through the wires going north, Margaret imagined Judith in her third-floor walkup on the Upper West side of Manhattan. Hopefully, she was home for the evening and relaxing in one of the bright and colorful caftans she wore as loungewear.

Judith's voice soon rang out with a melodic hello and Margaret felt a burst of pleasure at the sound of it. "Judith! It's been too long."

"Mags darling! How are you?"

The sisters settled into a comfortable chat to catch each other up on their lives. Margaret held back at first to hear about how the economic woes spilling over from Black Thursday, as they were now calling it, were affecting the arts on Broadway and Judith's life. Judith gave a glum summary and finished with, "...but I am holding my own, dear gal. As I am sure you are too."

Margaret couldn't wait to share the news of her day out any longer. "I've had the strangest day and...I may have found a silent partner for the farm."

"Oh darling. That's wonderful. I'm so glad for you. I know what that old sod means to you."

"And Judith, guess who it is?"

"Just tell me."

"Bill Miller!"

"Wait, Daddy's farm hand? Well, how did that come about?"

Margaret quickly filled Judith in on Bill's meteoric rise to success as an attorney after he had left Needham Forest.

"How ironic. That he started as a stable boy at Needham Forest, I mean."

"I know, life is like that sometimes, I guess. Early days yet but he is quite taken now with horse racing and has the capital to invest. But here's the thing that came out of all this…"

She paused until Judith prodded, saying, "What?"

"He said Daddy and he had conversations about a treasure."

Judith yawned aloud and then said, "You already found the treasure at Aunt Blanche's. That was a wrap as they say in the film world."

"No, no. He was very specific about it. Hidden here. At Needham Forest."

"What did he say it was?"

"Gold bars from the Confederates."

"Oh my…"

The sisters fell silent with just a crackle over the tenuous phone wire to be heard.

Margaret cleared her throat. "So do you remember Daddy— or Mother—ever talking about this?"

"No. Not at all. But my head was always more in the clouds than yours, Margaret. If anyone would know about it, it would be you. You were Daddy's confidante."

The specter of a jealous history and family dynamics rose up between them but Margaret quickly tapped it down. "Well, he definitely didn't confide in me about this. But…"

"But?"

"Maybe it's worth looking into."

"Mags, don't you think we would have found something like this? I mean, we were into everything all over the place when we were children. Remember that time we found the cache of hat pins with the pearled tips tucked behind the mantelpiece?"

"Yes, I agree. Especially when we played the hide and seek games and got more inventive with the hiding places but still…"

"How would you even go about finding this supposed treasure?

"I'll figure something out."

The sisters wrapped up their late-night conversation with Margaret left to muse about how to do exactly that—figure it all out—as she prepared for her bed and sleep.

CHAPTER THREE

The next morning, Margaret soaked in the peaceful quiet of her dining room. It was such a contrast to the barrage of images left over from the previous day at the horse event. She had barely eaten anything with the day's constant stream of people and ensuing conversations. That was a shame since the Maryland Horse Association laid out a magnificent spread.

Now, she tucked into the breakfast plate in front of her with gusto. It included eggs over easy, bacon from a nearby farm and Cassie's buttermilk biscuits with raspberry jam, all a welcome sight, prettily displayed on a flow blue china plate from her mother's wedding pattern. So far, she had been able to hold onto such family heirlooms even though the bills were again piling up.

Her gaze moved around the room to the peeling paint of the dining room ceiling. Triggered by the sight, Margaret couldn't stop the heavy sigh that slipped out. Necessary improvements and maintenance were on hold. But upkeep of a hundred-year-old house and farm demanded regular attention. She was loath to admit to herself that she could not keep up.

She had also been forced to let go of a couple of the trainers.

Her maid, Cassie, was now the only staff in the house aside from Cassie's husband, Albert, who pinched hit as Margaret's driver now and again.

A few months before the crash on Wall Street, Margaret just about managed to get finances on an even keel. Her no-good, soon-to-be ex-husband, Keith, had been hemorrhaging funds for years from the operation. An eleventh-hour inheritance from her Aunt Blanche saved the day and provided the farm with a much-needed resuscitation.

But, right on the heels of that, the unforeseen and unavoidable calamity of Black Thursday with its ongoing fallout occurred. Depression or not though, there were still people with money, some spending it on their pastime of choice, horses. Even FDR himself was from a family devoted to their horses. Margaret had only managed to stay afloat to date because horses were her business.

But she desperately needed more cash flow to spare Needham Forest the worst fate. Out of all the social whirl of the previous day, the stand-out was meeting up with Bill Miller. It held the promise and potential of a satisfying collaboration that might just get her out of the dicey economic downturn.

As she again gazed at the peeling paint and the room around her, she thought about the treasure that Bill mentioned. Could she even entertain the notion of it? That there was a gold cache somewhere around her very own house and farm? Surely, Bill Miller was mistaken. But, he was a sharp shooter, not likely to misremember something like this.

It seemed ridiculous, fanciful even. Yet what if it was real and not a fantasy? It could take care of a lot. In fact, maybe it could even get Needham Forest back on the map as a showplace, an operation known throughout not only the country but maybe the world. She owed nothing less to her father.

Sighing, she picked up a piece of bacon and concentrated instead on the satisfying crunch it made as she bit into it.

The phone rang in the hall and shook her out of her reveries. She could hear Cassie speaking in a low rumble. A few minutes later, the door between the dining room and kitchen swung open and Cassie strode in with a coffee pot in hand. Her usual cheery expression was replaced with a glower. "He's calling again."

Margaret exhaled heavily, understanding who "he" referred to. Keith, the soon-to-be ex. The one who had tried to bleed out Needham Forest. The one who was stonewalling her efforts to get their divorce finalized. Anger at him surged through her all over again.

"I put him off but he'll just keep at it." Cassie's voice was raised to a level that expressed her agitation at the situation. As she refreshed Margaret's coffee cup, she added, "He's a stubborn cuss alright."

Margaret put a hand up. "It's fine, Cassie. I'll deal with him."

Cassie left the room, mumbling and shaking her head.

After finishing her breakfast, Margaret knew she couldn't avoid it any longer. She sat in the hallway at the phone table and lifted the receiver. Keith answered on the fourth ring.

She headed him off at the pass. "Keith, you can't call here. You know that. All communication is through the lawyers now."

"Margaret, my dove. So nice to finally get through to you. Cassie might as well be wearing chain armor these days, blocking me from connecting with you." Keith's familiar velvety voice oozed over the line, sending with it an immediate feeling of revulsion.

"Well, just stop calling and—"

"I can't stop calling. The thing is, this has really gone too far now."

"What?"

"This laughable farce of a divorce on your part."

Margaret groaned inwardly as he went into his rant about how it shouldn't be happening. A loop he was stuck in, seemingly with amnesia because he was the one that brought this on himself.

She cut him off. "Keith, call your lawyer. We are done with these conversations." She placed the receiver down and lowered her head. What a mess. Her lawyer was supposedly one of the best divorce lawyers around. He laid out in no uncertain terms that Keith did not have a leg to stand on.

Keith himself could not even afford a decent lawyer for his countersuit against Margaret's assets. Instead, he was relying on an inebriated (most of the time) lawyer friend from the track. The same track where Keith almost gambled all of Needham Forest away. After being caught with money stolen from her aunt's estate, Keith had no basis to his countersuit at all.

If she had known how hard it would be to extricate herself from a marriage and a husband, well, sometimes she wondered if she would have ever gotten married at all. The fallout of her marriage made her question if any of it had ever been worth the while. But it did no good at all to dwell on that. As her father always said, "No use crying over spilt milk".

On the other hand, the companionship with Robert was exactly her cup of tea. Why, she could even envision it continuing just as it was indefinitely. A very modern solution. Although it would be nice to have him by her side in the evenings and, if she was being honest, in the mornings over coffee where they could share with each other plans for the day.

She was getting way ahead of herself. She couldn't even get out of her legally binding relationship with Keith yet. It did no good to fantasize about another situation. No good at all. Best plan was to concentrate on her business dealings.

As Margaret sat and pondered, the phone ringing right next to her made her startle. When she answered, a high pitched, sing-song voice rang out of the other end. "Margaret? Is that you?"

"Yes. Who's calling?"

"It's Jocelyn Miller."

Margaret held back a sigh. "Oh yes. Hello."

"I wanted to set our plan for meeting at Woodward & Lothrop this week."

Margaret mentally calculated when she might know for certain whether Bill Miller would actually become her partner. Robert was going to set up a lunch meeting when Bill had an opening. If that wasn't going to be the case, did she need to engage with this woman? On the other hand, it might be an edge with Bill when they did meet. "Ah yes. This week is a bit tight. But, I do have Wednesday open."

The other woman gave a little squeal. "That would be perfect! How about we meet in the lobby at noon?"

Margaret murmured her agreement and quickly ended the call by saying, "Must run, Jocelyn. See you then."

CHAPTER FOUR

Margaret walked briskly into the grand entrance of Woodward & Lothrop; the eight-story high department store favored by so many in the shopping district. It advertised itself as a "store worthy of the nation's capital", a stand-out with its dramatic Romanesque Revival architecture. With the store's veneer of wealth and glamour and its busy comings and goings, Margaret could almost forget the sting of the times they were in.

Margaret heard that department stores were trying to stay viable by offering entertainment. This store included a pianist positioned in the elegant entry foyer, tickling the ivories with light-hearted tunes. As Margaret looked away from the pianist, her eye was caught by the vivid red of Jocelyn's dress. She was waiting by a potted palm off to the side.

Margaret paused and assessed the other woman. The color red accented her hourglass figure and nicely contrasted with her blonde-colored hair. Her appearance danced just on the edge of an overt sexuality. Like many women trying to catch the eye of a gent or two, Jocelyn appeared to be packaging herself in a tried-and-true manner.

There was no doubt Jocelyn could capture the

imagination of the opposite sex handily. Yet, as Jocelyn gazed around with a vacant look, Margaret also sensed something wistful and childlike. Margaret suspected there was more to discover about Jocelyn, much more. Her eyes caught the other woman's and she gave a wave and approached.

Jocelyn immediately gushed out nervous chatter. "Hello, Margaret! So glad to see you. Shall we shop a bit first? Or get something to eat?"

Margaret noticed Jocelyn was carrying a few bags already. "Oh, it looks like you already beat me to it?" she said, pointing to the carrier bags.

"These? No, no. These are returns. I am buying and then returning all the time. It's just so much fun, don't you think?"

Ah, Margaret thought, so Jocelyn was one of those women: a habitual shopper making a game of purchasing and exchanging. It was the last thing Margaret herself found to be fun and she headed it off at the pass. "How about if we just head to the Tea Room? I am rather parched."

Jocelyn nodded. She then took the lead through the store, clearly at home in their surroundings, chatting all the while. She paused in her flow of talk to ask, "Shall we ride the elevator up or take the new electric stairway?"

Woodward & Lothrop had recently installed a new-fangled people mover design and Margaret had not yet tried it. "By all means, let's try the electric stairway," she said.

As they made their way up floor by floor to the seventh story, Margaret took in the sensation of moving on the automated stairs. It was strange, totally unlike the elevator banks. It also allowed for a glimpse of the hustle and bustle of each shopping level.

When they exited out onto the seventh floor, the Tea Room entrance was right ahead of them. Margaret found herself anticipating the specialties the place was known for: Wellesley Fudge cupcakes and chicken pot pie.

They managed to grab one of the last available tables in a room bustling with activity. The Tea Room upped the glamour of the shopping experience with its white-linen clothed tables and crystal chandeliers. They settled into seats with striped chair covers in rich ruby red and ivory. Margaret and Jocelyn sat amongst other women who had met up for shopping and socializing just like the two of them.

Conversation paused as a waitress gave them menus. Margaret just gave a cursory glance, already knowing her order. Both placed them down at the same time and looked back up at each other, an awkwardness setting in.

"Well..."

"So..."

Jocelyn giggled. "You first."

"Oh, I was just going to say I'm ordering my usual."

Jocelyn tilted her head. "What's that?"

"Their pot pie. It's always delicious. How about you?"

"I'm on a diet so just the tomato aspic for me." Her mouth formed a sad moue.

Margaret had no desire to plow through dieting talk with the "whys" and "what-fors" so she diverted the conversation tactfully. "I know a bit about Bill with his law career and his background with horses, but what are your interests, Jocelyn?"

Jocelyn moved a fork back and forth on the tablecloth as she pondered Margaret's question. Finally, she answered. "Well, I lunch with the ladies a few times a week. And, of course, shopping is my favorite of all pastimes."

The waitress stopped at their table and Jocelyn paused answering Margaret's question.

After they both ordered, she picked right back up. "I know my way around every department store in this city, Margaret. I can promise you that. Lord and Taylor, Garfinkel's, but my favorite is, of course, where we are today. All the sales girls know me so well. In fact, they pull things out special now for me to try on. They know my taste and set things aside. Now mind you, I do spend as much time returning items as I do buying!" She let out a raucous laugh.

"So, tell me..." Margaret's curiosity got the better of her and she just had to ask for Jocelyn's take on the story. "How did you and Bill meet?"

Jocelyn giggled again. "It was just a fluke really."

Margaret urged her to continue. "How so?"

"I was a cocktail waitress over at The Madrillon. Bill walked in one day and, aside from his age, he cuts such a fine figure of a man." A small smile curved at her lips. Margaret was taken aback how it was almost lascivious in nature.

"He wasn't my only choice, of course. But he wore me down until I just caved."

Even though The Madrillon was a restaurant frequented by some of the city's most important figures, Margaret wagered that William Ingleside Miller was most likely the biggest game afoot on that fateful day.

After their meals were brought to their table, Jocelyn continued to wax on about Bill's attributes. Margaret listened but mainly concentrated on the enjoyable taste of her pot pie meal. "...and he just drew folks to him like a magnet. What do they call that? A magnetic personality. That's my Buddy."

"Buddy?"

"He just always seemed like a Buddy to me, not a Bill. He didn't mind. And he calls me a nickname."

"What's that?"

"Mom."

"Excuse me?"

"He calls me Mom."

Margaret controlled her expression upon hearing the somewhat disturbing nickname. "Well...that's interesting. Buddy and Mom."

"Anyways, we had a whirlwind courtship."

"You did?"

"Yes, two weeks from the start of it to a marriage proposal."

"That's...really something."

Jocelyn nodded. "It is, it is. Now, two years later, here we are."

"He was a widower when you met?"

Jocelyn's mouth turned down at the edges. "Yes, the poor dear. He lost his wife shortly before then."

Margaret burned with curiosity about how short that time frame was but simply said, "Well, I'm sure it was his lucky day to meet you. A happy marriage made by all accounts."

"Indeed. I do love him deeply. It's just..." A frown came over Jocelyn's face. Then she spoke again. "The only thing we fight over is where we live."

Margaret tried to remember what neighborhood they lived in. "Why, it's Midcity, isn't it? That's always seemed very nice to me." Her mind conjured up the tree-filled streets and the sturdy brick rowhouses that filled several blocks in the northwest quadrant of the District.

"Oh, it's alright but...Bill is a famous lawyer. He deserves to live in a place more suited. Such as the new neighborhood up near the city lane. Chevy Chase. Now, those are houses deserving of the Miller name."

"Huh..." Margaret did indeed know Chevy Chase, a newly burgeoning suburban-style neighborhood where those with airs of grandeur scrambled for a spot. Many in the horsey set circles were doing that exact same, vying to buy into the place.

Margaret didn't, however, see Bill as that type. He was more down to earth, tied into his humble beginnings. Rooted in fact. Margaret could perfectly understand him staying where he was.

The meal wound down and conversation trailed off. Margaret was looking forward to its end, and she fervently hoped it would be a one-time thing.

As they paid their bills, Jocelyn smiled widely at Margaret and said, "Okay, shopping time!"

"Uh, I'm not really much of a shopper, Jocelyn. I'll just let you carry on if it's all the same."

Jocelyn lips spilled open in a pout. "But you said we would go shopping and have lunch."

"I did? Well..."

"Oh, come on, Margaret. It's no fun to shop alone. I thought we could pick out some nice things in the lingerie department."

Margaret was a bit flummoxed by the needy demand from the woman across from her. But she had to stay in good graces with Bill and, by proxy, his wife. And she did need some fresh night attire. Not seeing a way around, Margaret soon found herself on the way to the lingerie department with Jocelyn jabbering the whole way there.

"Ooooh, this just came in. Look at it!" Jocelyn pulled out a coffee-colored lacy number from a rack. It was meant more for a boudoir than a matronly bedroom in Margaret's opinion but she just responded with a weak smile.

As they waded through, Jocelyn stopped at a rack of peignoirs, all silk and much more tasteful than the lacy selections. "Now, this is the ticket." She held the hanger up and displayed it on the front of her bosom.

"Yes, quite, um, fetching."

"Margaret, I mean for you, not me." She looked slyly over at Margaret. "That shell pink color would go perfectly with your skin tone and hair color. I'm sure Mr. Brady would find it so."

Margaret cleared her throat. Jocelyn had pushed too far. "Jocelyn, I certainly don't understand what you mean."

Jocelyn tossed a coy smile over her shoulder as she continued on to the next rack. "Okay. But I'm telling you that color is a knockout on you."

Margaret paused and picked up the peignoir. It was actually quite nice, and in good taste too. It was not a color she would have ever picked out for herself. She hung it in front of herself and gazed into the standing mirror nearby. Her reflection caught the color mixed with her skin tone and she realized that Jocelyn had been spot on. It really did make her look...well, quite fetching. Maybe she would purchase it and treat herself to something after the months of worrying over every penny. Why not?

A half hour later, the two women stood at the checkout with selections in hand. Jocelyn glanced down at the shell pink peignoir in Margaret's grip. "That's the spirit, Margaret."

Margaret nodded and looked at the stack of hangers on Jocelyn's arm. Bill really did have his hands full, in more ways than one, it seemed.

Saying their goodbyes back in the store's lobby, Margaret noted that Jocelyn's carrier bags had doubled in number even after she had returned some items. She shook her head ruefully at the thought of Bill and what he had taken on in his young wife.

CHAPTER FIVE

Robert had arranged a spur-of-the-moment lunch with Bill Miller at his favored spot, The Madrillon. As Margaret walked by Robert's side through Foggy Bottom, the bustling financial district in the heart of the nation's capital, she just missed getting her heel tip caught in an errant sidewalk crack. Robert reached over to grab her elbow as she righted herself. "Steady now. You don't want to miss this meeting." Indeed, she did not.

As they continued on towards The Madrillon, Margaret said, "Tell me why this is Bill's venue of choice." She had dined at the lavish restaurant a couple of times but was curious what the draw was for Bill.

"Well, the Caliph Room has become the place to see and be seen for lawyers of late."

"The Caliph Room?"

"Yes. It's on the lower level—set apart from the other rooms. You know, the Spanish Village, the Mayan Room and the Moorish Room."

"Oh yes...I think I have only been in the Moorish decorated one. What is a 'caliph' anyway?"

"The head honcho. The chief or the ruler, in other words."

"So, a seat of power then? How fitting that all the lawyers in town congregate here." She threw a sly look Robert's way.

He nodded with a wry smile. "I guess so."

They reached the intersection of 15th Street and New York Avenue and Robert took the crook of Margaret's arm to cross the street. It stood in front of them, the Washington Building which housed The Madrillon, an ornate building with decorative friezes, arches, and fluted columns constructed at the tail end of the Twenties boomtime.

Margaret paused, lifting up her gaze to study the detail on the frieze with its pattern of fleur-de-lis and multiple gargoyle heads between pressed blocks. Even though it had only been constructed a few years earlier, it harkened back to a grander time. "This building really is something, isn't it?"

"Yes. Very appropriate for what they call this spot—The World Corner."

"Oh, how spoiled we all were. Do you think we will be able to get any of it back?"

"What?"

"Days of grandiose architecture for starters."

Robert followed Margaret's gaze to the magnificent detail decorating the building's facade. Then he spoke. "You know, maybe something will rise out of the catastrophe of last year. Something equal or maybe even better. That's how I like to think about it anyway."

Robert stepped ahead to reach for the huge brass handle on the overly large door and then swept an arm for Margaret to enter first. Once inside the massive entryway, there was an immediate sense of calm away from the frantic energy of New York Avenue and its financial doings. Margaret relished the quiet while gazing around the flamboyant and rich décor of The Madrillon.

A wall of tapestry in a rich brocade of exuberant colors loomed impressively behind the maître d' at the entrance podium. The burnished, oily gold hues mixed with deep, silky maroons spoke of exotic locales far removed from the city they were in. Robert spoke to the man who gave a brief nod, then gestured towards a wide stairwell to the immediate left.

They followed him as the staircase swept generously down to the lower level. They entered into a darkened space and Margaret blinked, her eyes adjusting to the change. The low lighting was paired with a décor of darker colors. The Caliph Room, more intimate and clubby, was a striking contrast with the upper level. Margaret assumed, in fact, it operated like a private club with the Prohibition loophole that allowed for serving liquor from well-stocked stashes. Although they couldn't purchase any new supply (in theory, anyway), they were able to pour out from their reserves.

As they waded through the room, Margaret took in the round tables covered by dark red tablecloths and the leather chairs encircling those tables, big enough to seat any sultans. Instead of sultans, they were almost entirely filled with men in suits that spoke to their profession, attorneys, probably one and all.

Margaret supposed they gathered here mid-day to share comradery amongst their ilk. But it felt like a lair in a way, a place for just them and them alone. The only other women were the cocktail waitresses bustling between tables.

Robert gave nods here and there while Margaret began to receive curious looks especially from the most pompous looking types. Her temper flared at the unspoken rule: the fairer sex was not afforded a role in this room aside from the waitresses with their tightly-bodiced bosoms.

A voice from one of the interior tables bellowed out to them. Bill sat back in his chair, clearly at ease in the setting. In fact, it looked like it could be his second home. He stood up with vigor and greeted them, clapping Robert on the back and giving Margaret a sort of bow. "Well, well, happy to see you folks made it. Grab a seat here."

The other men who had been sitting casually around the table with Bill discreetly excused themselves and took leave without too many words said. Bill must have made it known this was to be a private meeting.

Once they were all situated, Bill spoke. "This is my other office, you might say. Do you know, this is the spot right here where I had the good fortune to meet my beautiful bride? That's right. Two years ago, on this past Valentine's Day in fact."

"Jocelyn was here?" Robert asked.

"She was one in the bevy of the gorgeous waitress staff here. And the finest one at that." He paused to take a puff of a lit cigar then continued, "Now Bobby, I hear tell that a certain lawyer in your practice got his comeuppance from Judge Sourpuss the other day." Margaret held back a smile at him being called Bobby.

Robert grimaced. "Yes, you heard right..."

The two men began to go back and forth about a case. When a waitress came up to the table, she interrupted Bill mid-sentence, speaking to him in a familiar manner. "What will your guests have, Bill?"

Margaret studied her. Brunette curls in a bouffant wreathed her face, a cherubic one, which somewhat belied the skimpy costume that stretched her assets to an eye-popping point.

Unfazed by the interruption, Bill said, "This time of year is perfect for gin and tonic, I say. How about you, my dear?" He deferred to Margaret who nodded assent. "Bobby? The same?"

"Sure thing," Robert/Bobby said.

As the two men continued with their conversation,

Margaret began to imagine the day Bill met Jocelyn at The Madrillon. She could just about conjure up the scene... Jocelyn gliding towards Bill's table in all her blonde glory, outfitted in what the other waitresses now wore.

She may have interrupted like this waitress had done, saying something along the lines of "Gentlemen, is there anything I can get you?" Jocelyn standing there with her darkened eyelashes, rosy cheeks and that hourglass shape within touching distance must have been like a tall drink for a thirsty man. And the stage was set for him to want more after that initial meeting. His colleagues may have been surprised—even alarmed—at Bill, susceptible to the allure of a "skirt", so soon after the loss of his cherished Katie.

But Jocelyn had no doubt landed her sights on Bill, the recent widower. He had fallen hard under Jocelyn's spell and wasn't that just the way the world turned? Had this all gone down after the loss of Katie? Or, had Bill and Jocelyn met here long before Katie— Margaret shook her head ruefully at that thought.

"What are you thinking about over there, little Margaret?"

She looked up at Bill with his wide smile and big, soulful eyes, and set aside ideas about him and his marriages. "Well, I don't know that I'm that little anymore, Bill."

"Oh yes, my pardon. Margaret is a name that suits you, by the way. A strong name for a female I have always thought. So, let's talk horses."

Margaret sat up a little taller and cleared her throat. This was her chance to pitch Needham Forest and she was ready. She could feel Robert's eyes on her as she began her spiel and took a measure of confidence from his steady gaze. She did not intend to disappoint him.

An image of her adored father's face stayed with her as she

explained how Needham Forest had been during her father's heyday, finishing up with, "Daddy was a maverick—in the best possible way. As you might remember, he pulled himself up by his bootstrings. He found horse racing to be his passion in life and made it all happen. It's all thanks to him."

"Hhmm." Bill methodically tapped his cigar before speaking. Then he said, "Yes, I well remember Charley's drive and passion. And I know a little something about bootstrings myself. But how did you take off with it after his passing?"

With no small measure of pride, Margaret filled him in on the years after her father's death, inheriting the property, expanding it and bringing it greater attention. As she did so, Bill puffed on his cigar, listening intently.

After she finished talking, Bill gave an audible sniff then took out a fountain pen from his waistcoat. He pulled the cocktail napkin out from under his gin and tonic glass and gave it a shake. He flipped over the decorative side—a peacock with red feathers trailing off one side along with fancy script stating "The Madrillon, 15th and New York"—and set it on the table.

"Alrighty then. Let's scope this out a bit."

He began to scribble while telling her his intentions of his investment. She peered over by lifting her chin trying to eye up what figures he was writing but couldn't make them out.

When done, he lifted the napkin up and read it over and then nodded. "Okay now. See how this bottom line looks to you."

Margaret studied the figures he had penned out, feeling a quiver of anticipation. She looked up at him. "Very satisfactory."

Bill stuck out his right hand and Margaret shook it.

Robert said, with some levity in his tone, "Hey folks, shouldn't we get contracts to review this?"

"This is old school, Bobby. You know how I operate. But I

will let Margaret take these figures with her." He winked at Margaret as he handed over the napkin, the back with the figures and the front with The Madrillon emblem and peacock design.

"I jest. I know you and Margaret will have a swell partnership," Robert said.

Margaret gazed down on the pattern of red and black and then remembered. "Oh, Bill, there is one other thing."

"What's that?"

"I was hoping you could fill me in a little more about that treasure you mentioned."

"The treasure?" He sniffed and moved a bit in the chair. "Oh yes. Well, I told you everything I can recall about it. Charley talked about gold bars somewhere on the farm. But he never told me any particulars about whether he had hunted it down. Not that I remember anyway. To be fair, we were usually pretty deep into our cups during those discussions." He let out a rueful laugh.

"So, nothing else that you can..."

Bill had pulled out his watch fob, glancing at it. "So sorry, Margaret. I am cutting it close now. But how about we all meet for dinner soon? The four of us?"

Margaret wondered if Bill was leaving something unsaid about her father and the treasure but she dropped further mention. "Oh, sure. Yes. Maybe we could chat more about it then."

Robert began to pull out his money clip but Bill put a hand up. "Nah...this is on my tab today. And I thank you for joining me. A productive meeting indeed." His smile took in both of them.

Margaret agreed and felt satisfied with the figures she now clutched on the napkin in her hand. Out on the street in the bright light, they said their goodbyes to Bill and watched his tall figure lope away in the opposite direction. Margaret turned to face Robert with a wide grin. "Thank you."

"Of course. Come on, let's get you back to Needham Forest." He looped an arm through hers. On the walk back to Robert's automobile, Margaret felt a flush on her cheeks with the napkin in hand and the warmth of Robert's body pressed against hers.

CHAPTER SIX

Several days later, Margaret tagged along for a ride into town with Albert, Cassie's husband. Albert sold fall produce at the Saturday market near the courthouse square in Rockville which was the location of the county's historical society.

They pulled onto a side street where a charming, one-story brick building sat, housing the historical society. After Margaret got herself out, she leaned into the open window of the farm truck. "Thanks, Albert. I'll be ready in a couple of hours, I think."

"Alrighty, Mizz Margaret."

As Margaret gazed at the dust-covered rear of the departing truck, she made a mental note to set up her own transportation now that Keith was gone. He had provided her rides whenever needed in his fancy roadster. Now that the fancy roadster had gone the way of Keith, she no longer had a dedicated driver.

Margaret hadn't fought to keep the vehicle despite the fact her money had paid for it. She now regretted it, since Keith was fighting tooth and nail for every other asset. It was telling that this was her only regret about his absence. Sad too.

She shook thoughts of Keith and bad judgments on her part

aside and turned to face the Montgomery County Historical Society several yards in front of her. By her estimation, it might have served as a summer kitchen to the Federal-era brick mansion near it. Now, she suspected, it might be under the helm of blue haired denizens of a certain age.

She had been unable to gain entry on other recent jaunts to Rockville. The sign on the door stated hours on Tuesday and Thursday mornings and some Saturdays but with the caveat, "subject to change at any time". It apparently was the latter part of the sign that took precedence. If, once again, it was closed, she would meander down into the center of town to Albert's farmstand.

Margaret reached for the doorknob and felt it turn underneath her hand. *Finally,* she thought. She walked in and was hit with a mixed odor of old building, dust and mustiness. It was a welcoming smell, although her nose began to wriggle into a potential sneeze.

The church-like quiet room was dominated by floor-to-ceiling shelves crammed with books and documents. Margaret caught sight of a very small lady with a huge dome of snow-white hair at an almost hidden desk. She peered at Margaret above the half rims of her spectacles with sharp, inquisitive eyes. "Can I help you, madam?"

"I hope so. I'm so happy to find you open this morning..."

"Well, catch can as catch does."

Margaret kept her opinion on that to herself and said, "Yes. Well, I am searching out the history of my farm, Needham Forest. It was the Magruder..."

The other woman cut her off. "I know it. What is your interest exactly?"

"I am a Magruder descendant. In fact, the owner, and I'm seeking more information about it." She left it at that.

The woman nodded. "Fair enough. Take a seat over there–"

pointing to a small table tucked beneath the only window. "Mind you don't touch any of the documents on the table."

Margaret allowed herself an inward eye roll as she situated herself.

The lady got up and moved with a wobbly gait into a row of shelves. As she poked around murmuring to herself all the while, Margaret looked about the room wondering if any of the nooks held the answers to her puzzle, the treasure at Needham Forest.

"Aha, here it is!" The woman spoke aloud, jolting Margaret. Her slow shuffle eventually brought her to the table. She carefully placed a folder in front of Margaret and pointed to its label, "Magruder". "This should give you a good start." She then returned to her desk picking up whatever activity Margaret had taken her away from.

Margaret took a deep breath and opened the file. It was comprised of various loose papers all relating to some aspect of the family but not organized in any particular manner. After getting halfway through it, her eyes began to cross at reading the minute and tight script. She could barely make it out. When she looked up from the folder, her vision was blurry.

Margaret blinked for a bit and then went back to it. The final piece in the file was a family tree that began with the first Magruder in the county, a man named Zadok Magruder. It was all because of him that she was seated in the room trying to find an answer to a question. It was kind of astonishing really. She placed it down and closed the folder.

When she stood up by the small table in need of a stretch, a bone or two made a cracking noise. She was sore from a ride on her Arabian stallion she had taken the previous day—it was a good sore but she did feel it. The other woman still engrossed in her project did not look up at Margaret's creaky bones.

Margaret needed something more. She wished she could

just rip through the shelves by herself and be left to her own devices. That wasn't going to happen on this woman's watch, she knew that. It came to her in a burst of inspiration. She needed maps. How to prod this out of the fierce guardian of all here? She decided to take the straight forward approach.

"How about some maps?"

The lady looked over with raised eyebrows then directed a glance at the clock on the wall. "It's closing time now. You'll have to come back another time."

The "catch can as catch does" time, Margaret assumed.

The woman relented somewhat, asking, "What is it you hope to find here, dear?"

Margaret thought about the seemingly innocent question before giving a response. Rockville was the county seat but really just a small country town. Like every other of its kind, people talked and gossip spread like wildfire. If she told this woman what she was looking for, people would soon be lined up and down Needham Forest's drive with shovels and the like ready to find their own treasure. But, on the other hand, this paragon of the archives might just know something. Maybe old local lore handed down, maybe a clue.

"Really, I am just hoping to find out more about my home's role during the Civil War."

"Well, of course, all the old homesteads around here saw military engagement and action. Skirmishes and such. You can rest assured about that. And Needham Forest...now wait a minute. I do think there was something..."

The woman's gaze moved to the one small window in the room and she went quiet in thought. Then she spoke. "I was just a small child during the War between the States but I do remember all the strife and angst around me. There was a particular tale about your farm. It's just at the edges of my mind."

Margaret stayed silent waiting for whatever it was. Hoping that it was a memory about the gold bars as confirmation. But, instead of any confirmation, the other woman shook her head. "It's just not coming to me. And I do need to close up shop now. My granddaughter is going to take me to tea this afternoon." Her face brightened in a way that Margaret had not yet seen on it.

"Oh, okay. So, if it happens to come to mind..."

"Yes, yes." She pushed a piece of paper and a pencil towards Margaret. "Jot down your telephone line here."

Then she lifted herself up and ushered Margaret to the exit, leaving little room for any more conversation on the subject. Outside, Margaret stood, a bit put off at her abrupt ejection from the place. If this was any indication of those involved in history, it was going to take some finesse to bridge that gap.

Margaret glanced at her watch, realizing Albert would still be busy in the town center. As she headed along the brick walkway, she tried to dismiss the overwhelming frustration at her aborted task. She had gotten absolutely nowhere in the little building, except for maybe picking up the sniffles from the exposure to the dust-laden books and documents. A historian she was not. She needed to figure out some other way to get at the secret—if indeed, there was one.

Suddenly, it clicked into place. Leonard. Her farm manager. He had known her father as well as anyone. But would her father have confided in Leonard as he did with Bill Miller? Leonard had been hired long after Bill's tenure. The nature of their relationship was far different from that between her father and Bill. For starters, there was much more of an age difference.

She needed to have a sit-down with Leonard. It was possible that he could confirm or deny the story. Then she could let it go, or pursue it. She felt lighter in her step along the brick walkway and wondered why she had not thought of it right away.

As Margaret approached the commercial heart of the town, she walked past its most notable building, the imposing red brick courthouse, constructed forty years earlier. Its decorative, ornate fenestration added an upscale note to the little country town. This was followed by a row of lawyers' offices and then shops along Montgomery Street. The market was set up in an empty lot right beyond but still in the central area.

Margaret was heartened by the sight. It gave farmers from outlying areas an opportunity to sell their harvests and, more importantly, keep their farms as ongoing concerns during these times. The sights and sounds of the busy market filled her senses, allowing her to put all other thoughts aside. She strolled through the loose set-up of wooden crates and displays, noting the array of colors. It brought with it a soothing pleasure. She breathed in deep, releasing the leftover musty and dusty from the historical society.

She paused in front of one stand that displayed cartons of jet-black berries. She ran a finger over the cartons with a light touch, deciding on a purchase. Robert was coming over for dinner that night, just the two of them, and she wanted it to be very special. The blackberries conjured up a vision of Cassie's wonderful berry tart. Maybe Cassie could bake it using this purchase along with some of her preserves.

As Margaret handed over money to the vendor, she felt a strange crawling sensation on the nape of her neck. She turned swiftly around to see if someone was right behind her. But there was just the passing by of people shopping, nothing untoward to notice.

She turned back and took her bag, thanking the man in dirt-streaked coveralls, but still feeling a sensation of being watched in the crowded space. She headed towards where Albert stood with his wares, taking comfort from his tall, steady presence on the other side of the market.

Halfway there, she again felt a tingling like someone was behind her, right on her heels. She whipped around and there he stood with a ridiculous looking fedora pulled low on his brow in a poor attempt at being incognito.

"Keith! What exactly do you think you are doing?" she said, in between clenched teeth.

Keith put his hands up in a mock gesture of surrender. "Just going to the market, Margaret. Like you. Last I heard, it wasn't a crime." There was a glint in his eyes and an unattractive downturn in the corners of his mouth.

They were in a stand-off as the crowd moved around them. Margaret studied the man in front of her who she had been married to for thirteen years. He did not look well, not at all. He had slid further downhill since she had last seen him in the lawyer's office several months prior.

"You don't live out here anymore. You're in the city now. So, you don't fool me for a second. Just...just stay away from me."

He took a step towards her, a menacing expression coming over his face, an expression she could not recall ever seeing in all the years they had been together as husband and wife. She felt a frisson of fear. But hot anger overcame it.

Right before emotion made her do something rash, a steady hand grabbed her arm. "Everything alright here, Mizz Margaret?"

Albert stood at her side, looming over both her and Keith. A larger man than Keith, his physicality made clear the potential victor if it came down to a dust-up.

"Mr. O'Keefe was just leaving, I believe." Margaret shot daggers at Keith with her eyes, outraged at his attempt to intimidate her, to scare her. How dare he?

Keith sniffed. "This isn't over, Margaret. Not by a long shot." He turned on heel and slinked his way off into the crowd.

Margaret, with Albert still at her side, watched his departing back.

"Thank you, Albert. That was...unpleasant, to say the least."

"Anytime, Mizz Margaret. Sorry he's troubling you like that." His weather-beaten face was crunched into wrinkles of concern.

"Yes. That's the word for it. Trouble."

Margaret needed to shake Keith out of her life for good. *It needs to happen sooner rather than later,* she realized. Especially if he was now lurking about in the shadows, stalking her and even making veiled threats.

CHAPTER SEVEN

"I've got it, Cassie!" Margaret yelled as she strode out into Needham Forest's center hallway upon hearing a knock.

With a hand on the knob of the antique paneled front door, her heartbeat quickened with anticipation at seeing Robert. She was looking forward to a quiet and relaxing dinner for just the two of them, especially after all the unpleasantness in Rockville that morning. The black cloud that was Keith could be pushed aside for the time being. There was no need to burden Robert with the ongoing, pesky problem of her ex.

Margaret had planned for the evening to be a welcome change from a calendar chock-filled with social engagements. She had not had Robert to herself for quite a while. In fact, she was becoming resentful that she had to share him with so many others.

She pulled on the knob and there he stood, his back towards her. The last pinches of the setting sun over the fields were in front of him while crickets sang their songs off in the distance, signaling autumn's arrival. He turned to face her and she was taken aback by his expression, troubled with something clearly amiss.

"Robert, are you feeling alright?"

He leaned towards her and kissed her cheek. "I've had the strangest day."

"Let's get you a beverage." She grabbed his hand and led him inside.

Once in the drawing room, she gestured for him to take a seat and made her way to the credenza where the glass bottles of libations twinkled in the room's lighting.

"The usual?"

"Sure."

Margaret began to prepare two vodka tonics, placing ice cubes into both glasses as the finishing touch and giving them a little shake. As she did so, she glanced over at him, worried at his odd, distracted air—very unlike him.

She walked over to the gold-threaded brocade sofa and handed him his drink. She sat down next to him with her own drink in hand.

Robert took a healthy gulp and then looked at her directly. "So...I met with a client earlier today." He paused for another sip. "A doctor was present who will be testifying on behalf of the client when it goes to trial." He studied his drink before saying anything else.

"And?" Margaret said, pressing to figure out what was on his mind.

"Afterwards, the doctor was chatty and we continued out to the carpark where his car was, a smart convertible. Strangely, he asked me to get into the car's front seat. He said he had something to show me."

Margaret raised her eyebrows. "What? A bit odd..."

"I went ahead and did it. I mean, yes, it was odd but I didn't give it too much thought at the time. Next thing I know, he pulls out a large envelope from underneath the seat." He paused again, shaking his head at the memory.

"And?"

"He said he keeps a loaded gun in it."

"What on earth? Why?"

"Of course, I asked him that very question. His response was that he couldn't take any chances because he testifies on so many high-profile cases."

"I hope you got out of that car as quickly as possible."

"I did. And now, well, the whole experience just doesn't sit right with me."

"You don't think...you don't think he's unhinged, do you?"

"Maybe that's why it bothers me so much. Why is he running around town with a loaded gun?"

"Can you tell me who this person is? I hope it isn't any doctor I've ever encountered!"

He looked off to the side. "I can't tell you that, Margaret. I wish I could though."

Margaret nodded. "It's fine. I assume it's a breach of ethics to do so?"

"Something like that, yes."

Cassie came in and coughed a bit to interrupt the conversation.

"Oh Cassie, is dinner ready?"

"Yes, ma'am."

Margaret could feel Robert's mood lift, as did her own as they walked into the dining room, arm in arm. Lit candles along with the perfectly laid table lent a romantic tone. Cassie had picked up on Margaret wanting this dinner to be special.

They sat down across from one another and Margaret poured two glasses of red wine from a bottle opened earlier. It was one of the last remaining in her father's collection from the root cellar. She decided it was a special enough event, dinner with Robert, to open it.

"A toast," she said, raising her glass.

His mouth curved into a smile. "What is the occasion?"

"Just us. That's the occasion."

He held her gaze in his. What they had both danced around for some time was happening, a promise of more. Cassie walked back in with steaming plates and broke into the charged moment between them.

Attention diverted, they both tucked into a pot-roast dinner with new potatoes and turnips. The pot-roast was a rare treat these days with food prices escalating but Cassie had somehow managed to snag one. The small kitchen garden that Cassie kept behind the house had reaped enough for canning some summer vegetables. Those vegetables provided sides along with yeasty rolls and spring turnip greens. The last course would be the berry tart that Cassie had whipped up for dessert from Margaret's market purchase.

Over the meal, they talked about things other than Robert's disturbing encounter with the doctor and the gun. Instead, Margaret brought up her day at the historical society followed by the tale of her most recent foray to a horse auction up in Pennsylvania and the characters she had run into. She trailed off the story by saying, "...the people up there seem so different to me."

"Different how?"

"I don't know. Maybe just a different pace of life. Away from the District's rat race..."

Robert let out a chuckle. "Rat race? That's a new one to me. What does it mean?"

"I was reading it in the New York Times the other day. It means the constant struggle to get ahead that people put themselves through. Maybe the rat race is exactly why that doctor thinks he needs a gun?"

Robert shrugged. "That's possible."

Cassie made one last trip into the dining room with

refreshed water goblets. "Anything else you be needing tonight, Mizz Margaret?"

"No, this is all wonderful, Cassie. Thank you."

"Alrighty then. I know you need this nice time after the day you done had. Hmm-hmm." Cassie mumbled to herself as she left the room.

Robert gave Margaret a pointed look. "What is Cassie referring to?"

"Ah, it's nothing. Just a rude encounter at the market today."

"Rude encounter?"

Margaret looked down at her plate. She really didn't want to talk about it. At all. But Robert awaited her response and she just could not lie about it.

"Margaret?"

She looked back up and let out a sigh. "Keith was at the market today."

"What? Why?"

She shook her head. "I think...I think he was seeking me out. On purpose."

Robert's fork hung in midair as he stared at her. Margaret tried to downplay how it had been. "I mean, it might have been just my imagination but it was...it was..."

"Well, it sounds as though Mr. O'Keefe has upped the game. We will have to do something about that."

"How so?"

"I'll put a call in to his lawyer and make it clear this kind of thing is not acceptable. Don't worry, Margaret. I won't let you be threatened in any way." He reached over and took her hand.

She found immediate comfort and reassurance in the gesture. "Thank you."

The mood shifted again as they finished the meal. There was a silence that had snuck in with the weight of Robert's day, along with her confession about seeing Keith.

As he placed his fork down after his final bite, Robert looked over at Margaret. "So, it's just the two of us tonight."

Margaret nodded. "Yes. In fact, I told Cassie to take the rest of the night off."

He looked at her with a new intensity. "Well, then this night really has just begun, hasn't it?"

Margaret nodded, gazing at his handsome face and taking in his fine physique. She drank the final dregs from her wine glass but really no alcohol was needed to fuel her passion for the man that sat across from her.

"I'll bring out the dessert. Something special I picked up today at the market."

He stood and took her hand. "I think dessert can wait..."

———

The next morning, Margaret drew herself up with a languorous stretch. She felt the soft, sleek material of her new shell pink peignoir glide over her arms and wryly realized she had Jocelyn to thank for its purchase. Not something she would have chosen for herself normally but it seemed to have fit the bill for the previous night.

She gazed over at the empty side of her bed and then ran a hand over the silk sheet, now cool to the touch, where Robert had been until his very early morning departure. She didn't know what time it had been precisely but she had been aware of his leave-taking and the brush of his lips against her forehead.

Margaret assumed he was guarding her reputation and she stifled a laugh at that thought. As if a woman her age with her almost divorcee label merited such preservation of her status. She was at a point where she couldn't be bothered much anymore with the societal mores, just staying on the edge enough to keep her foothold with her business. Toeing the line to that point, yes, but there was a sense of freeing herself up, a sense of finding out who she really was in that freedom.

She did wonder though if the primary reason for Robert's early departure was that it was a Sunday. He was a churchgoer, attending Catholic Mass on the regular. His ties to the church and his upbringing were somewhat baffling to Margaret mainly because she did not have any such ties. They had not really touched on the subject too much and she had hoped it would not get in the way of their relationship. Yet, a bigger part of her knew that was probably wishful thinking on her part. His background came with expectations. The biggest one being that he entered into a fully sanctioned and lawful marriage under the eyes of the church. Whenever or if ever he chose to marry.

A barb of worry hit her. Would that interfere with their... arrangement? They had not really talked much about a future. Mainly because Keith was still so much in their immediate present despite the ongoing efforts to remove him. But Robert had to know she had deep feelings for him—didn't he? Maybe she should tell him in no uncertain terms. Her mind continued to wander about the territory of her and Robert as she rubbed a finger over the delicate fabric of the peignoir. Finally, she shook herself and stared at the color again. Shell pink. Who would have thought?

The sound of the back door opening and then closing signaled Cassie's arrival, and was soon followed by movements in the kitchen right below Margaret's bedroom. Judging from the late hour on the clock, Cassie held off arriving on this morning. Maybe she assumed Robert would not have left until then.

Everyone around Margaret, it seemed, was trying to shield or protect her...and there was no need for that, in her opinion.

CHAPTER EIGHT

After breakfast, Margaret headed to the stables with Oliver weaving in and out around her stride. It was a crisp day with a hint of winter in the air, just a hint—the best kind of weather to muck around with her horses.

As she made her approach, she caught sight of Leonard's figure in the distance. He was working on a Sunday—again—which was not right but did give her the opportunity she needed. "Leonard," she called out. "This is your only day off. You should be taking a break!"

Leonard leaned against one of the stable openings which allowed him to support his bad knee as he watched her approach. He had become the heartbeat of Needham Forest many years earlier. When Margaret had taken over the operation, there had been no question as to whether Leonard would stay on. His connections ran deep not only in the region's horse circle but well beyond also. He was really the one keeping the whole operation afloat, a seasoned veteran of all things in the horse business and someone, along with Cassie, she could not do without. All that said, Margaret did not expect him to work on a Sunday.

He shrugged. "You know me, Miss Margaret. I ain't no churchgoer. This is the closest thing to a church I got. And it's too fine a day to be elsewhere." He reached down to chuck Oliver under his chin.

Margaret looked at Leonard fondly. He wore his customary red plaid flannel shirt and dungarees. As usual, he held a smoke in one hand. The years of that habit also showed up in his heavily-lined face, a face framed by gray hair longish at the temples.

She couldn't agree more with Leonard's sentiment. She did indeed know that Leonard Snowden was no pious, church-going man. He shared that in common with Margaret and her late father. They all subscribed to the church of the outdoors instead.

"Let's have a seat. There's something I need to pick your brain about."

"Alrighty." His look gave nothing away, whether he was curious or not.

They headed into the stable hall and Margaret began to greet the horses, murmuring to each one, stroking their manes. She got a few whinnies and snorts by way of response. They made their way to the sectioned off corner of the barn where the farm office was situated. Leonard gestured for Margaret to take the chair behind the desk. But she demurred. "No, you take that one so you can prop up your knee."

Once they were seated, she began to tell him the strange tale about the gold bars. As she did so, she watched his face for what it might reveal. She went silent after finishing with, "...so in all the time you spent with Daddy, did he ever say anything to you?"

Before speaking, Leonard repositioned his knee with a slight grimace. "I did hear something one time. But I thought it was just the drink talking."

"What? What did you hear?"

He let out a breath. "I can barely remember now. Cuz I just figured it was a tall tale."

Margaret waited for him to cull through his memory banks to maybe remember whatever had been said—or done.

He shook his head. "It was something like the farm was going to always be okay because he could always fall back on finding the money somewhere on the property."

"Did you push for what he meant?"

"No. Like I said, it was a night of hard drinking after a big racing loss. He got real upset and hit the sauce in a way I had never seen him do before. He was morose but then perked up cuz he said what I just told you. That it would always be okay."

"Huh."

"So, you really think this might be a true story?"

She put out her hands in a helpless manner. "I just don't know. But I feel like maybe it's something I should try to find out."

In the pause of the conversation, their attention was snared by the loud purr of a car engine pulling up outside. Oliver, nestled in his dog bed, lifted his head and gave a sharp bark, followed by another.

"Who could that be?" Leonard said.

Margaret smacked her forehead with a palm. "Oh, I forgot! I have a guest visiting. Yesterday was so...well, it slipped my mind. But it's the man I was telling you about the other day. Bill Miller."

"The other lawyer fella?" Leonard gave her a wink.

"Yes, yes but you'll like him. He's one of the good guys, like Robert."

Heading out to greet Bill, she silently hoped it would be just Bill. He had not said one way or the other whether Jocelyn was to be included. His tall, lanky form emerged from his Packard and he bellowed out a "Hello there, little Margaret!"

Once closer, he clasped both of her hands and said in his hearty way, "Isn't this just a treat? I surely miss being around horses every day, I'll tell you what. And I haven't been out here in...well, I don't know how long." He gazed around as if he was taken back to earlier times, earlier memories.

Margaret beamed at him. She really did like the way he had about him. "Let me give you the cook's tour then." She looked back over at the Packard. "Is Jocelyn not with you?"

"Oh, we split ways on Sundays. I got Mass and she's got her folks to visit over in Mount Vernon. So, I keep busy in the afternoons and find ways to occupy myself—like driving up here today. Of course, we always meet back for Sunday supper and dine together at the end of the day."

"Well, come on through."

As she led him towards the barn, he paused and said, "Almost forgot to tell you. I saw our man, Bobby, at Mass earlier. He sends his regards." He gave her a wink after he said it but Margaret didn't mind. Just like she didn't mind Leonard's wink earlier. She was not going to hide what she and Robert had together from anyone.

Once inside the barn, Bill looked around nodding at the same time. It appeared that he was happy at seeing Needham Forest again even if he didn't say the words per se. They continued out for a walk around the other stables and the paddocks and finally stopped at the fence line. The view in front of them was the rolling fields and pastures that Maryland horse country was noted for.

"Remind me. How far does your property line go, Margaret?"

She drew an imaginary line with one finger left to right.

Then added, "All total, we have over one hundred and twenty acres."

He gave a low whistle. "It's mighty impressive. Mighty impressive. Always was and still is."

She smiled, feeling the pride she always had about Needham Forest. "Let me take you into the office to meet my farm manager."

Inside, Leonard still sat behind the large desk that took up the better part of the space. He stood up with a creak of complaint from his knee as they entered.

"Bill, this is my righthand man, Leonard Snowden. Needham Forest would just not function without him."

The two men grasped each other's hands for a shake and Margaret could see the silent sizing up that each took of the other. In the quick moment, she could also see approval from both parties.

"Well, let's sit and chat some more. Leonard, could you grab that bottle of Scotch we keep?"

Once the drinks were all set up, the conversation began with Bill saying, "Well, this is real nice. Just us folks."

As they sipped their drinks in a companionable silence, Margaret spoke up. "So, I'm curious, Bill. Why did you leave horses to take up law?"

Bill gave a chuckle. "You mean, when did I decide to move on from being a stable boy? That's what I was, you know."

Margaret smiled. "Well, we all start somewhere, don't we?"

Bill sat back in the chair a bit. "Worked around horses as a young 'un and then all the way through school. My pappy was a detective and there were stables down at his precinct for the horse patrol brigade. I hung around there as much as they'd let me. I found I had a way with them...well, I don't have to tell you two how that is, do I?"

Leonard and Margaret both gave a nod.

Bill picked the thread back up. "After I graduated high school—Central High over on O Street—you know it?" They nodded again. "Well, after that, I came out here and worked for your pop for a while. But then it came time for me to do my duty. Do the right thing. I signed up during the Spanish American conflict. You serve?" He looked over at Leonard.

"Yes, sir. Company D, 116th Infantry. European War," Leonard answered.

Bill nodded and continued. "Why, when I got back, only job I could get was working as a janitor over at the First Precinct. I'll tell you what, between learning from horses in my youth and then listening in at the precinct, I picked up all I needed to know about folks. I knew I had to take all that and apply it the law and that's what I did."

Margaret took another sip of her Scotch. "That's really admirable, Bill. I didn't know how far you pulled yourself up. How is it you chose criminal law?"

"Like I said, it was seeing and hearing what the horses and the people taught me. Natural order of things being what it is."

"Do you take on any case?"

"Nope. Only the ones that are truthful. The truth will out, I always say. Of course, Shakespeare said it first. *Merchant of Venice*."

Leonard's face scrunched up. "Well, how do you know right off the bat like that it's not a truthful one?"

"When the words don't match the face."

"Huh?"

"It's like this. A man might be telling me with a straight face a tale that makes perfect sense, but if his eyes don't look right to me, it's off."

"What would eyes not looking right be like?"

"Snake eyes, dark and cold."

Margaret felt a chill at the thought and looked over to catch Leonard shift in his seat as well.

Bill continued. "Now on the other hand, if the eyes and the story match, I'm a taker. And even if they don't have money to pay, I'll stand for them."

"So, let me get this straight. You do law for free for some folks?"

"That's right, partner. That's just the man I am."

Leonard nodded thoughtfully at the answer.

There was a lull in the conversation and Margaret stepped into it with the pressing issue that lurked around the edges of her mind. She cleared her throat first and then said, "So, Leonard and I were just chatting before you got here, Bill. About the gold you mentioned to me."

Bill nodded. "That's right. That's what your pop told me."

Margaret continued. "Leonard also remembers Daddy saying something about some money hidden around here but I'm having a time though trying to figure it out. Do you recall any other details at all?"

Bill sat back in the chair with a bemused expression. "You know, as best I remember about that time, the Confederacy was stockpiling gold with the intention of getting it down to Jefferson Davis for a turnaround of their side. They had ideas of using it to become the victors. So, there was always talk about hidden stashes around at collection points that they were going to retrieve and get to old Jeff Davis. Course that's not how it happened. It stands to reason that there were caches that they couldn't get back to, doesn't it?"

"Huh. And word got out somehow that there was a possible stash here at Needham Forest at some point." Margaret's words hung in the air.

All of a sudden, Bill fumbled for his watch fob. "Oh geez.

Look at me jabbering away. My bride will have a conniption if I'm not back."

"Oh..." Margaret said, taken aback at the sudden change in his demeanor. He had been so relaxed but now seemed almost nervous.

"Yes, and I've kept you good folks tied up too long anyway. Now, let me just pen this out for you before I head out." He drew out a checkbook from his jacket pocket and placed it on the desk.

"Oh, thank you, Bill. I didn't know..." Margaret was flustered at the sight of the check.

After signing off with a flourish, he waved it to dry and then handed it over to her. "You are quite welcome, my dear. I'm looking forward to standing right next to you in the winner's circle in the spring. Am I right?"

"Indeed. I'm thinking we will be well prepared in time for the Belmont Stakes with our winner. You agree with that estimation, Leonard?" Leonard gave a slow nod. "How does that sound, Bill?"

Bill gave her a wink. "Sounds like a great collaboration."

Margaret set the check discreetly off to one side of the desk. They both knew that Bill's name tied to a winning horse was the goal here. Along with a proven record at winning court cases, Bill was looking to show up as a winner on the track too. Margaret intended to keep her side of that arrangement with the influx of his funds.

As Bill stood up, he made quick work of smoothing down his hair and placing his hat on. Margaret and Leonard also stood up to join him with Margaret saying, "Let me walk you out."

The two men shook hands and Margaret accompanied Bill out. He moved at a much quicker pace than earlier and Margaret picked up again on a nervous energy. Once at his vehicle, he turned suddenly and said, "You know, Jocelyn had a wonderful time with you shopping. Couldn't stop talking about it."

Margaret smiled and nodded, keeping internal commentary to herself. Bill looked down at his tie and rubbed it between his fingers. Margaret sensed he wanted to say more.

He looked over at her with big, earnest eyes. "Something —Something—"

She was surprised that his usual verboseness had abandoned him momentarily. "What is it, Bill?"

He let out a sigh. "She's been acting funny lately, Margaret."

"Funny?"

"Yes. Hard to put a pin on it. She gets these blue moods at times. I was wondering, well, could you go shopping with her sometime again? Maybe sometime soon?"

Margaret felt her stomach sink. She did not want to go shopping with Jocelyn again. At all. But... "Of course, Bill. I'd be happy to...and I'll see if I can figure out what's troubling her."

Visible relief came over his broad features. "Thank you, Margaret. And I do thank you for the tour also. We are well on our way to a most excellent partnership."

As she watched his car pull away, Margaret felt conflicted by her thoughts. On one hand, she felt even greater admiration for the man who was now her partner. But she marveled that a man of his stature was so beholden to a woman like Jocelyn. And her distaste for Jocelyn increased.

She heard rustlings and looked over to see Leonard standing nearby also watching Bill's departure. He shook his head and said, "Don't seem right."

"What's that?"

"A man like that tied to his wife's apron strings."

Margaret held back a laugh, saying nothing. Of course, it wouldn't seem right to a confirmed bachelor like Leonard. But, he wasn't wrong either. Then again, who was she to comment on other people's marriages based on her state of affairs? Glass houses and all that. Instead, she said to Leonard, "You like him though, right?"

"Yup. He'll work out fine."

She nodded and set aside any doubts about having Bill on board. It was never him she had doubted though. Just his wife.

Back in the office, Margaret picked up the check and peeked at the amount. She let out an unladylike low whistle. It was more than they had discussed and more than she could have wished for. It would solve some immediate problems. She felt a lightness in her step as she walked out to the stalls where Leonard was working.

"I'm taking Moonlight out for a ride now," she said to Leonard. She intended to spend the rest of the glorious fall afternoon out in the place she loved best. Riding her prized Arabian horse, Moonlight, through the fields of Needham Forest. There was no other place on earth like it to celebrate this boon from Bill.

"You need me to tack him up for you?"

"Nah. You take the rest of the day off now, Leonard. It is Sunday after all."

After scooting Leonard off, Margaret went over to Moonlight's stall. A whiff of cigar smoke came out of nowhere. She sniffed and a memory of her father's preferred Cubans wafted over her. She looked around but, of course, there was no one. Could it be from the office? But Bill and Leonard had not smoked when they had their chat.

So, what was Daddy trying to tell her now?

Later that day, she placed a call to Judith, hoping she would still be in. Sitting at her phone table, she pictured Judith waltzing over to pick up the receiver.

"Hello, Mags! I'm just about to run out to the theater."

"I know but I'm glad to catch you. I just had to let you know that my investor—our old friend, Bill—is working out and the farm is back on track."

"Wonderful news!"

"Yes, it seems the gods are smiling down once again on Needham Forest. Daddy is pulling some strings perhaps. We'll do the Magruder name proud, won't we?" She paused and then added. "But there is one oddity."

"You mean the new treasure hunt?"

"Well, that. But also, this..." Margaret went into a description about Bill's marriage and his much younger wife and how it all rubbed her the wrong way.

"Well, she must be quite a looker, eh?"

Margaret begrudgingly admitted that to be the case. "Yes, blonde hair, big baby blues."

"Sounds a bit like that up-and-coming actress they are calling the 'Blonde Bombshell'."

"Huh?"

"Some upstart from Hollywood. Jean Harlow. You haven't heard of her?"

"No, but Jocelyn might be able to give her a run for her money."

The sisters promised to keep in touch and finished the conversation by making tentative plans for Margaret's next sojourn north to New York City.

CHAPTER NINE

Margaret had become accustomed to a weekly check-in call from Bill Miller. It was a couple months into their partnership and she couldn't be more pleased with the arrangement. It worked out even better than she had hoped: Bill provided a much-needed sounding board when she wanted to talk about the training and breeding of Needham Forest's roster. It came as no surprise given Bill's long-standing experience and savvy with horses.

One morning, she realized they had not chatted the previous week. She perched herself on the phone bench tucked off in the spacious center hallway of Needham Forest and dialed out. His secretary patched the call through and she said, "Hallo, Bill! Margaret here."

"Well, good morning, little Margaret." His greeting was per usual but she could hear something in his voice, something that was not right.

After they exchanged niceties, Bill cleared his throat on the other end. His out of character hesitation made Margaret nervous. Could he be having a change of heart about investing in Needham Forest?

"Is...is everything okay, Bill?"

He let out a big sigh. "No, Margaret. It's, um, well, it's Jocelyn."

Margaret felt relief. This was about Jocelyn, not Needham Forest. But the relief was followed by immediate chagrin. She had never followed up as he had wanted and scheduled another shopping outing with the younger woman. "Oh Bill, I just realized I never got in touch with Jocelyn. I'm so sorry. The time got away from me—"

He cut her off. "Nah, I understand. You are a busy woman. But things have taken a turn."

Margaret shifted on the bench and felt some worry. She did not need this boat she was on with Bill rocked in any way. "How so?"

"Well, she's been getting some treatment over at St. Elizabeth's. I got her set up with the best doc over there for the... for the blue moods she gets."

Margaret held back her surprise at Bill's pronouncement. St. Elizabeth's was the city's esteemed and reputable mental hospital, where all sought treatment for that particular arena of problems. Usually, such matters were kept within a family circle. It was unfortunate but, in Margaret's experience, society did not look kindly on people afflicted with mental health issues. She tempered her response. "Oh, that's good. So, it's better then?"

"Well, here's the thing. Better maybe but...different."

"Okaaay." Margaret dragged out the word, unsure how to respond.

"Could you go ahead and take that shopping trip with her now?"

"Uh, Bill, I don't know that—"

"Margaret, I trust and value your opinion. You're a real

sharp cookie. There's others around I could ask but I just don't have a comfort level with them. How about it?"

"Just to clarify, you want me to ask Jocelyn if everything's okay?"

"Yeah, sort of like that, but more like see if you can figure out what's different."

Margaret suppressed a sound of irritation and agreed to make a date to see Jocelyn. She could do this. Or she could at least give it a shot. After all, Bill was the primary reason Needham Forest was doing so well and back in good stead. It was just a damned shame he had to worry about such fickle matters related to his young wife.

Margaret contacted Jocelyn to make the arrangements and, this time, changed up the locale. Garfinkel's, a smaller department store than Woodward & Lothrop, was Margaret's preference. The two bastions, equally revered, vied for top spots in the department store hierarchy in the city. There were others of less prestige in the shopping district between 7th and 14th Streets along F Street but Garfinkel's, in Margaret's mind, was the most refined and elegant.

Its owner, Julius Garfinkel, prided himself on white glove treatment for all who shopped there and all who worked there too. He was an odd duck, short in stature and fastidious in his grooming, often seen roaming the store, meeting and greeting. In a few short months, a new building for the store was to be opened, upping the store's stronghold on glamour all the more. Setting up the plan with Jocelyn, the original store was just fine for Margaret's purposes, more subdued and usually less hectic than Woodward & Lothrop.

In the gold-toned lobby, Margaret spotted Jocelyn, waiting. Upon sighting Margaret, she waltzed over and began talking as if they had already been in the middle of conversation.

"I'm on the hunt for a bright pink brassiere, Margaret."

"Oh..." Margaret managed a smile at the unusual mission. "Well, let's see if we can find one, shall we?"

Jocelyn talked excitedly and in a more agitated way than Margaret recalled before as they found their way to the lingerie department in Garfinkel's. The area was an open room with various counter spaces and displays with a private back corner holding brassiere inventory.

A small bird-like woman dressed in black approached them as they entered the space. "Good morning, ladies. How may I assist?"

"I need to see all your hot pink brassieres!"

Both Margaret and the sales clerk cast their gazes aside, embarrassed at the statement. Was this what Bill had meant when he described his wife as "different"?

"Well. Let's take a walk over here."

They followed the much smaller woman to the display of available brassieres. She sorted through the rack and pulled out one that looked slightly pink, definitely not hot or bright pink.

"This is one right here." The clerk lifted the bra out, surreptitiously passing a discreet eye over Jocelyn's substantial bosom. She added, "I think this size might work for you."

Jocelyn's mouth moved into a small moue of disappointment. "That's all you have?"

"I'm afraid so, madam. It's not necessarily a color in much demand."

Jocelyn sniffed. "Well, I guess it will have to do. I'll try it on."

While Jocelyn was in the changing room, Margaret idly wandered through the section picking up an item here and there, not much interested. She looked at her snakeskin wristwatch realizing ten minutes had passed. The sales lady exchanged a look with her, maybe wondering if Margaret was as strange as her shopping companion. It felt disconcerting to be lumped in the same category as Jocelyn.

Finally, Jocelyn emerged all flustered with her outfit slightly askew. She handed it over to the clerk, saying "Wrap that up for me, will you?" Then she smiled brightly at Margaret. "Where to, Mags?"

Margaret was completely taken aback. Mags? Only her sister, Judith, called Margaret that—and she barely allowed Judith to do so. Bill was right. Jocelyn was acting differently. "Uh, how about we get some lunch now?"

Once seated at Garfinkel's tearoom with their orders placed, Margaret thought carefully about how best to probe Jocelyn about her issues and provide Bill with a modicum of insight. Maybe one way would be to find out more about their beginnings as a couple.

"Jocelyn, I never heard about your wedding to Bill. Was it a big affair? Tell me all about it."

This time, it was Jocelyn who seemed taken aback. "Oh, it wasn't much. Just a small event really. Mother and Daddy don't have much. Also..." She hesitated.

"Also?" Margaret prodded.

"Well, the truth of the matter is they had strong feelings about me marrying Buddy."

"Why was that?"

"I don't know. A couple of things, I guess."

"Like what?"

"They don't hold much stock in Catholics, and, as you know, Buddy is a dyed-in-the-wool member of that flock. In fact, he's such a stickler that I had to sign up for it as well. I don't care much either way."

"What else?"

Jocelyn let out a sigh. "They—well, really my brothers—made a big stink about the age between us. So silly..."

"Oh really?" Margaret played naïve. "What is the difference in age between you?'

"Well, he was just turned fifty when we got married and I was twenty-five. He calls himself a late bloomer." She giggled.

Margaret sat back, thoughtful. "Isn't part of being Catholic having a lot of children?" In the back of Margaret's mind, she was also thinking about Robert and this issue.

Jocelyn nodded. "Sure is. But..." She lowered her voice and leaned in closer to Margaret. "I don't have any such notions. I grew up in a family of nine kids. I was never going to do that to myself."

Ah, so this was a girl cleverer than she let on. "So, how do you...how do you make sure no such blessed event occurrs?"

Jocelyn gave a self-satisfied smile not minding Margaret's nosy questions one bit. "I found a woman in the area. Old school, you know. With the right herbs and what not, and some careful attention to business, you can stop it from happening."

"And Bill hasn't pressed further, like wanting a doctor to find out why it wasn't happening?"

"Oh, he has. But I just assured him that doctor said it was not meant to be." She winked at Margaret. "Of course, I didn't go to an actual doctor. I really don't hold any truck with most doctors, tell you the truth."

Margaret tried to stem the aversion she felt for the woman in front of her. Ironically, Margaret shared similar thoughts about doctors, no love for them and their ways. She could agree with Jocelyn about that—but Margaret was not in cahoots with lying to a marital partner. Like Keith had done to her.

Jocelyn, in fact, exemplified some less than desirable qualities of their shared gender. Yet, Margaret had to hand it to her for setting up the life she wanted: rich husband, no children and leisure time to spend as she saw fit. Jocelyn had clawed her way to the top that was available to her. A part of Margaret could understand it even if she didn't necessarily approve of it.

It was time to probe more, to find out about her treatment at St. Elizabeth's. Margaret lobbed another foray. "So, do you go see doctors for...anything?"

Jocelyn turned the corners of her mouth down a smidgen. "Well..." She went silent. Margaret waited it out.

Jocelyn let out a huge sigh. "Bill insisted recently that I go to, um, to St. Elizabeth's."

Margaret responded in what she hoped was a bland manner. "Oh?"

"Yes. You see, I get the blue uglies sometimes."

"Blue uglies?"

"That's what I call them. You know, how sometimes at a certain time of month you can get in a real funk. I guess he just can't stand seeing me like that so, I humored him about it."

"How did it go?"

She looked off into the room and a secretive smile slipped over her face. "I am under the care of the top doctor there. I mean, the very best. And he has done wonders for me."

She looked back at Margaret and her eyes positively sparkled. Again, Margaret wondered if this was "different" too.

Curious, Margaret said, "I actually know a doctor over there. What is the name of yours?"

"Dr. Michaels."

Margaret held in her expression. Michaels was a psychiatrist that she had encountered a year prior when trying to get her Aunt Blanche freed from an institution called Blue Plains. She knew, in addition to running Blue Plains, he also served at the nearby St. Elizabeth's as the head of psychiatry. It had been immediately evident to Margaret on first meeting that the "good doctor" was not so much into the business of helping people. Rather, he was more into the business of bettering himself financially. He even had the gall to ask them for donations from her aunt's estate.

Margaret kept all of that to herself and said, "Well, that's good you are getting the care you need."

"Oh yes, he is just so calm and so easy to talk to. A real sweetheart." Jocelyn gushed out.

"Sweetheart?" Margaret couldn't keep the incredulity from her tone. That would be the very last word she would use to describe the man that she remembered as self-serving and opportunistic. She stopped herself from saying any more and changed tack. "Uh, so have all the blue moods straightened out then?"

"Yes, I feel fantastic!" Jocelyn arched her body forward as she said it and a sultry expression came over her face. Margaret could barely take it in. It was as if Jocelyn wanted to make it perfectly clear that a certain area of her life was impressive. An area that people never spoke about in polite company. But Margaret had realized early on that Jocelyn did not really fall under the category of "polite company".

Margaret didn't know where else to steer the conversation as it trailed off. She didn't think she discovered anything enlightening for Bill either. As they finished the last of their meals, a feeling of toxicity came over the table and Margaret was eager to escape.

A small piece of crumpet still sat on Jocelyn's plate and she toyed with it with one perfectly manicured fingernail rather than finishing it up. It would be impolite to not let her finish but Margaret was now itching to extricate herself and make her departure.

The waitress came over with a silver coffee urn offering refills. Before Margaret could respond, Jocelyn glanced down at her diamond encircled wristwatch and gave a little gasp. "Oh, look at the time!"

Surprised, Margaret said to the waitress, "No coffee, just the check please." Then she asked Jocelyn, "You have another appointment?"

Jocelyn was gathering her packages up in a distracted manner and becoming almost frantic. She stood and hastily slung her mink stole around her neck saying, "Yes...yes. I have a ride waiting for me. And I need to pop out to the powder room first."

Margaret, while surprised at the abruptness, was also relieved. "Well, I've got the bill. You go on ahead so you won't be late."

Jocelyn gave her a bright yet flustered smile and said in parting, "Thanks ever so much, Margaret. I just can't wait to do this again."

With that, Jocelyn swiftly headed out leaving Margaret to stare after her somewhat flummoxed. After paying the bill, Margaret stood and made her way to the front of the department store. She had no desire to shop and really just wanted to get out of the city, back to Needham Forest. She liked the city but always became antsy when away from the farm for more than several hours.

The doorway was now busier with people, mostly women, purposely striding in on whatever shopping mission brought them there, with the cold air of November whipping back and forth through the entrance's constant opening and closing. Margaret squeezed her way out to the sidewalk. She came to a sudden halt at the sight of the golden head of hair on the edge of the sidewalk near the curb. She didn't need or want to engage with Jocelyn again.

Margaret edged back towards the doorway and watched as Jocelyn peered into a car after it pulled up alongside the curb. A man exited out of the driver's side and quickly came over to Jocelyn. Before opening the passenger door for her, he leaned in towards her, whispering something in her ear. She simpered in that coquettish way she had and Margaret could see her face lifted towards his with that same come-hither look that she used on Bill.

Except that this man wasn't Bill. In fact, it was a man that Margaret recognized too well. It was Dr. Michaels. And there was clearly a familiarity here that went well beyond a doctor and patient relationship. Well beyond.

As Margaret watched the doctor's snazzy black convertible coupe pull away from the curb and enter into the steady stream of city traffic, her head whirled with what she had just witnessed. How exactly was Jocelyn entangled with the most noted psychiatrist in the District? How could Bill, a man Margaret admired and respected on so many levels, be a party to this? Margaret didn't know what was worse in her mind: if Bill didn't know...or if he did know.

CHAPTER TEN

Margaret stared at her reflection in her vanity. She sighed and picked up her powder puff gently patting it over her made-up face. She finished primping by dabbing her favored perfume, Chanel No. 5, behind her ears and on her wrists. She breathed in the familiar, comforting scent with its rose and jasmine notes and took a measure of confidence from it.

The dinner out with Bill and Jocelyn had already been scheduled and there was no way to get out of it. But it couldn't have come at a worse time. She had been struggling with what she had seen in front of Garfinkel's a few days earlier—the affable Bill Miller being hoodwinked by his young bride. She just did not know what to do with the information she had seen with her own two eyes. Why, oh why, had he lassoed himself with a woman like Jocelyn?

She had not told Robert anything about it, hesitant on several levels. Nor had she telephoned Bill. It did not sit well with her, not at all. She couldn't stop dwelling on it, Bill being made the fool. Then again, was it really any of her business?

She gathered her belongings and walked down the staircase. The bottom stair tread made its comforting creak, what she considered her "lucky" creak, as she stepped into the hall. Maybe she could count on that "luck" to get her through the dinner with the Millers.

She walked into the drawing room to wait for Robert. They were driving down into the city to a restaurant Bill had suggested, the Tabard Inn off Dupont Circle. Bill had pushed for them to go out as a foursome for some time. It had not been possible to put him off any longer despite misgivings about time spent with Jocelyn. Now, though, the idea of it was far more off-putting.

Margaret was restless and paced around the room until she heard the smooth hum of Robert's new Roamer Roadster come up Needham Forest's drive. She grabbed her bag and wrap and went out to meet him. He was already out of the car when she opened the front door.

The roadster was a recent purchase, a well-deserved splurge after winning a big case. Margaret encouraged him to buy the automobile, one of the last built models for the company. It suited him, gunmetal gray in color and sharp in style. He reached out for her hand.

They headed out and made their way down the curvy rolling country road where Needham Forest was situated, eventually reaching River Road, which ran loosely along the Potomac River. The new macadam surface kept Robert's car from bumping and rattling and soon brought them to the city's edge.

Robert broke into the peacefulness of the drive. "Well, this is a nice night out. Driving downtown and meeting up with Bill...and his wife too, of course."

Margaret shot him a look.

"What? Oh, that's right. You just saw her the other day, didn't you?"

"I certainly did." Margaret's tone came out clipped sounding.

"Not a pleasant outing?"

She turned and gazed at Robert's handsome profile. She didn't want to mar the evening but she couldn't keep it in any longer. In fact, it felt duplicitous not to share her thoughts on the young Mrs. Miller with Robert. "I didn't get a chance to tell you before now but..."

As Robert drove and looked straight ahead, Margaret relayed, blow by blow, what she had witnessed in front of Garfinkel's. As she told the tale, she could see a muscle moving slightly in his jawline. He did not comment after she finished, deliberating over it. They drove in silence passing by the changing colors of the new season.

Finally, she couldn't help but burst out, "What do we do about it? Bill is being made a fool. We can't be the only ones who know what she is up to. I mean, it was in broad daylight on the curb of F Street for goodness' sake."

Robert still remained silent.

Margaret continued and said, "If you had a wife who did this, wouldn't you want to be told?"

"My wife was doing that."

"What? What wife?" Margaret braced herself with hands pressed on the bench seat, shocked by Robert's comment.

Robert stared straight ahead. "I was married once. It was annulled. For the very reason we are talking about."

"Annulled? Like it never happened?"

"That's right, except it did."

"Robert, I— You never said anything."

"It's a chapter of my life best forgotten. But this brings a lot up for me."

Margaret let out a whoosh of breath. "Of course. I can see why. So, you would want to be told?"

"Oh, yes. Even though I might just hold it against the messenger."

"Great. So Bill will hold it against me?"

"Not you. Me. I'll do the telling."

"Robert, that's chivalrous of you but I'm a big girl. I can handle it."

"I know that, Margaret. But let's keep Needham Forest and you separate from this awful news Bill has to face. And it won't be tonight. The man deserves a nice enjoyable night out. One last night with the pretty picture of his marriage that's not so pretty. We owe him at least that much."

"Alright then. Agreed."

The dinner arrangements included swinging by Northwest, D.C. to the Miller's townhouse in Midcity, so that Bill and Jocelyn would not have to bother with a cab. Another piece of the evening that Margaret wished was not so. She began to steel herself as they parked alongside the Eighth Street address.

She recalled Jocelyn complaining about their residence the first time they had met at Woodward & Lothrop. She had railed on about wanting to move to the new Chevy Chase subdivision that was all the rage up on the border of the city where it met the Maryland suburbs.

As Robert edged his roadster into place, Margaret looked over at the benign townhouse, its details illuminated by a nearby gas street lamp. It showed a bit of age with some dowdiness around the edges but, aside from not having the sparkle and shine of a Chevy Chase address, it was perfectly respectable all in all.

Robert was also gazing over at the beige brick townhouse. Finally, Margaret turned to him. "Shall we?"

At the entrance, Robert lifted up the brass knocker and let it knock down twice.

The door opened and Bill stood at the other side with one of his welcoming and beaming smiles. "Well, there you are! Come on in for a moment. Jocelyn's still powdering her nose and such."

They walked from a dark hallway into the main room, a small living area. As Bill and Robert chatted about a case that was making the news, Margaret took in the space. The décor was, in a word, dated, with wallpaper from a more austere era covering the walls. She knew that Bill had lived there with his first wife, Katie, before she had passed on. Katie Miller must have been the original decorator of the place. The question in Margaret's mind was why didn't Jocelyn just redecorate the place to her own taste instead of complaining about it?

Footfall on the staircase filtered in and Jocelyn made her entrance with a flounce and a vapid smile. She wore a royal blue silky number that stretched tautly in the bodice, showing off, as usual, her assets. The blue color offset her blonde hair and Margaret did need to give her props for presenting herself always in the most favorable of ways. After greetings were made (with Robert almost visibly bristling at the sight of Bill's wife), the men picked up their conversation and Jocelyn moved closer in to Margaret.

In a not too disguised whisper, she said, "Now you can see what I am up against with this place, Margaret. I mean just look at it. And is it any wonder? It's over fifteen years old now." She frowned looking around the room.

Margaret asked her point blank, "Why haven't you changed the wallpaper out? That would really spruce things up, just doing that alone."

"Oh Margaret. I don't want to mess with these old crumbling walls. I just want a blank canvas to work with. A brand-new place."

Margaret hoped that they would not have to hear about it the entire dinner long.

After the flurry of putting on coats and getting out of the house and into Robert's roadster, the drive from Midcity to the Dupont Circle neighborhood was a quick one. The roadster took the curve around Scott Circle with its statue of General Winfield Scott gleaming in the street light. Once off the circle and into the wealthier Dupont Circle neighborhood, there was a shift from the Miller's stodgier and middle-class environs into a more upscale, tonier setting.

But Margaret sadly noted that even the wealthy Dupont Circle area had lost some of its luster since the market had plunged. The buildings gleamed a little less, it seemed.

Robert let them all out in front of the Tabard Inn on N Street and headed off to park nearby. As the three of them made their entrance with Jocelyn chattering on, Margaret focused on the elegant exterior of the Tabard. It harkened back to an older style. Margaret recalled some of the history she knew about the place. A woman named Marie Rogers had established it some years earlier and had taken the name from the Canterbury Tales, supposedly. When Margaret had dined there once, it had an English tearoom feel to it—but it also served international cuisine of some repute known throughout the city and even beyond.

There was a bit of jostling once inside the restaurant and some confusion about the reservation. Bill stepped forth and, as usual, his presence immediately commanded attention. They were quickly sorted out and escorted to an intimate table for four in a corner by the windowfront.

Before she took her seat, Jocelyn paused. "Silly me, but I need to take a trip to the powder room. I'll be back."

Margaret sat as Bill stared after his wife. Then he sat down. He turned to Margaret with a troubled expression. "How did it go the other day, Margaret?"

She thought she had prepared herself for this question but

she became mute, not knowing what to say. "I think fine, Bill. I think she's fine."

He looked at her with his brow raised. "Something you're not saying?"

"Um..."

Robert appeared at her side, after finding his way in. "Everything okay?"

Bill cleared his throat. "Ah yes. Needed to ask Margaret about a horse we had been eying up the other day..."

Once Jocelyn had returned and they were all settled at the table, Bill threw a satisfied look around their little group. "Finally. All four of us here, together."

Margaret and Robert both nodded politely. Jocelyn was gazing wide eyed all around the room. In a way, Margaret did not blame her. The room did charm with an old-world flavor that included Flemish-style paintings, colorful wallpaper, and tasteful place settings among other more subtle accents.

"Geez, Buddy. How come you never brought me here before now?"

"Well, Mom, I was saving it to surprise you. It's even better sharing it with our special guests tonight."

Robert and Margaret shared a quick glance at each other upon the use of the Millers' unusual nicknames. She couldn't recall if she had shared that piece of Miller lore with him. But it was indeed even stranger to hear them used aloud.

The waiter with a pencil-thin mustache discreetly approached their table and handed Bill a list. "May I recommend our special vintage monsieur?" Happily for all, the restaurant provided wine in "medicinal" quantities for those diners interested.

"Sure, why not?" Bill waved him away and then turned to Robert. "Bobby..."

Jocelyn turned to Margaret and said, "I did so enjoy meeting you the other day. We need to make it a regular weekly thing, don't you think?"

Margaret did not think that but just smiled in return. Jocelyn began to prattle on about a dress she had in mind and wanted to go back for.

In the customary way of couples socializing, Margaret knew she would be relegated to one-on-one conversation with Jocelyn while Robert and Bill talked shop. She also resigned herself to the fact that there would not be an opening to query Bill some more about the Confederate gold bars. She gave the appropriate nods and "huhs" along the way but one ear was tuned into what the men were discussing.

She turned to their side of the table abruptly when she heard Bill say, "That God durn Dr. Michaels was in the courtroom the other day. Testifying again. The man is a real burr in my side when he gets involved in a case. I mean, I give him some leeway as he's recently widowed and all that but I'll tell you what: he's something."

It was as if Bill just laid down a loaded weapon at the table.

"How do you mean?" Robert looked at Bill with a strange intensity. Margaret was jolted as she suddenly put two and two together. Could Dr. Michaels be the doctor who had shown Robert his gun?

Jocelyn, Margaret realized, had stopped her chatter. She too was looking intently at Bill.

"Well, he just always is right at the edge of right and wrong in my opinion. The best criminal defense as you know..."

When the topic changed to something else, Margaret gazed around at her dining companions realizing that they were a tableful of secrets. Her secret was keeping what she had seen at Garfinkel's from Bill. Jocelyn's was carrying on an affair maybe. Robert's was holding back which doctor had shown him a gun.

Margaret waited to see if the other two, Robert and Jocelyn, would chime in with anything of their own about Michaels. She halfway expected and hoped for it, for some of it at least to come out. But they did not.

The only one who talked about Dr. Michaels at the table was Bill, seemingly the most guileless of their little group. Or was he? He was a razor-sharp man who had saddled himself with a woman taking him into some dark places. Surely, he knew more than he was letting on.

A lot of the time, truths were difficult to come by.

Back at Needham Forest several hours later, Margaret and Robert lounged on her comfortably cushioned sofa, her feet in his capable hands for a massage. "Well, this was quite a night."

He nodded, deep in thought.

"I think there's something else aside from being married before that you haven't told me," Margaret said pointedly.

"You figured it out."

"Yes. Michaels is the one with the gun."

He nodded slowly.

"What should we do about it?"

"I'm working that out in my head."

"Bill has to be told, Robert. About all of it."

"He does. And he will be told. I just need to figure out how to do so."

"How could a man like Bill be with a woman like this?"

Robert shook his head.

CHAPTER ELEVEN

A week after dinner at the Tabard, Margaret and Robert were settled on the sofa in her drawing room, drinks in hand. Robert had driven out after a long day in the city. A day that included finally having a private chat with Bill Miller.

Margaret broke into their companionable silence. "How did it go?"

Robert took a long, thirsty pull from his vodka tonic before answering. "Not well. As you can imagine..."

"Did he not have any inkling at all?"

"He didn't say but I have the sneaking suspicion others had tried to let him in on it. But when I told him what you had seen directly...well...it hit pretty hard."

"Of course, it did. It's just so angering what this...this... strumpet has set up for him to deal with."

Robert sighed heavily. "Look, I think it would be nice if we took him out to lunch at The Madrillon. Get his mind off it somehow. Maybe...I don't know...talk shop about horses over some drinks."

"Absolutely. Should I set it up or..."

"Let me. Like I predicted, he's not happy with the messenger right now. But that should lift, I hope, by next week."

"That's so unfair that he would hold it against you, Robert."

He shrugged. "It's just human nature. An age-old tale. But someone of his intelligence won't let it stand like that. I'll give it a week and then reach back out."

They went silent, each mulling over Bill's terrible plight. Margaret spoke up, breaking into their thoughts with a stab at some levity. "Well, since Bill is otherwise occupied, I guess I need to start up the hunt for the gold bars again, eh?"

"Can't hurt to try," Robert said with a wry note. "I thought you hit a dead end with that though. Did you ever hear anything back from the lady at the historical place?"

She shook her head then added, "But I didn't expect to. She made it clear I was a bother. But I'll go again. Maybe someone else will be there next time."

"You know, after you told me about all this, I ran it by a colleague in the office who fancies himself a Civil War expert."

"You did?"

"Yes, and he did recall a story about missing gold in this area. Supposedly, there was always talk that it tied into a train heist that occurred up near Monocacy, a little south of Frederick, followed by a small skirmish afterwards nearby."

Margaret sat up to take in Robert's story better. "Really? So, this train heist—and then the nearby skirmish—could be connected to a possible gold stash here at Needham Forest?"

Robert shrugged. "Maybe it's a reach or maybe it's something? I mean that train junction at Monocacy is roughly ten miles or so from here."

She eyed him with an appraising glance. "You could very well be onto something, Robert."

"Well, it's not conclusive proof of anything, but seems too coincidental, doesn't it?"

Margaret reached over and clinked her glass to his. "Yes, and I, for one, do not believe in coincidences."

Margaret tried to focus on the paperwork in front of her but the figures on the bills of sale blurred. She was thinking about Bill Miller again—and getting anxious. More than a week had now passed since either she or Robert had contact with Bill Miller. It was partly due to the ruckus of the holiday season rushing in, but the larger cause was down to Robert revealing the truth about Jocelyn to Bill.

Margaret had put a lot of items on hold that needed Bill's input with his investor hat on. She had grown to value and appreciate his astute advice and was missing it. It was a situation she just did not know how to handle. The only saving grace was that Jocelyn had not been in touch. Margaret already decided if Jocelyn rang, she would just put her off.

Cassie gave a light rap on the door and poked her kerchief-covered head in. "Leonard out in the kitchen for you, Mizz Margaret. Should I send him in?"

"Of course." Margaret stood to stretch out the kinks that had gathered in her neck, evidence of the stress she was under. She walked over to the window and gazed out.

Leonard cleared his throat, announcing his presence in the doorway. Margaret turned to greet him. "Oh hello, Leonard. Is everything okay?"

"Yes, ma'am. I just wanted to give you this." He held out several large rolls of paper.

She reached for them, asking, "What are these?"

"I was doing some organizing. Some of those shelves had piled-up papers and I came across these. They look to be floor plans of the house. Thought you might want to keep them up here."

"Oh yes. I had forgotten about these. They were done up when Daddy had started the plans for the addition right before —" She stopped and didn't continue. Leonard nodded with a solemn expression.

Her father had died of a sudden heart attack in the prime of his life, snuffed out so unexpectedly. His ambition had driven him each day to accomplish, to achieve. One of his pet projects was building a showcase addition to the house. He felt it important to show off the house to its full potential where he could entertain the horse set with frequent gatherings and events.

Margaret remembered how he had vetted the one of the premier architects in the region, Jacob Garmong. Her father's desire was that the historical nature of the house and farm be an integral aspect of the addition and shown in the best possible light. The plans were shelved immediately after his death and she remembered only glancing at them once throughout the years. Her grief had eclipsed any interest in the project.

"Thank you. Yes, I'll keep them up here in my files."

Leonard nodded and remained still. He apparently had something else on his mind. "I remembered something else when I found these plans. Your daddy used to study them something fierce down in the barn office some nights." He shook his head. "I can still see it in my mind. Late night—when I would check in on things—he would be there with his cigar and a drink just all caught up in them. I don't know if that means anything or not, but I thought I'd mention it."

"Huh. I guess he was just so excited about the project maybe?"

"Maybe. Or, could be he thought they held an answer somehow for...well, you know."

Margaret frowned. "What do you mean?"

Leonard shrugged. "They might tie into that cache of gold somehow. I don't know. Just thought it worth mentioning."

"Oh goodness. Of course that makes sense." Margaret shook her head ruefully. "Leonard, where would I be without you?"

He grinned in response as she added, "Especially since I have absolutely nothing else to go on. I don't have to tell you how much those mystical gold bars would come in handy about now." They had gone over the recent financials together the previous day and the figures had been a stark dose of reality.

Leonard grimaced. "I know it. I surely know it."

After Leonard left, Margaret sat back down at her desk, the rolled-up plans in front of her. What was it her father had divined from the plans, if anything?

No time like the present. She stood and rolled them out, the paper now brittle after twenty years or so of haphazard storage at the stables.

Margaret grabbed paperweights to place on the corners. The ink was a mix of blue and black, not too faded, on the delicate paper, with the architect's distinctive signature at the bottom right, Jacob Garmong.

She examined the drawings, trying to view them from her father's eyes. An hour went by and she was no closer to deciphering much with the exception of one thing. They revealed a footprint of an original dwelling place buried underneath the current house. She looked up from the plans and stared out. How did she not know this about the house she had resided in almost her entire life?

She bent back over them to try and make sense of it. The architect had penned notes along the side of the building's outline which mentioned that the current house was probably constructed about fifty years after the original. The house became what was now standing, a Federal-style house exemplifying a monied residence of the early 1800s.

The notes went on to reveal that the original footprint had possibly been a log house. Margaret envisioned a prototypical, backwoods-style log cabin. She glanced around and thought about where exactly the original building would have been before it was expanded.

The phone ringing in the hall snapped her out of her thought process about house footprints. She hustled out to pick it up so Cassie wouldn't have to.

Robert was on the other end. "Margaret, he finally took my call," he said without preamble.

"Oh, thank goodness. How did it go?"

"He's not doing so great, but he's willing to meet—to meet both of us, in fact. I know it's last minute but what do you have on for this afternoon?

"Meeting you and Bill if that's a go."

"Definitely a go. Let's meet at his office. Can you get to the Appeals Building over on E Street?"

"I'll take the train and then a taxi."

"I'll be waiting outside for you."

They said their goodbyes and Margaret stayed in her seat at the phone table for a beat, working up the nerve to go and meet Bill Miller.

CHAPTER TWELVE

Margaret stepped out of the taxi and spotted Robert in front of the Appeals Building, standing diagonally from the statue of Abraham Lincoln. The sun reflected off the statue darting a beam in Margaret's direct line of vision, obscuring Robert.

Behind him and the statue, the three-sectioned building sat squatly. Its Greek Revival style gave it a formality in keeping with Judiciary Square, where much of the legal business for the nation's capital was conducted.

As Robert walked towards Margaret, she finally saw him clearly and gave him a big smile. He grabbed her hand and intertwined it in his, saying, "Are we ready?" She nodded.

Inside the building, they walked through the marbled hallway to Bill's office suite at the western end. His secretary, an older woman with white hair pulled back in a low chignon, looked up with a somber expression that quickly switched to a smile at the sight of Robert.

"Hello, Miss Stanwick." Robert introduced Margaret and they exchanged niceties and then he continued. "We made arrangements to meet Bill for lunch."

She nodded slowly and then stood up almost as an

afterthought. "Please wait for a minute." She tapped on the door behind her desk and paused. Then she walked into the inner chamber. Within seconds, she emerged and said, "He's ready for you, Mr. Brady, but..."

"But?"

"Just, he's not really himself right now."

Robert held the door for Margaret and she almost let a gasp out upon the sight of the man standing in front of her. His suit hung off his shoulders loosely as though draped off a hanger. His face bore a gray pallor. Since the night of the dinner at the Tabard, only a month prior, Bill had become a shadow of his former self, disheveled and despondent.

Margaret couldn't stop herself. "Oh Bill, I just hate to see you like this."

He wiped a hand over a bristly chin, normally so well-shaven. "Margaret, I know you tried your best with her."

Margaret drew back a little in surprise. She hadn't done anything at all about Jocelyn. "Well, I..."

Robert stepped up and broke into the interaction, grabbing the other man's hand in a shake. "Bill, it's good to see you. Let's get you out for a bit. Margaret and I thought we could all have some lunch. How about at The Madrillon?"

Margaret shot a sharp look at Robert and interjected. "Or someplace else, of course." Robert immediately looked sheepish upon realizing too late that The Madrillon was loaded with memories of Jocelyn.

But the gaffe was overridden by Bill's answer. "I can't show my face there. Not right now anyway."

It wasn't the association with Jocelyn, Margaret realized. It was more that Bill was too humiliated to show up at his regular haunt. A place where he had "held court" for all the years it had been open probably.

Robert spoke up. "Well, I know where we can go instead.

An out of the way spot that none of the lawyer crowd knows about. A best kept secret really. What do you say? Come on. My treat."

Bill hesitated before looking back up at them with a hangdog expression. "Alright. Let me grab my hat." As he reached towards his hat atop the coat stand, he moved like a very old man. He had aged so much since their last meeting and it crushed Margaret to witness it.

He stopped all of a sudden in his tracks, hat in hand. "Oh wait... I need to say today's novena before we head out. Join me, will you?" His gaze moved to the corner of the office where, amidst all the stacks of paper and books, there was a cleared off area. The set-up looked like an altar. A clean white handkerchief had been stretched atop a hall table. White candles sat on top decorated with what appeared to be the Virgin Mary.

Margaret looked to Robert for guidance. He too seemed taken aback but said smoothly, "Yes, of course."

Bill lit several candles with a shaky hand and a smell rose up, a smell Margaret could not pin down. But she didn't like it. Their trio stood in front of the small, makeshift shrine and Bill began to speak some Latin which was complete gibberish to Margaret. Robert, on the other hand, mumbled the words under his breath as if they were coming from another person. Margaret stood off to one side, uncomfortable with the proceedings but not moving away from it.

When Bill was finished, he said in passing, "I got those candles blessed by Monsignor Ferguson over at the Immaculate Conception the other day. I just got to keep at it. I'm almost finished with my first nine days of petitions. Then it will start over again. He said to keep up with them and that she'll mend her ways."

As they walked back through the main hallway, Margaret

couldn't help but notice others making a wide berth for their threesome. Almost as though reading her mind, Bill said, "I know I've been acting like a madman ever since finding out. Folks don't want any part of it. I can't blame them. Times are tough enough without this kind of nonsense to get tangled up in."

Margaret could hear a bit of Bill's customary vim and vigor in the words. If only he could take those words to heart and act on them. Disengage himself from letting a girl as silly as his wife run him into rack and ruin. She wondered what could make him see this.

Outside, Margaret breathed in crisp, cold air wiping out the smell of Bill's candles as the three of them walked, mostly in silence, into the next neighborhood over. Eventually, they turned into an alleyway where a hanging sign with an image of a white lighthouse with black stripes jauntily announced The Lighthouse Grill. It operated as a speakeasy at night which meant drinks were really available anytime.

Robert led the way down three steps into the basement of the older commercial building that housed offices on the upper floors. Inside was dark and dim, exactly the kind of place to have a private and confidential conversation. A barmaid gestured for them to seat themselves and Robert led the way again, this time to a round table in the corner. Once situated, Bill looked up at them, his soulful eyes like wounds on his visage. It was almost too much to bear, to absorb his expression.

They got drink set ups, gin and tonic for Bill, vodka tonics for Margaret and Robert, and then sat with an awkward silence between them. Robert nudged Margaret. "So, Margaret, tell Bill about the new foal at the stable...how that's been going..." His voice trailed off.

Margaret perked up. "Oh yes. Bill, you must come out and

see. It's just a bitty thing but I have high hopes we'll have a winner soon enough."

Bill absentmindedly fingered the lining of his tie. He wasn't really listening to Margaret, judging from his somewhat vacant expression. She paused and another strained silence crept in.

Finally, Bill pulled his head back up, his gaze taking in both Margaret and Robert. "I guess I'm now the spitting image of a cuckold, aren't I?'

"Now, Bill, don't say that!"

"Well, if the name fits..."

Margaret couldn't hold back any longer. "Did you not know, Bill? No suspicion at all?"

He fiddled with the tumbler in front of him, not taking a sip as of yet. "I accidentally picked up the extension line upstairs one time. Michaels was talking to her in a...well, a too familiar tone. Telling her to get some rest or some such nonsense. But I figured it was his bedside manner at the time. Now, of course, I know different. But other than that..."

"Look, are you planning to divorce her?"

Bill reeled back from Margaret with a look of horror on his face. "Divorce her? I love her. I would never do such a thing."

"Well, but what is she saying?"

He let out a huge puff of air. "We fight a lot these days. She throws things. Yells and such. But it's not too unlike when she gets the blue uglies. The reason this whole kerfuffle started. But she just won't agree to give him up. Doesn't want to."

"Oh my." Again, Margaret was amazed by the gall of Jocelyn. Who did she think she was?

Robert, who had been silent, interjected. "Bill, have you approached Michaels man-to-man about this?" Margaret knew right away that the gun was on Robert's mind. He was trying to cipher out what exactly the level of recklessness might be between the two adversaries, the two rivals for Jocelyn's heart.

Bill gave a snort. "Of course I have. I confronted him right outside the courtroom the other day. I told him to leave my girl alone."

"What did he say?"

"He laughed at me, if you can believe it." His mouth moved into a rictus of pain.

Robert continued. "Do you think...could he be a physical threat at all?"

"To Jocelyn?"

"No. To you."

"Nah. I could take him down easy if he wanted to try anything. But he's a threat in other ways...if he manages to take my sweet girl, my sweet Jocelyn, away from me. I just don't know how I'd live without her."

Margaret had a couple of thoughts about that but kept them to herself.

Bill spoke again. "I don't know what it is about that man. It's like he has cast a spell on her. These alienists...I'll tell you what, just between us, I've never much cared for any of their types. I guess they got a fancier name now. Psychiatrists." He sniffed aloud and then continued. "Shifty as all get out. They change their tune to match whatever the story is in my experience."

Margaret couldn't disagree with Bill on the subject. Especially when it came to Michaels. She had disliked the man upon her first encounter with him. And now this episode really boiled her blood. An affair with a patient was against every code in the book.

Bill turned directly to face Margaret with more pain leaching from his big, expressive eyes. "I've begged her, Margaret. Could you talk to her again?"

"Of course, Bill. Anything you need."

Bill's face crinkled into the start of a smile, just a start. But it heartened Margaret to see it. She added, "I can try to get her to change her ways." At the same time, she felt duplicitous saying so because she knew something about the human heart. It couldn't be told what to do. Ever.

Bill sat back in his chair and finally lifted up his drink for a sip. Then he said, "Next time, we'll be at The Madrillon again. I'll get this thing straightened out. Just watch me."

Margaret and Robert both nodded, avoiding each other's gaze. Then Bill leaned forward closer to look at them. With some intensity in his voice, he said, "You two are the best. You're good people. Don't forget that."

They walked Bill back to the Appeals Building and parted ways after lending him some more words of encouragement.

When it was just the two of them again, Robert edged closer towards Margaret and said, "How about you stay in the city and, after I finish up at the office, I'll take you out for a surprise. Something to get our minds off this awful business."

Margaret thought about it for a moment. There was a new art exhibit at the Corcoran Gallery of Art she was interested in viewing. "Alright. It's a deal...or a date."

They worked out where they would meet a couple of hours later and Robert leaned over to kiss Margaret on the cheek. She felt the usual electricity flare between them. As she watched him heading down the block to his office, she hoped that spark would not die any time soon.

CHAPTER THIRTEEN

Robert pulled his roadster up to the corner of 17th Street and Pennsylvania Avenue where Margaret waited with the Corcoran looming behind her. The art collection, housed in a magnificent Classical Revival building constructed almost sixty years earlier, was top notch. Margaret had been especially enchanted by one of the traveling exhibits, just the distraction she had needed.

After Margaret hopped into the car, Robert maneuvered back into the teeming late-day traffic. "Do I need to be dressed up more for wherever we are going?" she asked.

"Nope." She felt the warmth of his gaze as he took her in. "You are perfect just as you are."

She smiled and sat back in the comfort of the leather-cushioned seat, breathing in a whiff of Robert's cologne. As Robert navigated the city traffic and headed in a northerly direction, she said, "Can I get a hint of where you are taking me?"

"Sit tight, Mrs. O'Keefe. We will be at our destination shortly."

She knew he was saying it in jest but suddenly "Mrs.

O'Keefe" didn't sound right anymore to her. She did not want to be Mrs. O'Keefe. And she definitely didn't want to be married to Mr. O'Keefe anymore. She let a sigh escape at the thought.

"What's in that head of yours?"

"I was thinking about divorce."

"Bill Miller's?"

"What? No, I don't think he has any intentions of divorcing. In fact, I would venture to say he will fight that to his last breath if necessary. No, I was thinking about my divorce from Keith."

"Oh. How is that progressing?"

"It's not. He has gummed up the works again, apparently. Stalling on signing something or another. I was just thinking, I don't want to be Mrs. O'Keefe anymore." Her voice trailed off and an odd silence crept into the space. She regretted it had slipped out—especially because she didn't want Robert to think that she was pushing to be Mrs. Brady. Or did she want to push for that?

The silence was broken when Robert said, "We're here."

Margaret looked out her passenger window. "Where...oh, it's the Tivoli!"

"Yes, I heard through the office grapevine there's a good show on this evening. So how does dinner and a show sound, Mrs.— I mean, Margaret?"

"Sounds wonderful."

The Tivoli Theater, taking up a city block in the Columbia Heights neighborhood, was known as "the temple for the arts" in the city. It had ties to another theater, the Knickerbocker, and Margaret couldn't help but recall that horrible tragedy in the winter of 1922. A large snowfall had caused the roof to collapse while patrons were inside with almost a hundred lives lost.

While the crown jewel was the theater, smart shops were sprinkled along its stretch of 14th Street. Right next door to the theater was a little café. Robert and Margaret snagged one of the last tables available in the busy theater and shopping complex.

Over a light meal, they chatted. Margaret told Robert about the exhibit and he told her about his afternoon court session. Both were purposely avoiding the unavoidable: Bill Miller's predicament. Also, Margaret did not broach something else weighing on her mind. She had hoped Bill might offer her another check, but he had not. Given his condition, there was no way she felt comfortable bringing it up during their lunch conversation.

When they were served after-dinner coffees, Margaret stirred a teaspoon of sugar into hers. Then she said, "What was all that about novenas and nine-day petitions?"

Robert's expression became grim. "I am worried about him and his behavior."

"It was such an odd scene, Robert. I mean, the way it was laid out like an altar. And the chanting. But you knew it too?"

He nodded. "It's Latin. It's what we recite in Mass every Sunday. Well, some of it anyway. Other parts are just rote from attending parochial schools, I guess."

"Well, do you think it's okay to go along with that? Let him think it will win Jocelyn back or get her to stop what she is doing?"

"I don't know, Margaret. But it felt like we had to humor him at the very least. I've heard from others that he's been roaming the halls a lot at his office building. Walking back and forth aimlessly. I mean, it can't go on like that forever."

"I guess next up is me trying to reason with the girl." She shook her head with disdain. "But I don't hold any faith that will change a thing."

"Well, it's worth trying, don't you think? Maybe approach it like you would a pouty child?"

"I've never had to deal with a pouty child. But...you're right.

If I view it like I need to engage a child and talk her out of her foolish, foolish actions, maybe she might see reason." She again shook her head. "I just don't know how Bill puts up with it. Any of it."

They sipped on their coffees, both in their own heads about how to help the man they considered a good friend.

"Well, look who it is."

Both Margaret and Robert looked up at the woman standing by their table. Tall and elegantly attired with a mink wrap draped around her neck, she smiled at Robert. Margaret's vantage gave her a direct view of the little claws of the mink that hung down from the wrap.

Before Robert stood up quickly and leaned towards the woman, kissing her cheek, Margaret caught a flash of his expression which seemed to convey surprise but also something else...maybe dismay?

He spoke after the kiss saying, "What a surprise. Are you here just on your own?"

"No, no, the gals are in the powder room and I just caught sight of you before joining them there. But you're being rude. Who is your friend here, Bobby?" Her gaze down towards Margaret was a weighty one.

"Oh, yes. Pardon me. This is, uh, this is Margaret O'Keefe."

Margaret, by turn, waited to find out who exactly this woman calling Robert, "Bobby", was.

"And Margaret, this is my sister, Meredith O'Connor."

"Delighted to meet you," Meredith proffered a gloved hand for a gentle shake. Margaret sized up Meredith, taking in her poise and confidence, as they shook hands.

"Please, won't you join us?" Margaret gestured to the chair next to her. Meredith nodded and took the chair offered.

Once seated, she asked, "I only have a minute but tell me, how do you two know each other?" Again, her smile seemed veiled. Margaret could see a faint family resemblance through the eyes. The woman had never heard of Margaret and Margaret only recalled a vague mention of Robert's sister.

"Well," Robert said as Margaret said, "We..." The three of them chuckled and Margaret waved a hand at Robert saying, "Go ahead..."

"Margaret and I worked on a case together. You remember it. The Blanche Magruder case. Blanche was Margaret's aunt."

"Oh, I do remember it. Quite something..." Meredith raised her eyebrows and added, "And you've kept in touch since then?"

It was a loaded question and Margaret let Robert take the lead on it.

He said simply, "Yes. Yes, we have."

An awkward pause took over before Meredith spoke again. "So tell me, Margaret. Do you live here in the city?"

"No, no. I'm a country mouse. Out towards Rockville in horse country."

"Ah yes. That explains why I don't recall seeing you at Immaculate Conception."

"Seeing me— Oh, I'm not Catholic."

An almost imperceptible freeze came over the other woman's face. "Ah, I see." She glanced at her wristwatch. "Well, the others must wonder what has become of me." She stood and again gave Margaret a bland smile. "Nice to have met you, Margaret." Then she looked pointedly at Robert. "Dear brother, we are overdue for a coffee sometime. Alright?"

Robert stood and said, "Sure, sis. Enjoy the show." He sat back down and they both watched Meredith depart as she made her way through the crowd.

Margaret looked at Robert. "Did I sense a cold shoulder when your sister found out I'm not Catholic?"

He cleared his throat. "She's a bit protective. You know,

older siblings and all that. But let's not bother with it. Come on." He grabbed her hand. "We also have a show to get to."

With Robert's hand in hers, Margaret tried to shake the scene with Robert's sister. Meredith was clearly not enamored with the idea of Robert spending time with Margaret, for more reasons than one it seemed. As she felt the warmth from Robert's hand, Margaret wondered if what they had was more tenuous than she let herself believe.

CHAPTER FOURTEEN

Margaret headed up the electric stairway in the middle of the crowded store—too crowded for her taste. The initial thrill of the new-fangled stairway had already diminished and was on its way to becoming "old hat". She exited onto the floor with the lingerie department.

People, not too unlike horses in Margaret's opinion, tended to be creatures of habit and it was Jocelyn's habit to go shopping most days of the week. Margaret gambled on spotting Jocelyn at her favorite department store, Woodward & Lothrop, on one of the biggest sale days of the year, Remnant Days. Items were put on clearance with deep discounts after the hoopla of the holidays wound down.

Jocelyn seemed to have a penchant for the lingerie department and possibly a fascination for brassieres so it stood to reason Margaret would find her there. Margaret's vague plan was to approach her in her element like she would a high-strung filly in the paddock. Then, somehow, she would have to get this girl-woman to see reason.

Margaret approached the area, set off in a corner, where frilly, lacy, silky and satiny fabrics hung from circular racks awash with many colors. It set a mood, in fact, a mood that was a departure from other, more practical sales departments. It called out like a siren song to a certain breed of shopper, Margaret thought.

Through the flurry of activity, women rifling through sales racks and chit-chatting in excited voices, Margaret sighted Jocelyn positioned at a rack of girdles. With slow, measured steps, she headed straight for the confrontation.

She studied Jocelyn whose movements were frenzied as she whipped through one item after the next almost as if unaware of her actions. When Margaret was directly across from her, she caught Jocelyn's attention.

Jocelyn let out a gasp of surprise. "Margaret! What are you...why are you here?"

"Same as you, Jocelyn. Shopping. Isn't this one of the best sales of the year?"

"Oh...yes. It is."

"But I have been meaning to call you."

"You have?"

"Yes. Could we take a break and go to the tearoom? Maybe grab a coffee to fortify us?"

Margaret could see the wheels spinning in the other woman's head. "I don't really..."

Margaret pressed the issue, expressing sympathy and concern she in no way felt. "I just wanted to see how you are doing."

"Well, I guess I could take a short break."

They walked together to the electric stairway, neither saying anything. After they were able to grab one of the last available tables in the busy tearoom, a constrained air sat between them. It was a vastly different dynamic between the two women from their previous meeting. Margaret was somewhat heartened that at least Jocelyn must understand the gravity of her actions at a minimum to be acting so differently from her normal flighty self.

Margaret again reminded herself how she would approach a gun-shy horse before she spoke up. "Well, Jocelyn. It appears things have become a muddle."

Jocelyn avoided eye contact with Margaret and her gaze skittered off to one side. "However do you mean?"

"Everything is out in the open now. Isn't it?"

"What?"

Margaret felt a wave of extreme irritation but clamped it down. Jocelyn was going to try and play innocent. She changed tack. "Bill is such a lovely man."

Jocelyn's mulish expression softened. "Of course, he is. I know that, Margaret."

"It's very painful to watch him go through this."

"You've seen him?"

Margaret nodded. Silence filled the space between them again.

Finally, Margaret couldn't keep it in any longer. "Jocelyn, my dear girl. You need to stop this. You need to give up whatever it is you think you have with Dr. Michaels."

"I can't."

"Why not?"

"That's, um, that's what's hard to explain."

"It shouldn't be. Tell me."

Jocelyn leaned a little forward and, with a plaintive tone, said, "I owe him. He's made me feel like a new woman, Margaret. Like I've never felt before really."

Margaret waited, saying nothing. Jocelyn continued on with another rationale. "And...and...he's in some debt so he needs me to help him. With money, I mean."

Margaret's jaw dropped before she could curb herself. Now this silly woman was funneling Bill's hard-earned income to this joke of a doctor. "Jocelyn, why would you need to give him money? I'm sure he does quite well in the medical field."

"No. He, uh, well...it's all a bit confusing. I just..."

Margaret took in the full measure of the woman across the table from her. Her visage had taken on a sulky expression, like the face of a child in a toy store being told to put back a sparkly, shiny item but balking at doing so.

"Have you talked to anyone else about all of this?"

"That priest at Bill's church. He came over to the house. Boy, does he think a lot of himself." She almost spit out his name, "Monsignor Ferguson."

"What do you mean he thinks a lot of himself?"

"He had the nerve to tell me that what I was doing was wickedness. Can you believe it? Wickedness." Her gaze was one of innocence.

Margaret steeled herself once again. "Well, Jocelyn, don't you think what you are doing is...wrong? I mean, it's very basic. Cheaters never prosper, do they?"

Jocelyn shifted in her chair and looked up at Margaret with a slyness in her big, blue eyes. "I don't know about that. You never cheated at anything, Margaret?"

Margaret was jarred by the comment. She suddenly felt exposed and inwardly questioned herself. Had she cheated and been untrustworthy in her own life? At times, yes, she had. In a way, wasn't she being duplicitous at that very moment? Feigning concern for Jocelyn when really, she couldn't give two hoots about the girl herself. It was Bill she cared about. And who was she to tell this girl what to do? But she plunged on, changing up the conversation once again. Clearing her throat, she asked, "Why is it you think the doctor is better for you than Bill? What is it about him?"

In a sudden transformation, Jocelyn's face crumbled. She

began to weep with loud and unseemly sobs. Other patrons were turning and openly gaping.

Embarrassed, Margaret handed over a napkin. She waited a beat for the sobs to dissipate some. Again, she dug deep into her experience with horses and how to calm them, applying the same technique in choosing her words. Because, when it came right down to it, Jocelyn really was acting like a skittish mare. Like handing over a sugar cube, Margaret tempered her tone and said, "Let's see if we can figure this all out, Jocelyn."

Jocelyn gave a loud sniff and lifted her gaze back up. "I don't want Bill to be hurt. I really don't. But I'm putty in Donald's hands. Oh, it's all such a tangle." Another sob loudly escaped from her.

"Well, here's how you untangle it. You tell him in no uncertain terms that it is over. That you love your husband. That you respect and honor the vows of marriage that you took a couple of years ago."

Jocelyn gave another sniff followed by the slightest nod.

"Surely you can see that you need to make this right. As soon as possible. Today even." Margaret gauged Jocelyn's expression which had turned from recalcitrant to defeated and she added, "Really, you can't hesitate here. Things need be cut off immediately with Dr. Michaels...Donald. I know he's very persuasive and that's challenging but the way forward is clear. Can you do it?"

A contrite expression came over the other woman's face, now mottled in red splotches. "Yes, I can. I'll do it."

"Good. Now I do need to get back to the farm. And you should go home. Right now. Leave shopping for another day and tend to this." She raised a hand to flag their server down. "This was my treat. I'm just glad we bumped into each other and had this little chat."

She corralled Jocelyn to the exit noting the other woman

tossed a backwards, longing look at the lingerie department. Outside, she helped Jocelyn to find a cab home. As she watched the back of the cab with Jocelyn's bright head of hair bobbing in view, she wondered if any progress had been made, if she had gotten through to her at all. She fully recognized her motives were selfish in part. Getting Bill back on track meant that Needham Forest could also get back on track. But it also gnawed at her to see Bill in these dire straits with his horribly knotted-up marriage.

Margaret walked in the direction of the electric streetcar line. Taking that back to Rockville was longer than the train ride due to all the whistle stops along the way, but she needed the distraction and wanted to do so while she still could. There was recent talk that the vexing economic downturn may lead to severe changes to the lines, possibly the one out to Rockville.

Once on board, the weather was pleasant enough to take in the sights and sounds of the northwest quadrant of the city as the streetcar made its rocky and bumpy way through neighborhood by neighborhood. But instead of being a distraction from her meeting with Jocelyn, the city streets became a blur as Margaret sifted back through the disturbing discussion. Now she questioned whether it had been productive or not in getting the girl to see the wrongs of her ways. Had Jocelyn truly been contrite by the end of their meeting? Or was it all just an act? Margaret wanted to take it as a change in the other woman but it was quite possible that "change" was really only surface-deep.

She let out a big sigh which made the passenger sitting next to her turn and stare. Only time would tell what was to happen with Bill and Jocelyn. Time would tell.

PART 2

CHAPTER FIFTEEN

A WEEK LATER

The Washington Star was spread out on the table in front of Margaret, splattered with the horrific event of the previous day. Bill Miller had shot Donald Michaels inside his car at point-blank range in broad daylight at the intersection of 11th and G Streets. Evidence of Bill's actions was graphically displayed in photographs and in the newsprint details. The chilling term used repeatedly was "in cold blood".

A part of Margaret still thought it was all a dream, that it just couldn't be the reality that Bill had done this. Her partner, almost a father figure to her in some ways, could not be the same man who'd carried out such a dastardly deed. Could he?

Cassie interrupted her mindless staring at the newspaper, walking in with a coffee pot in hand. She made a clucking noise as she eyed the most egregious photograph; the doctor inside his car, slumped over, blood dripping down the side of his neck. "Just awful business, Mizz Margaret. Just awful."

"Yes, Cassie. It's...it's beyond awful. I just can't wrap my head around any of it, really."

As Cassie poured more coffee into Margaret's mug, she said,

"Such a nice man when he came out to visit here. I guess the devil works his ways on anybody. Just goes to show."

"Hmmm..." Like a hangnail, one of the more salacious details in the article was catching at Margaret's attention. Jocelyn was known around town as "Dr. Michael's girl". Margaret provided a delayed reaction to Cassie's comment saying, "The devil? Well, in this case, if anybody is the devil it's that jezebel of a wife he has, pitting him against the doctor like this."

Cassie let out a long sigh. "Just ain't right, is it?"

"No, it's not."

Cassie wandered out of the room as Margaret continued to study the words and the images, trying to make some kind of sense of it. According to Robert, all of Miller's brother-lawyers had banded together to come to his aid. That was encouraging at least.

The arraignment was scheduled for that morning. Robert was in the maelstrom of the chaos that had immediately kicked in. He promised to call Margaret with any new developments. She forced herself to close the newspaper and push it aside. She sprang up knowing she had to take her mind away from all of it. And she had just the ticket.

After changing into her riding apparel, Margaret strode down to the stables with Oliver yipping and twisting around her legs. She herself prickled with nervous tension and energy at each footfall. She tried to focus on the beauty of the morning, the sunlight that cast shadows off the old bank barn in the near distance with its stone foundation and its upper frame part painted in a bright red. It was a touchstone, her bank barn, like others that dotted the landscape throughout central Maryland.

Leonard stood up in his slow and careful manner upon Margaret's entrance into the farm office. His presence was always the calm in whatever background storm was going on in her life.

"Miss Margaret. How you keeping?"

"You've heard the news?"

He nodded, his mouth a grim line. "Sure did. Hard to fathom."

"It is." She exhaled audibly and then added, "I'm taking Moonlight for a ride."

"You want me to saddle him up?"

"No. I've got it."

As she entered Moonlight's stall, the stallion gave a whinny of greeting. Margaret rubbed his nape in return, murmuring, "Hey there, boy. You up for a ride?" He snorted in response.

She began to lose herself in the methodical process of grooming the Arabian first before placing on the tack. Once prepped, she lifted the saddle off its hook on the stall wall. Its leather scent immediately hit her nostrils and she paused as a memory of Bill came over her in full force.

He had talked to her about a horse he had owned as a much younger man. A horse that seemed to know exactly how he felt, whether he was up or down. She shook her head. She wished that horse had been around when Bill needed him the most. If he had been able to take a horse out like she was now doing with Moonlight, maybe, just maybe, it would have kept his emotions in check better. Kept him from—

Margaret shook her head again. She needed to stop thinking about it.

She finished arranging the tack and then opened Moonlight's stall door to lead him out into the paddock. Once out, she held the reins and looked towards the open fields feeling a glimmer of hope at the sight. She hoisted herself up into the saddle and, once up on her mount, positioned her seat better.

When she let loose the reins and gave Moonlight a slight kick, they moved out into the landscape and away from all the images in her head. Needham Forest was mostly comprised of fields sprinkled with small copses. She passed by the old stone quarry and the traces of its river crossing. Stone piers remained —the bridge deck long gone.

They moved into some swales amongst the hills. When she stopped to catch her breath, she heard fresh birdsong filling up the woods. She noticed how, at the top of a hill, two trees formed a heart shape.

It had been too long since Margaret had come out with Moonlight for a jaunt. It revived her to traverse the farm with new sights for her world-weary eyes. She never tired of her land with its constant enchantments. When both the horse and its rider were finally spent and sweat-covered, the exhilaration of the ride was a reminder to Margaret—to not let that much time go by again.

In the distance as the stables neared, she could just about make out a figure leaning against the paddock fence: Robert. A part of her wanted to direct Moonlight back into the woods and the fields, away from whatever it was that he had come to tell her.

Once she was near him, Margaret brought Moonlight to a halt and lifted herself off the mount. She held the reins and rubbed Moonlight's forehead. Then she looked over to Robert. "It's more bad news, isn't it?"

He shook his head, a terse expression on his face. "Bill is facing the chair."

She closed her eyes briefly. When she opened them, she could see in Robert's eyes the same anguish she was feeling. "It's all such a travesty. What happened? How did this come to be?"

Again, he shook his head, not finding any words to reply.

They moved together towards the stable. Leonard was at the open doors watching their approach. "I'll take him for you."

"Thanks, Leonard," Margaret said, handing over the reins and giving Moonlight one last pat on the rump.

Robert reached a hand out to Margaret's. Before she took it, she warned, "I'm sweaty."

"I don't care," he said and they walked with clasped hands up to the house.

Once Margaret had freshened up, she met Robert back in the drawing room where he sat staring out to the farm. She plopped down with a big sigh. "So, the arraignment must have been a mess."

"It was. The reporters were clamoring about outside. We had to herd Bill in through all of that. And then..."

"Then?"

"Well, the judge made the call and announced no bail. So, prison time until the trial. When that happened..." He gulped. "When that happened, Bill fainted straight away. Fortunately, the bailiff caught him in the nick of time and spared him from cracking his head open. Just a terrible, terrible time."

"Oh Robert! Well, where is he now? Did they stick him in jail like that?"

"No. That's maybe the one break. They took him to a psychiatric facility near Baltimore."

"He'll stay there until the trial?"

"Unknown. But I did wrangle a bit and got us on the guest list to visit him."

"Oh my. Another psychiatric institute to visit together." Visions of Blue Plains where Margaret and Robert had first met while helping her Aunt Blanche flitted like ticker tape, the dismal gloom of the place coming over Margaret like a shroud. "But at least Donald Michaels isn't at this one." Margaret caught herself. "I meant... Oh that didn't come out right. I didn't mean I'm happy he was killed. Of course, I'm not."

Robert stopped her. "It's alright, Margaret. I know what you mean. This is such a strange business all around." She moved closer towards him and he grabbed her into a tight embrace.

When they separated, she asked, "Do you know any more details? How this all came to happen?"

"It's...it's confusing as hell. The charging documents really did not give that much more information than all those sordid details that you already saw in the papers. You read all the articles out, right?"

Margaret gave a slight nod and then Robert went on to explain more about the bits and pieces he had been made privy to. "Apparently, Jocelyn was getting into Michaels' car right on G Street. Bill ran up and tried to pull her out. There was a scuffle between the two men and then gunfire. Michaels took two bullets, one to the temple, the other to the chest. Both were from Bill's gun."

Margaret let out a whoosh of air. "I guess either shot would have done the job."

"Yes. Bill is claiming self-defense. That Michaels was going to shoot him."

Margaret asked, "Was that the case?"

Robert threw his hands out in a "who knows" gesture. "There was a gun found on the seat of the car half hanging out of an envelope. Of course, my thoughts go back to when I saw something similar in that car."

They both fell silent then Robert continued. "The documents laid out that Bill shot Michaels in a murderous rage. There are conflicting accounts from the eye-witnesses there too. It will all have to play out in the courts."

"Ugh, what an ungodly mess it all is!"

"Yes. There's a lot of work ahead of Bill's defense team. To sort it all it."

"I'm just sick about it, Robert. Why did Bill do this?"

"As best I can figure so far, it seems that it was a sudden snap with reality for Bill. All the stress of the past month or so I guess. It built up to a level his mind—and soul—he just couldn't take any more. He hit the breaking point. Bill said that Michaels went for the gun in his car to draw it at him."

"Bill said? Do you...do you think that was not really the case?"

"At this point, it is considered 'alleged'. I'm in lawyer-speak right now."

"Oh, okay. Because surely Bill would not make up something that wasn't the truth."

Robert nodded. "Anyway, I've got to get back. But I wanted to come out and... Well, I guess I just wanted to see you." He took her hand again and they gazed at each other. Margaret felt the warmth of his hand and his gaze.

He continued. "As soon as we are allowed, I think we should go and visit him."

He stood up and Margaret did the same. "Of course. Of course, we'll go and visit."

They embraced again and said their goodbyes. At the open doorway, she watched his departure as the roadster spun dust along the long driveway of Needham Forest.

When Margaret closed the door behind her, she immediately moved to the phone table. She needed to talk it out with someone. Judith was the one. She looked at her watch and saw it was past noon. That was no guarantee that Judith could take the call if she'd had a late night but it was worth a try.

Judith answered after ten long rings. Upon hearing it was Margaret on the line, she grumbled, "Mags, it's a little early, isn't it?"

It apparently had been another late night. "Two o'clock? I wanted to make sure to catch you."

"Well, you caught me alright. This is practically getting up with birds, for heaven's sake."

"Well, I think the birds have been up for a while now and might argue that point. Anyway, I couldn't wait."

Judith made a loud show of yawning in an exaggerated fashion before saying, "Go ahead. You got me on the hook now."

"There was a murder in front of Woodward & Lothrop. Did you read about it in the papers?"

"What? No, why would I have seen that?"

"I'm sure it will be spread out into the national news shortly because...the thing about it...it was Bill Miller."

Judith gasped. "Oh no...Bill was murdered?"

"No, no. He's the one that did it. He killed Dr. Michaels."

"What? Why? Start again. I haven't even had a cup of coffee yet."

Margaret sighed and then carefully explained the goings-on of Jocelyn and the love triangle. Then she stopped. Repeating the tale made her realize even more what a bizarre circumstance she had become involved in.

"Oh my. That is really quite a story, Mags."

"Yes, it's a lot."

"Dare I ask how this plays into the help you were getting from Bill?"

"You can ask but I don't have an answer. I just don't know what will happen next."

"And here you thought you had the plan all wrapped up to spare Needham Forest from financial ruin. I'm so sorry." A silence filled up the line. Then Judith spoke again. "Now, look though. You do have something."

"What's that?"

"Those magical gold bars supposedly floating around

somewhere on the farm. And you love a good treasure hunt. Just do that instead for now. There's not really much you can do for Bill at this point anyway."

After ending the call, Margaret knew that Judith was right. There was not anything more she could do—not only about Bill but about Needham Forest's financial situation. She resolved to get back into finding out if there was a map or anything. Maybe it was chasing a chimera or maybe it wasn't. But it would get her mind off her problems.

CHAPTER SIXTEEN

The following morning, Margaret grabbed a ride from Albert since he was going into town. As Judith had aptly reminded her, she needed to get her mind off Bill Miller's catastrophe and onto anything else as a distraction. Hunting down more historical information about her house and the gold bars was the very thing.

As they approached the commercial hub of downtown Rockville, Margaret could see the town bustling with activity. Tuesdays, designated "Court Days", were busier than other days with more folks coming in from the surrounding areas. Farmers, Albert included, set up impromptu stands in a nearby empty lot with fresh produce on offer.

After Albert dropped her off in front of the historical society, Margaret crossed fingers and walked to the door. She felt a lift in her spirits when it opened. Apparently, it was a "catch can" day. As she entered, Margaret hoped for a different white-haired denizen manning the desk. But, just as before, the same little lady sat at her station engulfed by books and documents.

Margaret plastered a smile on her face and rang out a "Hello".

The lady looked at her. "Oh, it's you."

Margaret found that to be a strange and discouraging greeting but merely replied, "Yes, hello again. I—"

"Took you long enough to get back here."

Margaret forced a weak smile on her face. This woman really had an unusual manner. She wondered if it went with the territory—people drawn to historical matters and family trees being unusual. Since she herself had never felt the pull of it, she had never had any dealings with these types. And she had left her number for the woman to call her but apparently that had been disregarded.

Margaret began again, "Well, I—"

"I remembered what the rumor was."

"The rumor?"

"Yes, yes, the rumor," the woman said in a tone laced with irritation. "It was about the rebels in our area. In fact, very near your farm. Walter Mandeville lived near there and he was the one who told me."

"Oh, okay. What was it? The rumor, I mean."

"Mandeville said—he was sweet on me by the way, that's why he told me—anyway, he said there was a minor skirmish. So minor that it barely made the news."

Margaret realized that Robert had been on the right track if this was, in fact, the incident following the train heist. But it was difficult to get the woman to parse out information. She cleared her throat and then asked, "I had heard of gold being stolen from a train further north. Could that be the source?"

The woman gave her a bracing glance. "Dear, of course that was the source. The North used the railroad to transport gold down to the Capitol and had stopped at Monocacy."

Margaret decided the best approach was to act dumb. "Why did they stop there?"

"They were going to unload it at the train station into wagon transport that would take it south into D.C. But that didn't happen."

"It didn't?"

"No, dear. A band of rebels held up the train, stole the gold, and headed out. Presumably south towards Richmond since that was the capital of the Confederacy."

"So then, according to Mandeville, there was a skirmish for the gold down here, near or on my farm? Do you know where exactly?"

"Well, how am I supposed to know that? I've never walked your land."

Margaret held in a rising exasperation with the other woman but kept it at bay and instead asked, "Okay, so, no other details then?"

"Just one."

Margaret waited her out. The woman almost seemed to enjoy withholding the detail, dragging it out with a gleam in her eye. If Margaret wasn't mistaken, it might even be a teasing gleam.

The silence grew awkward but still Margaret waited. Finally, the other woman broke it. "He said, if my memory is correct that is, he said that in the middle of the skirmish there was a tree that served as a landmark."

"Huh. A tree. Any uh—"

"I was just getting to that if you would let me finish." She gave a noise of aggravation. "It was a black walnut tree and stood alone on a slight incline. But what really made it stand out was a cleft in its middle. Now, who knows if it still stands or not, but there you have it."

"Well, that is very helpful. Very helpful indeed. And, um, thank you for remembering."

The woman puffed up a bit. "I knew it would come to me. My mind is razor sharp."

"Ah yes. Well, today I thought I would take a look at the maps of the area—if that's okay."

"Alright. If you must. Sign in here in the guest book please and I'll go get them."

As the woman tottered off down one of the cramped aisles, Margaret signed in and stifled her annoyance with the woman's manner. She would need to play the game—for a little longer at least. After she signed her name, she glanced at the page of prior visitors and went motionless.

In fanciful cursive, there was his name in black and white: Keith O'Keefe. A noise escaped from her mouth. What in the world would he have been in here for?

When the woman returned hefting two big and overfilled folders, she caught Margaret examining the book. "Dear, that's not really information for you to look at."

"Can I ask, do you remember this man being in here?"

With a frown, the woman looked down to where Margaret pointed. "Nope. Thursday is not my day. Lucinda is here then. Here, could you please help me with these?" She handed the folders over to Margaret and then added, "Sit at the table and please go through them very carefully."

Margaret did as she was told but she couldn't concentrate much on the maps and other miscellanea in the folders. Her mind was on Keith. There was no reason for him to be at the historical society other than following in her footsteps. He would not waste his time charming little old ladies unless it was worth his while. She needed to figure out exactly why it might be worth his while.

Once back at Needham Forest in the afternoon, Margaret sat at her desk in the room always called "the library" which she now thought of as her study; a smaller, more private space across the center hall from the drawing room. She tapped a pencil to a rhythm only she could hear. The historical society's map folders, while interesting, had not provided anything of use. And she was in knots about Keith and what he had been doing there. She was pulled in all directions; scattered thoughts, scattered energy.

Eventually, her brain settled on one image: a black walnut tree. She took out a portfolio that her family had owned forever of flora and fauna in the Mid-Atlantic region. It contained beautiful drawings by a nineteenth century artist whose life's mission was to pursue the topic. As she leafed through, she remembered childhood afternoons spent doing the exact same.

Margaret would sit on the settee nearby while her father worked right at the very same desk where she currently sat. She would become absorbed in the artwork and in learning about the various trees, plants and animals. Doing it now brought it all back to her. Those wonderful days of being a child without a care in the world, with her dear father nearby.

She kept at it in the hope that one of the folios would depict a black walnut tree—because she could not recall it from those earlier years. In luck, she found it. It appeared to have darker bark and, without leaves, took on a gothic look with branches fingering outwards. It provided a distinctive fruit, of course; a black walnut encased in a hard, dark shell.

Margaret looked up from the book and gazed out the window, scanning through her mind where on the property she had seen such a tree—or trees, if there was more than one.

Three areas cropped up in her mind and she stood up with determination. She would take Moonlight out and see what there was to see. There was still enough daylight to find those trees.

In the barn, she concentrated on quickly getting Moonlight ready for the ride. She gave a start when she heard Leonard's voice in the stall. "Oh Leonard. I'm sorry. I'm a million miles away."

"That's alright. I just said it's kind of late in the day for a ride, isn't it?"

"Yes, but I need to go out and find... Well, I'm looking for black walnut trees."

He gave her a quizzical look. "Why's that?"

"It's just something to do with possible hiding places. Anyway, do you recall where any are?"

He scratched his head. "Well, my grandpappy used to have some on his farm in Carolina. I remember he always said they stand alone."

"How come?"

"Something about the tree's roots. They don't let nothing grow around them is my memory. Like they kill any other plant around trying to get in."

"Interesting. So that means they will be obvious on the landscape."

"Well, yeah that. But also, you could look for any black walnuts left on the ground. If the squirrels haven't gotten all of them." He gave a gravelly smoker's chuckle.

"Oh yes. Of course. I can look for that too."

"My recall is that there is definitely one over in the southernmost corner and then maybe another on that hill that goes over to the Jacksons' property. And they're old, mind you. They can live for hundreds of years I think."

"Okay, good clues. Those are the two places I remember. Also, I think there is one at the top of where the old stone quarry was."

Moonlight had begun prancing his hooves up and down and chomping down on his bit as Margaret and Leonard chatted. He was just as eager as she to get out into the fields. Margaret finished the conversation saying, "I'll be back soon."

Once in the saddle, she let the reins out so Moonlight could gallop to the southern part of the property. She pulled the reins in once she spotted a black walnut tree in the distance. Leonard had been correct as the tree stood out on the horizon all to itself.

She brought Moonlight to a halt, dismounted the horse and walked around the tree. There was the barest skirting of leftover leaves from the previous autumn along with a few walnuts at the base of the tree, now shriveled and moldy. She picked one up and studied it.

It really was remarkable that the tree had probably stood during the Civil War and still produced nuts like this. But was it the location of the supposed skirmish? She looked all around beyond the tree not seeing any evidence of such a thing. Then again, how would it be evident? Also, while the woman at the historical society had been irritable, she had also been specific about the details of a cleft and an incline.

Margaret got back on the horse and headed to the other area Leonard mentioned. Again, she was able to clearly distinguish the black walnut tree on the hill near the Jackson property line where it stood starkly outlined on the horizon. She examined the tree and its surrounds but it ended up being a blank. Like the first tree, there was nothing distinguishing it or nothing indicative of anything special there.

She was running short on daylight but headed to the last place in mind. When she approached the old quarry, Margaret looked around at the top of the hill not seeing anything. Maybe she had misremembered. A copse stood to one side and she circled Moonlight around the back side. There she found it, the black walnut specimen she recalled being there.

She leapt down from Moonlight and took it in. It was clearly the oldest one of the three and worse for wear with a beat-up appearance. As she stood back from it, she could see a lightning strike at some point had taken off part of its top. This area made a bit more sense as the site of the skirmish with its protection from the woods—assuming the woods had been the same during the war. Out of the three locales, she had a sense this was the one—if there was any truth to the rumor at all.

As she circled around to the side that faced the copse, she saw that the tree had a long and narrow keyhole in its trunk. A deep cleft in fact.

Margaret stared at it as her nerves kicked with a buzzing sensation. Could it be a hiding place? She moved closer to the opening and looked down into a tight and dark nook. It wasn't possible to see inside.

With her riding glove on, she reached down with a tentative hand. She could only feel blank air and emptiness. But there was a bottom to it, a bottom that she could not see or reach. She would need to come back and bring Leonard or Robert or maybe both of them with tools. It might hurt the tree but if there was the slightest chance of something in there, it might also save the farm.

The sun was setting as she got back to the stables and took Moonlight to his stall. Leonard had left for the evening so her news about the black walnut tree would have to keep until morning. It was also up to Margaret to care for the horse and put him to good stead before tending to herself.

The horse let out a grunt when she removed his saddle followed by the blanket underneath. "Well done, sir, well done," she murmured to him. Taking out the curry brush, she brushed him down. She was alone in the stables and alone in her thoughts as she methodically moved the brush across the horse's broad back.

The stable became dark and she interrupted her doings to turn on the one bulb that hung overhead and created a murky light. All was quiet with just some random noises from the other horses. Moonlight stayed still as she worked on him. But, all of a sudden, the horse jerked under her hands and whinnied. "What? What is it boy?"

Margaret felt prickles along her spine. What now? She moved away from the horse, throwing the brush down and walking into the center aisle. "Who's there?" she yelled out. No one answered.

She walked up and down the aisle but saw nothing. She sniffed the air hoping to smell cigar smoke and feel the reassurance it always gave her. But there was no whiff of it on this night. She hurried through the rest of Moonlight's care with him cooperating and not complaining again.

As Margaret dashed her way out into the now dark night, she shook her head at her foolishness. *Everything is starting to get to me*, she thought. *I need to keep a level head.*

Once safely back inside Needham Forest, she made her way upstairs straight away and drew a long, hot bath. She sank into the large, porcelain tub gratefully and stayed there for some time.

When Margaret finished her toilette, she found the dinner that Cassie had set aside and moved into the dining room with it. After she ate, she fixed herself a much-needed martini. As she sat with it in the drawing room, some of the day's tension began to ooze out.

By the time she heard the hall phone ring, she was much more relaxed. She drifted into the hall and picked up the receiver at the phone table. Robert's voice on the other end combined with the effects of the martini gave her a warm glow.

After they discussed the latest on Bill's situation (nothing much to report, all on hold for the time being), Robert said, "But tell me what you've been up to."

Margaret hesitated before she spoke. She didn't want to burden Robert with the Keith problem right now. He had enough on his plate. Plus, she needed to find out more first. Instead, she brought up the clue about the black walnut tree. Finishing the story, she said, "So I need to get back out there with Leonard. And I thought maybe you too. If you have the time..."

She could hear the chagrin in his voice as he answered. "There's nothing I would like more but this Bill Miller situation has left me neglecting all my other work. I can't take any more time this week."

"I understand. It's fine. Leonard and I can get out there tomorrow. I just thought..." She stopped.

"You thought?" he prodded.

"I thought...well, if there is the off-chance, we find something, I would love for you to be there for that."

"I'm honored. And, of course, I would want the same. But it is kind of a long shot, isn't it?"

Margaret gave a rueful chuckle. "Of course, it is. Maybe I'm more of a dreamer than I ever thought."

"There's nothing wrong with dreams, Margaret." His words seemed loaded with more than one meaning. Or maybe she was imagining it.

They finished the call by making plans for the weekend when Robert might finally have a free moment. The plans involved a ride out towards Baltimore to visit Bill Miller.

After the call ended, Margaret made another martini tossing in an extra olive for good measure. As she sat with her second drink, she pondered the part of her day that she had not divulged to Robert. Keith's doings at the historical society. She resolved that she would track down this Lucinda when the place was next open that Thursday, supposedly Lucinda's day to volunteer. She couldn't let this go on, Keith stalking her or whatever it was he was up to. Robert did not need to be dragged into that—yet.

CHAPTER SEVENTEEN

With a slight fogginess from the martinis but one cup of coffee in, Margaret wandered down to the barns bright and early. There was no time like the present and the weather was also cooperating with a sunny day. Leonard, who always got up with the birds, was working in one of the stalls when she got down there.

He looked up at her with surprise upon her greeting. "Well, look at you, Miss Margaret. Up so early today."

"Yep. And here's why..." She quickly filled him in on finding the tree and what she wanted to do, finishing with, "So we need to pack some tools, ride out there this morning and get into this cleft or knothole, or whatever it's called, to check if anything's in there."

Leonard cranked himself up to a stand with a slight wince. "Alright. We can do that. Let me go root around for tools we might need. Meantime, you wanna saddle up Moonlight and I'll take Bessie here?"

Margaret nodded and the two of them separated to take on the tasks at hand. As Margaret worked with Moonlight, she breathed in the refreshing morning air mixed with the pungent odors from the horse stalls. It was good to be out here so early with any residuals of the uneasy atmosphere of the previous night gone.

When all was ready, they mounted their rides and headed out in a northwesterly direction to where the old stone quarry and the copse lay. The morning sun hit at points and blinded Margaret's view with its light, in a good way. Again, a rush of happiness came over her at being out on her farmland with its opportunity to toss all anxieties aside.

They got off the horses and Leonard grabbed his saddle bag off Bessie. They walked around the tree and Margaret pointed out the knothole. Leonard squinted and eyed it up. "That's a big one alright."

"Right? It seems like it could be the perfect hiding place, don't you think?" Margaret could hear the fanning of hope in her voice.

"Well, it's worth a shot to have a look-see, for sure. Now, let me just think on this for a moment."

Leonard peered into it then stood back and scratched his head. After a moment of consideration, he began to pull out some tools from the bag. As he laid them out on the ground nearby, Leonard spoke. "I've done a lot of work in my day but, fair to say, I ain't ever been asked to open up a tree knothole."

Margaret laughed. "And not just any knothole—a hundred or so years old black walnut tree knothole." He chuckled in return.

Margaret stood to one side and watched as Leonard worked at the base of the cleft with a small hand saw. It took some time and effort to open up the area more. Once he had done so, he pulled out a pocket size lamp from his bag.

"Oh, that's clever of you to think of bringing that, Leonard. I wouldn't have gotten too far without you on this caper."

He nodded. "Alrighty now. Let's see down there."

Both of them moved as close as possible to the keyhole. But it was obvious they had to take turns to look down. "Ladies first," Leonard said as he stepped back and handed the pocket lamp to Margaret.

She took in a big gulp of air, excitement stirring in her. "Okay…" She moved the light from the lamp in as far as she could. She stood back up straight and shook her head. "I can't see anything."

"Let me try." Leonard got as close to the tree trunk as possible and then slowly moved the light around. He stepped away and said, "Well, I got one more trick."

He pulled out his riding crop and worked it into the trunk. "Let's see if I poke around and hit anything here with this."

Margaret kept the flare of hope going as she watched the concentration on Leonard's face, one eye in a squint. He eventually stepped back again from the tree.

"Nothing in there?" Margaret asked the obvious. This time, it was Leonard that shook his head.

Disappointment seeped through Margaret but she checked herself. She was being ridiculous. This was really not much more than a lark and the sensible side of her knew that. "Well, thanks for humoring me, Leonard."

Leonard sniffed and then began to put the tools back into the saddle bag. He spoke up as he did so. "One time, I was just a young'un and we had a bunch of momma cats. Every spring, they all had kittens. They hid those kittens in the craziest places and me and my sisters would go hunting around to find the places. So, after we did our chores, we'd spy on those mommas and see where they would go off to."

Margaret didn't know why Leonard, usually more taciturn than chatty, was talking about cats. Maybe he was trying to take her mind off of her disappointment. She mustered up a response. "Oh, that must have been fun."

He nodded and continued, "Sure enough, one time a momma cat hid them in the bottom of a tree trunk with a big hole in the bottom not too much different from this one. We would go up to it and hear these little mews like real little baby cats do. I'll never forget that."

"Well, there's no kittens here—or treasure for that matter."

"Now, don't give up Miss Margaret. Don't give up."

They rode side by side in a steady clip back to the stables. The sun was now fully up and the day fully begun. Once back at the barn, they dismounted and began to separate out the horses to their stalls.

"Thank you again, Leonard." She hesitated but then asked what she had been wanting to ask him for some time. "Leonard, this may sound odd but...do you ever smell cigar smoke down here sometimes? Just randomly?"

Leonard looked off to one side before answering. "Your daddy used to come out here late some nights. I could see the tip of his cigar lit up and he would walk around. You remember how he liked to smoke those Cubans."

Margaret nodded. How well indeed she did remember. Leonard continued, "Restless, I always thought. But maybe..."

"Maybe?"

"Could be he was poking around for what you're looking for now. I don't know. I was just young then. Didn't know too much about things."

Leonard had not answered her question so she pressed on. "But do you ever smell the cigar smoke these days? At all?"

"Nah, can't say I do." He paused then added, "I'm heading over to the supply store tomorrow morning. Anything you been hankering for?"

Margaret shook her head. Leonard was not comfortable with her question and she needed to just let it go.

"No. I'm sure you have that all sorted out. But..." She

remembered that the historical society was open the next day with, she hoped, Lucinda volunteering at the desk. "Could you drop me off in Rockville? I need to get back to the historical society." They worked out the particulars of the time and then parted ways.

The next morning, they headed out in Leonard's Ford Model T runabout. They were mostly silent on the drive, each taking in the new day, each in their own thoughts. Margaret did have to wonder if her question about the cigar smoke had unnerved Leonard in a way. Did it sit like an odd note between the two of them or was it just her imagination?

When Leonard pulled up to the historical society, he looked over at it with a dubious expression. "You sure this place is open?"

She followed his gaze to the empty-looking establishment, the same as it always looked. "It's fine, Leonard. Just swing by when you're done at the farm store."

At the historical society door, she pulled the knob and found it indeed locked tight. This day apparently was going to be a day of not catching them in. She sighed and then walked around the rear. She edged her way over to the brick manor house associated with the place. A garden lay off to one side and would be a nice spot to sit and wait for Leonard. The neighborhood was all quiet, sleepy even.

As she approached the fenced-in area, she could see a man with a hoe working in the enclosed space. He was elderly with a coif of gray hair kinked closely to his skull. He looked up and proffered a nod her way.

"Hello," she said. "The garden is looking very fine."

He nodded again and went back to hoeing. From around

back, a dog came running over to Margaret, barking and tail wagging. She reached down to pet him. "Well, look at this handsome fellow."

It appeared to be a beagle, but with unusual coloring. Instead of the typical tricolor of tan, white and red, he (she noted it was he) almost looked yellow and white.

She looked up from the beagle and made another foray with the gardener. "I was hoping to get into the historical society. But I guess they are not opening today?"

He looked back up and stared at her with cloudy eyes in a weather-beaten face.

"I had heard it was Lucinda's day there. Maybe she hasn't made it in yet?" She posed it as a question in the hopes of getting a response from him.

His voice came out in low gravel. "She done live right over there. Mizz Lucinda does." He pointed to a small cottage right across the street. He added, "That's her dog. He'll take you on over there."

"Oh, thank you. I'll try that." Margaret felt uplifted at the stroke of luck getting this bit of information out of the gardener. The dog did indeed lead the way across the street and Margaret followed behind its jaunty tail.

She walked up onto a porch after the dog. She lifted up the knocker and rapped. She heard movements coming from somewhere inside the house inside, and waited. When the door swung open, a woman of indeterminate age stood in front of Margaret. "May I help you?" she asked, a question on her face and a trowel in one hand. Then she looked down at the dog, a smile coming over her face. "Chauncey, did you make a friend?"

Margaret took in the crepe-like skin on the woman's face, creased and, like the gardener, weather-worn. She stood taller than Margaret, who was tall herself for a woman. Her gray hair was cropped short and lay flat around her face in some defiance of the style generally acceptable to women of her era—long and coiled up into a bun.

"I hope you don't mind me interrupting your day but I was trying to catch you at the historical society..."

"Sorry, my dear. But it's not my day there."

"It's not? Oh, the lady—I don't know her name—she's very petite..."

"That's Sadie."

"Yes. Sadie mentioned it was your day."

"She gets confused sometimes. But why did you want to talk to me?

"I had a question about one of your visitors...um..." Margaret suddenly realized how awkward this was without the guest book nearby.

"Come into my backyard. I'm finishing up some repotting. You can help me." The woman spoke in a decisive tone. A tone that brooked no dispute.

"Are you sure it's not a bother?"

"Not at all. Come along."

Margaret was not a gardener but she was game if it gave insight into what Keith was playing at. She followed Lucinda's tall and rail-thin figure off the porch along with the dog, Chauncey, past the side of the house and into the back yard. At the sight of it, Margaret came to a halt and said, "Oh!" Lucinda looked over at her with a smile.

It was a stunning garden that was in no way obvious from the streetscape. It had been landscaped to perfection and included stone sculptures and a little fountain in the mix.

"This is my true work, back here," Lucinda said.

"I can see that. It is just amazing."

Lucinda walked over to a potting table and handed a pot to Margaret. "Here. Start with this one." As an afterthought, she gave Margaret a pair of gloves. "Put these on so you don't mess your manicure. These roots need to be planted. Between this and the historical society, I find that I run out of time most days. But I'm not complaining, mind. I have always loved to be busy."

Margaret, taken aback, nevertheless followed the other woman's lead. After she pulled the gloves on, she began to copy Lucinda. A sort of calm came over her as she worked her gloved hands through the soil and they made small talk. Chauncey curled himself up and began to snooze off.

"Your dog is quite the character and I don't ever recall seeing a beagle that color."

Lucinda nodded. "Yes, it is a rare one. They call it lemon-colored. He was the only one in his litter that shade. Now, what is it you need to find out?"

Margaret collected her thoughts and then began. She found herself revealing first her reason for being at the historical society and then, without realizing it, she began confiding in the woman about her divorce and the struggles with Keith. She stopped herself and said, "I'm sorry. I don't know why I am being too personal like this."

"Say no more. I had a no-good one myself earlier in my life. Happy to help you out, but I don't really understand how I can."

"Well, the thing about it is... he was at the historical society on one of the days you were there. At least Sadie said it was one of your days. I was hoping— hoping that you could remember why."

"Huh. Describe this fellow again."

Margaret had not described him at all yet but she said, "He's about medium height, light eyes, usually dapper in his attire..." She trailed off, suddenly uncomfortable at describing the man she had been married to for so many years.

"Ah yes. I do remember him. He could charm the birds out of the trees, I'm guessing. No wonder you were caught by him. And not bad on the eyes either."

Margaret couldn't help the laugh that came out of her. "Yes. It's true. But in recent years he has become... I guess dissolute is the word for it. He gambles at the track and just his lifestyle..." She ran out of words to describe Keith. "Anyway, did he tell you why he was there? Do you remember?"

"I do indeed. Because it was rather strange."

"Why?"

"He wanted to track down old deeds because he said someone was trying to take his land away from him."

Margaret's hands went still in the pot. Her mouth dropped open.

"Yes. Like I said, strange. He went on to say the deeds would prove he was the rightful heir or something like that. I did find it rather far-fetched but I humored him and brought out documents that included the early deeds of the county."

"Well, did he get an 'a-ha' moment?" Margaret heard the bitterness in her tone but couldn't keep it in.

Lucinda shook her head and said, "No. In fact, his demeanor turned cold by the end of his visit. The charm was clearly a veneer. I remember thinking that."

"Yes, you definitely got that right." Margaret went silent musing on what Keith thought he could possibly swing with this effort. Maryland, like many other states, considered inherited property to be separate property. Keith had no control over the farm that Margaret specifically inherited from her father. Nor was it a part of the divorce settlement between the two of them.

"So, are we to assume he is going after your farm somehow? Or that he thinks he can?"

Margaret nodded very slowly. "He thinks he can disprove a land deed that has been in my family for over a hundred years. My family. Not his. It makes no sense whatsoever. I have to wonder..."

"Wonder?" Lucinda prodded.

"Wonder if his brain has gotten completely addled by the drink, or something."

The potting was now complete and Margaret became aware that she was overstaying her welcome with Lucinda. She shook herself and said, "I really am grateful for you sharing this information with me. I'll get out of your hair now."

"No bother at all, my dear. I am curious though. What are you going to do with this knowledge now?"

"Well, that's just it, isn't it? I don't know how to stop him; how to get him out of my life once and for all."

Lucinda held up a small root to the light, narrowing her eyes. Then she turned back to look at Margaret. "You'll figure it out."

CHAPTER EIGHTEEN

Robert was in the driver's seat next to Margaret, right where she wanted him to be. Finally, it was the weekend with an opportunity to be together despite their unfortunate destination, the sanatorium where Bill was being housed for the time being. Although the weekend did revolve around the unpleasantness of the Millers' situation, it felt like a get-away, an escape from Margaret's nagging worries about the farm and Keith.

The scenic countryside whirled by as the roadster took them for a spin through central Maryland's rolling farmlands. The drive from Montgomery County into neighboring Howard County included traversing the old National Road for a spell. After they had been traveling for an hour, Margaret spotted one of the roadside parks in the distance. "Look, Robert. There's a place up ahead to pull over. Let's take a break."

Cassie had packed them an overflowing picnic basket filled with some of Margaret's favorites to sustain them for the road trip. Fried chicken, potato salad and a blueberry buckle. She had also included a restorative carafe of iced tea that still retained some of its chill to refresh them.

There was just enough room for Robert to edge his car in

safely. "Oh, how nice," Margaret pointed towards a tree beyond where a small wooden table sat with benches on either side. "Now we won't have to muss up your leather seats. We can spread out the food over there."

Once out of the car, Robert pulled out the basket from the back and they walked over to the spot. As they set up the provisions, a few cars whizzed by but, for the most part, it was a peaceful and quiet respite. A bright sun cut the edge off any of late winter's chill in the air.

After they ate for a bit in companionable silence, Margaret brought up their mission for the day. "Tell me more about the sanatorium where Bill is staying, Robert. I've never heard of it."

"It's called Patapsco Manor. A secluded and private hospital that apparently only takes care of a small number of patients. Under twenty, I believe."

"How did Bill... I mean, how was Bill allowed this as an option?"

"His law firm was able to pull some strings and get the judge to rubber stamp it. For now, anyway. That could change any time, of course. But it sounds like quite a decent place. Nothing like the mayhem, of say, a Blue Plains-type establishment."

They both went quiet remembering the horrid place where Margaret's late Aunt Blanche had ended up under the purview of Dr. Michaels. They had spent too much time there for their own liking when they had visited. Margaret gazed over at Robert knowing that as horrible as that experience was, it created a bond between them. In fact, it led them to where they currently were—together.

Margaret picked the thread of conversation back up. "It's in Ellicott City?"

"Yes, a little outside of the town proper."

"Have you ever been there?"

He nodded as he finished chewing on a chicken leg. "Yes.

I'm well acquainted with the town. A wealthy great aunt summered there when I was a child. It was popular then as a resort, a place to escape from the heat. But I haven't been back in ages. How about you?"

"A couple of times, I think. I just remember it the most for —" She stopped mid-sentence.

"For?"

Margaret just recalled knowing a few couples from the horsey set who made the leap into quickie marriages at the county seat's courthouse. Maryland was a popular place due to no wait times unlike other surrounding states that imposed blood tests. Some towns in particular, such as Ellicott City and Elkton, had become designated "marriage mills". In the case of Ellicott City, as far as Margaret understood, discretion was the draw. A small country town was an opportunity to avoid attention, such as mention in the public papers or being sighted by big city eyes.

A nervous laugh slipped out as she didn't want Robert to think she was suggesting anything. "Well, as you may know, it's a place where couples run off to get married. If they want to do it quickly, I guess."

"Oh, yes. That's right. Can't say I know anyone that has done it there. Gotten married, I mean."

The turn in the conversation seemed to introduce an uncomfortable air. When Robert stood up in a brisk manner, Margaret had to wonder why the topic of marriage was so off-putting to Robert. He took out his watch fob and said, "We should probably press on."

Margaret stood too and brushed herself off. They wrapped up the trash and Robert carried the basket as they walked back to the car.

"Everything alright?" she asked, looking over his way.

"Yes. Absolutely." He gave her a crooked smile and her

heart gave a lift. They were fine. It must be all in her imagination that the mention of marriage was awkward.

Within the next half hour, they crested the top of a hill above Ellicott City. From that viewpoint, the hub of commerce was displayed in front of them. The roadster snaked its way along the packed thoroughfare that ran through the center. Margaret took in the tight buildings lined along either side of the street, a twirling mix of stone, frame and brick. It was a compact area but appeared to have every commerce imaginable from Kraft's Meat Market to Easton's Funeral Home with many taverns in between, a little world unto itself.

Above the noise of the car's engine and the bustling town, Robert spoke loudly to be heard. "So, this town is known for its seven hills. We'll be putting the roadster to the test. I well remember trudging up from the river with my fishing pole."

"Fishing pole?"

"Yes, the Patapsco River is at the bottom of this hill—well, you can see it now in front of us."

Margaret could just make out the glint of the sun off a river ahead through an opening in a thick stone archway. Above the arches of the stone bridge lay train tracks running parallel to the river.

Robert continued. "It's a scenic river actually. I spent a lot of time there exploring during those summers."

A vision of Robert as a young boy passed through Margaret's mind and she gazed over at his profile with affection. She wished she had known him then.

"Here we go up one of the seven." Instead of crossing over the river, Robert took a hard right, maneuvering around a curve and then up an even steeper hill. They passed by a row of small houses that looked to be workers' dwellings. The town was also known for its mills that could also be seen lining the river in the near distance.

Margaret spoke up. "Isn't it Rome that's known for seven hills?"

"Yes, but this is Ellicott City. Not Rome." He threw her a wink.

Once they reached the uppermost hill, the road leveled out and, in short order, the sanatorium appeared off to the right side, sitting high above the quaint little town. A sign that read "Patapsco Manor" hung at the edge of its driveway and Robert made the turn into a horseshoe-shaped drive. From her vantage, Margaret was reminded of a mountain resort.

The compound held a cluster of buildings all done up with decorative wood shingles and chunky cobblestones scattered over a large plot. The centerpiece was substantial and sprawling, rising three stories tall. It seemed to be of recent vintage with a shiny shingled roof and copper flashing along the eaves and gutter spouts. Other smaller stone buildings with a cottage-like appearance were peppered around the large main one.

As they walked towards the entrance, Margaret noticed that the lively activity in the town below was unseen and unheard. There was an almost eerie sense of calm and stillness. Robert picked up on the same saying, "I've heard this whole area called Little Switzerland by some."

"I was just thinking that it feels like we are at a mountain cottage colony. It is rather charming, isn't it? If I didn't know better, I could almost imagine that we're visiting friends at their European estate."

Robert shook his head ruefully and said, "Well, let's hope the indoors has at least a nuance of the outdoor setting."

They made their way up the generous masonry steps leading to the doorway. Robert reached in front of Margaret to pull open one of the double doors. Both of them stopped right after crossing the large threshold. "Ooohh..." slipped out of Margaret.

Right in front of them, atop of the reception counter, sat what appeared to be a small, live lion. A longish-haired, orange-hued, striped coif ringed its massive head. Tufts of black fur puffed out of its massive paws. A middle-aged woman in a white nurse's frock stood behind the reception seemingly unbothered by the animal next to her.

"Is that a..." Margaret mused aloud, "A little lion?"

The woman smiled. "Not a lion. We get asked that often. This is our resident kitty, Manor. Go ahead and pet him. That's what he's here for."

Margaret and Robert exchanged a quick glance and then Margaret approached the cat who was intimidating in size and appearance. She reached an open palm forward to let the animal sniff. The cat leaned towards her palm, studying it with some curiosity. This was immediately followed by the loudest purr she had ever heard along with a nudging of her hand. "What a nice gentleman."

"He certainly is. Our big boy. Almost twenty-two pounds at last weigh-in. Now, what can I do for you folks?"

Robert cleared his throat, recovering from the unusual cat sighting. "Ah yes. We have an appointment to see Bill...uh Mr. Miller."

"Oh, Mr. Miller. What a lovely man he is. Let me just see." She checked through some papers. "I know he has a designated set list for visitors." She looked up from the papers. "Your names again? Mr. and Mrs.?"

Margaret and Robert both spoke at once over each other. "Oh no." "We're not."

Margaret, flustered, started to explain but Robert cut her off, somewhat abruptly, saying, "Mr. Robert Brady, Esquire, and

Mrs. Margaret O'Keefe." Margaret glanced at Robert's expression but he was unperturbed by the exchange.

The nurse's finger stopped halfway down a sheet of paper. "There you are." She stood up behind the desk and said, "Very good. Follow me this way."

As they followed the nurse, Margaret shook off how Robert made it crystal clear they were not a couple, almost curt about their status. She was being too sensitive and rustling up problems where there weren't any. Instead, she focused on her environs as the walk took them through a broad hallway painted a bright greenish-blue.

"This color on the walls...it's quite vibrant," Margaret said aloud.

"Yes, studies have shown turquoise to be a very cheerful color. It helps with mood regulation."

"Huh." Being cheery wasn't a bad thing. In fact, Margaret hoped that the attitude of the place was helping Bill's morale.

Yet, the hall was quiet, almost too quiet. It made Margaret nervous. Had they drugged all the inmates to the gills like at Blue Plains? Or was it just a better run establishment?

The nurse came to a stop at the very last door in the hall, a closed door. "Here you are. Enjoy your visit." Again, Margaret compared her experience at Dr. Michaels' institute. A complete contrast from the get-go.

They knocked and heard a voice from inside, recognizable as Jocelyn's, say, "Come in."

The room at first blush was as elegant as the rest of the place. The bed dominated and Bill was propped there in a seated position with a barber style cape over him. Jocelyn stood next to the bed, combing out his thick, white head of hair. In her other hand, she held scissors. She paused the combing at their entrance and looked at them with mouth slightly open.

Bill didn't look over at all at their entrance. He continued to gaze out the large window with a view of the grounds. Margaret had the errant thought pass through her mind how lucky Bill was with that thick mane of hair at his age. Then she shook herself. A man in his current position could hardly be called "lucky".

Jocelyn found her voice after her initial surprise at seeing them. "Well, looks like we got company, Buddy."

As astonishing as it was to see Bill in this condition, it was almost equally astonishing to take in Jocelyn's appearance. A matronly transformation had occurred seemingly overnight with drab apparel hanging off her figure. She also looked to have dropped a noticeable amount of weight in the brief period since Margaret had last seen her. All in all, her new wren-gray persona was in direct contrast to the bright, colored walls that surrounded her.

Bill shifted underneath the cape that was catching the hair from the trimming. He looked at Jocelyn with a childlike wonder in his eyes, waiting for her to direct him it seemed. She nudged him. "Say hello to Robert and Margaret."

Instead of doing that, he playfully swiped at Jocelyn's backside where there was still enough to swipe. She batted her eyes coquettishly at him. "Oooh, Buddy. Leave me be now."

Robert threw a nervous glance at Margaret at the jarring scene and then spoke. "How are you feeling today, Bill?"

Bill finally looked over at them and they could see it slowly register who they were through the film of whatever drugs he had been given.

"Buddy!" Jocelyn placed hands on hips in a scolding manner. "I told you to say hello."

He hung his head. His helpless demeanor was so out of character. "I'm sorry, Mom." He tried to rally as he turned to them and said, "Well, hello there, folks. When did you get here?"

"We've only just arrived, Bill. It was a nice country drive out from Needham Forest," Robert said.

Bill said nothing in return and a quiet took over, an uncomfortable quiet. Margaret broke into it by pulling a box of chocolates from her satchel. "Here you are, Bill. I brought you those chocolates you like."

He looked at the box of candy in confusion. "Chocolates?"

"Yes, we had them at the farm one time."

"The farm?" Bill said.

Jocelyn quickly interjected saying, "Let's open them up, Buddy. I can finish your haircut later." She made quick work of sweeping away the cape and collecting the tools off to one side. "Here folks. Grab some chairs and let's have a sit-down."

Robert and Margaret looked around, spotting chairs in the corner of the room. Robert pulled them towards the bedside. Jocelyn sat next to Bill, her high heels dangling off the edge of the bed, and placed the box of chocolates between them. Jocelyn opened it up and handed one over to Bill, then offered the box to the visitors who both passed on the offer.

"Well..."

"Here we are..." Robert and Margaret both started talking at the same time again. It seemed they were doing a lot of that lately. Margaret nodded at Robert to indicate he should continue.

"How are they treating you here, Bill?"

Bill was still jawing on a chocolate and swallowed before speaking. "Just fine and dandy. Nice people here. And, of course, I got my honey by my side."

His gaze towards Jocelyn oozed with emotion, an almost unseemly level of emotion. It gave Margaret pause. It was a bit unsettling that after all that had happened, he now had Jocelyn exactly where he wanted her—right beside him.

"So, Jocelyn, are you driving back and forth from the District every day?" Robert asked.

"Oh heavens no. I don't even know how to drive and taking the train would be much too long. I'm boarding down in the town. Right above the grocery store they rent out some rooms... to people like me." She gave a little grimace at the indicator of what she herself had orchestrated with the chain of events. She cleared her throat before continuing. "It's a nice little town, really. It suits my needs for now."

The awkwardness crept back in and Margaret again broke into it. "Well, it is nice to see you, Bill. We've been so very worried about you after..." She stopped. "I mean, since everything that has happened."

"What's happened?" He looked at Margaret with innocent eyes, completely innocent. Jocelyn caught Margaret's eye and gave a head shake.

Margaret didn't dare bring up how he felt about the trial that was scheduled to begin the following week. But he hardly seemed in any shape for it. "Oh...I mean just you being here like this."

His face cleared. "Ah...yes. But don't you worry Margaret. I'll be out of here in no time."

A noise at the door, which stood slightly open, interrupted the conversation. They turned to look as the little lion from the reception desk sauntered in with a tall and twitching tail.

"Oh, there he is!" Jocelyn's voice changed and her face brightened at the sight of the cat. "Come on, little friend." She patted some space left on the bed next to her. The not so little friend, Manor, jumped up in a nimble fashion despite the considerable heft to him. He landed his large-boned frame with a grunt on the bed. Both Jocelyn and Bill began petting and cooing at him.

"Well, this is unusual, isn't it? To see a house pet at a place like this...I mean, this place." Robert mused.

"He's not just a regular house pet, Robert. The house doctor brought him back from a trip to Norway. He fell in love with the cats over there and just had to have one. They are very special," Jocelyn said.

As if on cue, a strange, chatty sound came out from the cat. Margaret and Robert looked at each other, sharing a glance of surprise.

"Hear that? This breed of cat chirps like that. Isn't it delightful?" Jocelyn said.

"Yes...delightful. But, why is it here exactly?"

"Why, he's a comfort animal to the patients. Like a soothing balm. Here, come over and pet him. You'll see."

Margaret demurred. "That's okay. I got to know him when we checked in. But from Norway? That's um, really something."

As they watched the Millers pet the cat, Margaret raised her eyebrows to Robert to convey that they needed an exit strategy. Just then, there was a knock on the door.

Jocelyn called out, "Come in."

A short, bald gentleman in a tweed jacket walked in. "Hallo, hallo, all. Time for the day's checkup. Oh, you have visitors I see." He reached over towards the bed and picked up Manor in one fell swoop. As he held up the animal, his tweed sleeves revealed patched and covered elbows. The doctor was almost dwarfed by the large animal as he began to croon in the cat's ear.

"Yes, these are our very close and personal friends, Margaret and Robert," Jocelyn said.

The doctor smiled and nodded at Margaret and Robert. They needed no other excuse to take their leave.

Robert spoke up first. "Well, we will be on our way. It's

been great visiting with you, Bill...and Jocelyn. Glad you are doing so well." More goodbyes were exchanged and, without too much confusion, they made their way back out into the wide and silent turquoise hall.

CHAPTER NINETEEN

Once outside, Margaret took in a huge breath of air. Then she turned to Robert. "That was just...just outlandish. Really."

"Yes, I have to agree—rather a strange scene. Especially that cat from Norway as a therapy strategy. So unusual. Bill seems...um..."

The sound of the double doors opening interrupted Robert. They looked behind to see Jocelyn bustling down the stairs. Margaret's stomach sank.

Once Jocelyn stood in front of them, wringing her hands, she said, "Could I... Could I talk with you two about a few things?"

"Is it okay for you to leave Bill?" Margaret asked.

"He's fine. With the doctor still. I can leave him for a bit."

Robert looked between the two women, gauging the best plan of action. "Well, we could drive down to town maybe?"

It was the last thing Margaret wanted to do but she managed to say, "Yes, of course. Robert's car is right over here."

As they drove back down the hill, Jocelyn said, "There's a coffee shop that I've been grabbing meals at. We could sit and talk there?" Her voice raised it into a question.

"Yes, that's fine," Margaret said, her tone coming out sharper than intended.

Once in town, Robert pulled into a spot and parked. He hopped out to open up the car doors for his two passengers.

Jocelyn said, "It's right down here." She led the way with her heels clicking along the walkway.

The street bustled with people milling around, purchases hanging off arms. The tiny downtown heart, while shabby and a bit gritty at its edges, held an innate allure of yesteryear. Margaret found herself rather charmed by the place with its old-world flavor. It reminded her slightly of Georgetown in the District where her father was raised, although it did not have the same veneer of money overlaid.

They soon walked halfway down the strip and stood in front of a glass-plated storefront where a few diners could be seen on the other side, seated at window tables.

"Here it is." Jocelyn then waved a hand vaguely in the opposite direction. "The boarding house is over there, above that shop. That's where I'm staying." She paused and looked up above the building front. "And over there you can see the courthouse steeple. That's where folks can get quickie marriage licenses. That's where Bill and I..." She stopped.

"You and Bill got married here?" Margaret pressed.

Jocelyn nodded, a conflicted expression on her face. Then she added, "Later, we went to his church for another ceremony. But I had to finish all the rigamarole first."

"Rigamarole?"

"You know, all those papist requirements."

Margaret could almost feel Robert bristling next to her but he said nothing about Jocelyn's obvious dislike for his church. Instead, he reached forward to open the door and then held it for them. Inside, the one room space was tight and crammed with tables. But, as it was late afternoon, there were plenty empty to choose from.

A voice yelled out from behind the counter, "Grab a table, folks. Be with you in a minute."

They positioned themselves automatically with Margaret and Robert facing Jocelyn. The body associated with the voice came out, a tall man wearing a smudged apron, apparently running the whole show. "Welcome! Oh hello there, Jocelyn. Didn't see you at first."

Jocelyn smiled up at the man as he began to hand out menus. Robert stopped him by saying, "We're just here for coffee actually."

Jocelyn chimed in, "But I'll add a slice of that apple pie if you still have it, Sam." A coquettish expression flitted over her face in a brief flash of a moment. Sam pushed his mop of dark hair over to one side, grinning back at her.

Margaret felt a stab of outrage. Apparently on a first name basis with the cook, Jocelyn appeared to be flirting, unable to curtail her ways even now, in the midst of all the calamity.

When Sam walked away to get their coffees, Jocelyn became uncharacteristically silent. Now that she had them as a captive audience, what exactly did she want? Margaret tapped down a lid on her frustration, cleared her throat and began. "So, Jocelyn, you wanted to ask us some things?"

Jocelyn moved the cutlery in front of her around and then came out with it. "Robert, what do you think Bill's chances are?"

"Chances?" he queried.

"Yes, chances of being done with all of this business and getting back home."

Robert waited to respond while Sam placed the coffees and a slice of pie on the table. Then he said, "Well, it's difficult to say at this point. I think we'll know more when his lawyer establishes how strong the evidence is against him—or for him—during the trial next week."

"But Robert, you can see how he is. It's not fair to make him stand trial in his current state. Can't you do something?" It came out as a whine.

As both Margaret and Robert sat back in their chairs against her outcry, Margaret felt another rush of vexation towards the woman. Jocelyn dared ask Robert to fix something that she herself had set in motion with her foolish choices.

Robert shook his head. "There isn't really anything I can do, Jocelyn. Other than support Bill as a friend at this point. And, of course, testify and attend the trial." He included Margaret in a gesture as he added, "We'll be in the courtroom, just like you."

"Whatever will I do without him?" she cried out.

Margaret couldn't stop the words that came spitting out of her mouth. "Shouldn't you have thought of that a long time ago, Jocelyn?"

Jocelyn reared back as if struck. After some silence, she spoke again. "Oh, Margaret. I tried to stop it. I really did. I took your advice but Donald was so powerful. He had such a pull over me. I never even told you, or anybody, the worst of it."

Robert put a hand up. "Jocelyn, that's something you should confide in Bill's lawyer. Not us."

"I just have to tell somebody. I have to let it out."

Sam came out to the counter. "Everything okay here, folks?"

Margaret had not realized how loud their table had become. Well, how loud Jocelyn had become. "We're fine, thanks for asking," she said.

Jocelyn too looked over. She gazed guilelessly at the cook and parroted what Margaret had just said. "Everything's fine, Sam."

Margaret went stony silent at Jocelyn's performance. Was this all a ruse on Jocelyn's part? Was her sad sack demeanor a complete cover-up, a disguise? Margaret shot a glance at Robert to see if he was picking up on it. But he was looking out the window, maybe on purpose.

Jocelyn went back to it. "I'm going to tell you something and you can tell anybody you want. I don't care now. It doesn't need to be a secret anymore."

Margaret deferred to Robert. If this was a law issue, he had to make the call. It was not in her lane to do so. He turned his gaze back to the woman in front of him and, this time, did not stop what she was going to say.

Jocelyn first wiped around the corners of her mouth. Then she spoke. "I had to keep seeing Donald and stay in his good graces because..." She paused and Margaret wondered if it was again an act, if she was pausing for dramatic effect. "Because he said he would shoot Bill's old white head off if he tried to get between us!"

Robert sighed and said, "Jocelyn, why haven't you told this to Bill's defense team?"

"Because everything became such a jumble. It was all happening so fast. Don't you see though? I was trying to save Bill's life!" She paused again seemingly to gauge their reaction.

At Margaret and Robert's granite-faced expressions, she burst into histrionic sobs, not unlike the episode at the department store tearoom that Margaret had endured. Sam again popped his head out from the rear, eyeing their table with suspicion. Robert waved a hand, indicating it was all under control.

They let her sobbing wind down until it finally trailed off into loud sniffling with gaps in between.

Robert began to talk once again. "So, Jocelyn, I advise you as a, uh, friend—not your lawyer—let me be clear on that point. I advise you to contact the defense team from Bill's firm. Joe Patterson heads it up. Has he talked to you already?" Margaret could tell from the muscle moving in Robert's jaw that he was trying to suppress his ire at the woman.

"Yes, I talked to him. I just blocked all this part out, I guess. Especially after the nasty look he gave me."

"Why did he give you a nasty look?"

"It was after I told him about the pink brassiere."

Robert shifted, uncomfortable right away at the mention of female undergarments. Jocelyn had a way of pressing the boundaries of polite discussion.

Margaret sighed and knew she had to be the one to follow up. "Pink brassiere?"

Jocelyn nodded and then spoke again. "Yes. Donald insisted that I had to purchase and wear one. It was none of my doing. I don't even like the color pink."

"Really?" Margaret raised her eyebrows, remembering too well the hunt at the department store when Jocelyn had announced to her and the sales clerk her need for a hot pink brassiere and how mortifying the exchange had been.

"No. Never liked it. Anyway, it took forever to find one. I hunted throughout all the stores downtown. And then, wouldn't you know it, he said it didn't fit right." She threw her hands up. "So that's why I had to return it that day. That's the only reason Bill saw me on the sidewalk getting into Donald's car. And if it hadn't been for that, none of all of this would have happened."

Her tone became even more pleading as she doubled down on the claim. "He controlled me, Margaret. Can't you understand? None of this was my doing!"

"Well, dwelling on how it came to be is not helping Bill. Best right now to figure out a way forward," Robert said, disdain obvious on his expression.

Margaret knew the conversation would drag on in the same vein so she said in a stern manner, "It's time for us to get back on the road, Jocelyn. It's been a long day."

With that, she stood and Robert followed her lead. Jocelyn took her time standing up, clearly reluctant to leave the diner and go back to Bill.

As they drove Jocelyn back up the hill, Margaret turned to look back at her. Jocelyn appeared somewhat deflated, shoulders slumped against the car seat back. Whatever she intended to happen, her big reveal had not worked out like she wanted.

As Robert helped Jocelyn out of the car, Margaret made her goodbye a reminder. "You need to get in touch with Mr. Patterson right away."

As they navigated their way back through the town, Margaret was confounded by the day and what it all meant, not only for Bill but for her own future. Jocelyn had muddied the waters even more. Margaret pondered the pink brassiere contretemps, wondering if it was thrown out by Jocelyn as an excuse or a distraction. It was all so very coarse really.

Mid-way through town at a fork in the road, a shiny new gas station was perched at the cleft between two hills. "Just the opportunity we need," Robert said.

He swung in deftly but barely fit into the tight space in front of the gasoline pump with its cheerful red Pegasus emblem for Mobil oil atop of the glass cylinder. The gas jockey leaned in the window and asked, "Fill 'er up?" Robert gave a nod of assent.

As they listened to the glugging sound of gas filling the tank, Margaret could not wait any longer to say it. "It's all an act. Jocelyn. You know that, right?"

Robert spoke with no hesitation. "She's pure deceit."

Margaret, while concurring with his statement, was taken aback by the venomous tone, so unlike him. But Jocelyn seemed to have a knack for bringing out the worst in everyone. "You know, I have to say she's gotten into the habit of using her wiles and it's always worked for her. Now, it's not working anymore and her world is crumbling." Margaret sighed and then continued, "I could almost feel sorry for her."

They looked at each other and both said at the same time, "Almost."

"But, on the other hand, maybe, just maybe, some of what she has held back can be used to sway the jury," Robert said.

"Speaking of which, Jocelyn was right on one point. How can Bill possibly stand trial next week like...like he is now?"

Robert shook his head. "I don't know. Maybe they can wean him off whatever drugs he is on?"

The attendant came back to the window and Robert handed over some cash. He shifted the gear crank. As he looked over to Margaret, his face softened, all traces of his earlier tone gone. "Shall we?"

She nodded and they headed up the last hill out of the little town and back to Needham Forest.

CHAPTER TWENTY

Margaret swirled the last bit of coffee in her cup trying to ignore the pile of bills that waited for her attention. She had pushed them off to one side of the desk but that didn't mean they were not there to contend with. Especially the one that concerned unpaid taxes.

The calming solitude of the farm was in complete contrast to the inner turmoil she was feeling. After she finished the dregs in the cup, she set it down hard and sprung up from the chair. She paced the room as she thought over the day before with all its portents. She had to face it head on: the fact that Bill was no longer a viable partner in her horse business. Even if he made a complete recovery, even if he somehow dodged jail, or worse, for Dr. Michael's murder and even if things eventually and magically went back to just as they were, too many days would go by without the cash influx necessary to keep the farm a going concern.

When her gaze snagged on the blueprint rolls propped up in the corner of the room, Margaret stopped mid-pace. In all the chaos since the murder, she had neglected the exercise of hunting for treasure caches. The house plans had been set aside after her energy was expended on the black walnut tree escapade. She stifled a giggle at the memory of poor Leonard with the handsaw in the middle of the field.

She walked over to the corner and picked the plans up. She blew some dust bunnies off and carried them to the low, wide table in the middle of the room. Maybe if she studied them again, she would get some inspiration. Something might come to her. It was all she had at this point.

As Margaret laid them out, she again noted the architect's blocky signature on the bottom right of each sheet. After sorting through a few, she settled on one that detailed the original footprint of the house, the log cabin section. Like before, she mused about where exactly that section could now be buried. As she examined it, her finger caught on the bottom of the sheet and she realized there was a smaller sheet stuck underneath.

After she carefully peeled off the old and brittle paper, she laid it flat, apart from the larger plans. The paper displayed sectional drawings of the hallway and the staircase showing elaborate details of the woodwork. It displayed a different signature, distinctive cursive in the corner with the name, Nathan Magruder. She knew him. He was the great-great uncle who had owned Needham Forest as the very last in a long line of Magruder males.

Nathan had died suddenly and his maiden sisters retained residence. Margaret's father, Charles, reconnected with those sisters, distant relations, after becoming involved with the horse business. One thing led to another with her father eventually inheriting the house from the sisters and moving in with his young family; Margaret, Judith and their mother.

Margaret looked around the room. She vaguely remembered hearing that Nathan had fancied himself a gentleman architect. He made furniture, and enjoyed woodworking as a pastime. But she didn't realize that some of Needham Forest's finer architectural details might have been created by him.

At that thought, she leapt up and over to the bookcase which held the family bible. She flipped the pages until she found Nathan's information. Born in 1810 and deceased in 1870, he thus had been the owner during the time of the war.

Margaret sank down into the loveseat in frustration. The rumor of the gold had to have started with him. And he was a craftsman...there just had to be a link between those facts somehow. But how? She moved to the plans again tracing the footprint of the original dwelling with her forefinger. Where exactly was it now?

"A-ha!" she said aloud. The center of the original dwelling was covered by the present-day staircase, the very same staircase that Nathan Magruder had trussed up with elaborate woodwork. When he designed the house's expansion, was it possible he rolled something into that space? Something along the lines of a treasure niche?

A knock at her study door interrupted her musings and Cassie poked her head in. "You want some lunch, Mizz Margaret? Something to keep you going?"

"Oh, Cassie. What's the time? I got immersed in this..."

"It's done gone past noon."

"Goodness. No, don't worry about it. I'll come out to the kitchen in a bit."

Cassie gave a nod and left the room.

Margaret shook her head and blinked several times. She had no idea that much time had gone by. She walked into the hall and sat back down at the phone table. When the call connected down to the District and Robert's office, she felt warmth as she always did at hearing his voice on the line.

"Robert, I think I might have stumbled upon something. Can you come out here tonight?"

He was silent for a pause. "Margaret...I really have gotten behind. And..."

"And?"

"Bill's defense team contacted me."

"What? Why?"

"It's too much to go into right now but can this wait?"

She was taken aback at his brusqueness. "Yes. Yes, of course. I, um, we can discuss it later."

Their goodbye was even more wooden. Margaret hung up the receiver and sat with confusion. What had suddenly shifted? Their goodbye the previous night had been as passionate as ever. Maybe she was just reading too much into his tone. She could show Robert the plans the next time, whenever that would be.

She stood and headed back to the study to somehow figure out which unpaid bills could be stalled and which ones absolutely could not. But, in the back of her thoughts, was Nathan Magruder, the staircase and the gold bars.

As the day drew to a close, Margaret still worked with the mountain of paper but had made little headway. She pulled out the most glaring debt and stared at the not insignificant figure of three hundred dollars owed to Graystone's Hay and Services. She leafed through the other bills and thought about which ones to put off so that Graystone's could be paid. It was a bit like robbing Peter to pay Paul but she had to juggle it all somehow. The horses needed to be fed first and foremost.

The noise of a car's approach could be heard on Needham Forest's drive. She jumped out of her seat and looked out the window to see Robert's roadster. Given their earlier conversation, she was more than a bit surprised. She made her way into the hall and caught a glimpse of her appearance in the antique gold-rimmed hall mirror. She fluffed her hair and pinched her cheeks. It would have to do.

By the time Margaret flung the door open, Robert was standing with one arm up mid-knock. He reached forward and grabbed her into a fierce embrace. She pulled back after a few seconds. "Robert, what is it now?"

"Can I come in?"

"Of course."

They walked together into the drawing room. Without asking, she began mixing him a cocktail while he sat down on the sofa. The silence that filled the space was not a comfortable one. There was tension in the air and it bothered her. She couldn't place it; whether it was all from Bill's situation or if it had somehow leached over into their relationship. But maybe she was overthinking it once again and he was just collecting his thoughts.

As she twirled the drink with a spoon, Margaret let some relief rinse through her that at least his brusqueness from earlier was not evident. It couldn't be that he was pulling away from her. Because he was here now. She handed him the drink and joined him on the sofa.

He spoke up without any preamble. "The meeting with the defense team has me very concerned, Margaret. Concerned about Bill's fate."

Margaret's stomach roiled immediately at a hideous vision of Bill in the electric chair. It had recently become the preferred method over hanging for executions in the city. Either choice didn't bear thinking about.

Robert continued. "I shouldn't be confiding in you like this but..." He stopped and she waited. "The team has concerns about that gun that was on the front seat of Michael's car."

"What kind of concerns?"

"They think there is some kind of proof that Bill planted it."

Margaret gasped. "Oh no! Bill would never do something like that!"

Robert bowed his head. "I don't know, Margaret. I don't know."

"Oh Robert." Margaret wrapped her arms around him and felt some of his tension loosen.

After some time, Robert released himself and looked deeply into her eyes. "I'm sorry about earlier. When I was curt."

"Don't give it another thought. This is all overwhelming."

"There's something else."

Margaret braced herself. "Yes?"

"If things don't go well when the trial gets going, they want me to be a surprise witness for the defense. For Bill."

"Why? What would you be a witness to?"

"Well, I am already on the docket—along with many other of our lawyer friends and you—as a character witness, of course." Margaret nodded. "But they want something more from me. And I just don't know...I just don't know if it's..."

Robert's harried manner upset Margaret. She interjected, "Robert, you can only speak to what you know. You just tell the truth if they call you up, right? What is it they will be questioning you about?"

"Do you remember when Michaels called me to his car that day and showed me a gun?"

"Of course, I do. I was horrified and that was before I even knew who the doctor was."

"Right. So, the thing is he didn't actually show me the gun inside of the envelope. He just showed me the envelope and said there was a gun inside."

Margaret shrugged. "You assumed it was in there?"

"Yes, but they want to present it in such a way that it is definitive there was a gun in the envelope. And I just do not know if I can be a party to this. Call it Catholic guilt, call it what you will. On the other hand, it could be the piece that saves Bill from the chair. The proverbial, 'smoking gun'..." His voice trailed off and they fell silent once again.

"Well..." "But..." They both spoke up at the same time.

"You first," Margaret said.

He sighed and said, "I just don't know how this is going to play out. There's a gray area here between hearsay and—"

Cassie burst into the room speaking, "Mizz, you better eat something now—oh!" She stopped in her tracks upon the sight of Robert and Margaret nestled closely together on the sofa. "I surely didn't know you had a gentleman caller. I's sorry for busting in on you..."

"It's fine, Cassie. Look, I'll sort some dinner out for us. Why don't you take off now?"

Cassie bobbed her head and said, "Alright. I'll see you tomorrow. And you too, Mr. Robert."

They grinned at each other amused by Cassie's antics. It had lightened the mood and Robert said, "Enough of this. Tell me what you wanted help with tonight."

Margaret pressed all thoughts of smoking guns, financial woes and treasure aside. "It can wait. I'd rather just relax and take a breather tonight. With you. Hang on." She lit up from her seat and poked her head into the hallway. When she turned back towards Robert she said, "Cassie has left. It's just us."

They fell into each other's arms finding a much-needed escape from the chaos that swirled around them.

Margaret was in the middle of a delicious dream when her sleep was interrupted by the sounds of Robert getting up and preparing to leave. She reached over, grabbing his arm. "Don't leave. Stay."

Moonlight flooding through the windows made his eyes shine brightly as he gazed down at her. "I-I can't."

"Why Robert?"

He looked away over towards the window. "Did you know this moon is called the 'mourning moon'?"

She pulled herself up to a seat. "Uh, no. I did not."

"Not like early in the day 'morning'. Like grieving 'mourning'."

"Oh. Robert, are you trying to tell me something?"

He stood up and began pulling on his pants. "It's probably better that we have this conversation in the light of day."

"What conversation? There is no time like the present. You can't just leave me like this."

Now fully dressed, he sat back down at the edge of the bed. "Margaret, you know how I was telling you about my guilt about the gun and what exactly they will ask me to testify to?"

"Yes. You called it your Catholic guilt, I believe."

"That's right. Well, I have a similar sort of guilt about us. About this. That's why I can't stay here."

Margaret felt suddenly disoriented and fumbled for words. "You feel guilty about this? About us? But why?"

"Margaret, come on. We aren't exactly acting within the acceptable boundaries of society, are we?"

"I don't care a fig about that, Robert! And you shouldn't either. Don't we have something good here between us?"

He clutched the sides of his head with both hands. "Yes, yes of course we do! But it also seems wrong."

Margaret slumped down, stunned. "I had no idea you felt like this." But that wasn't really the truth. Niggling thoughts had been building up and bothering her. She just hadn't wanted to face them head on.

"Margaret, you're still a married woman. Married to another man."

"But you know I am working as hard as I can to untangle that!"

"Are you?"

"Yes! How can you question that? You know I want nothing more than Keith to be out of my life—our lives—forever." She stopped, biting back how Keith was attempting to stalk her and take Needham Forest back.

Robert stood again. "Look, Margaret. Maybe it's best to take a pause."

"I can't believe this is happening. Is it...is it your religion? Because I'm not a Catholic?"

"No. Yes. I don't know. I mean, I don't even think you could ever get an annulment in your situation."

"An annulment? Why would I— Oh, I see. We could never marry. In your church anyway."

"I'm leaving now, Margaret. But we'll see each other at the trial next week."

She stood up and pulled her wrap on. "I'll see you out."

There were no more words between them as they made their way to the front door. He looked at her once before getting into the roadster, an intense but inscrutable gaze. Was it a gaze of longing or a gaze of goodbye? She didn't know.

As Margaret watched the roadster become small in the distance, an incredible feeling of loneliness overcame her. When she could no longer see the car's tail-lights, it might as well have been that she was the only one in the entire world. All was quiet, not a noise to be heard.

She turned her gaze up to the almost incandescent light of the moon. She couldn't focus on its beauty, though. She could only think about what Robert had called it. As if she was entering a mourning phase and the moon mirrored that. What would she do without Robert in her life?

She walked back inside and closed the door, shutting out the world behind it.

CHAPTER TWENTY-ONE

Margaret tossed and turned for the few hours left of the night. She felt unmoored, a foreign feeling. Flashbacks of times spent with Robert competed with an overwhelming anger that everything had abruptly unraveled between them with the barest of explanations. She finally gave up on sleep when dawn made its appearance through the slits of her blinds.

She got out of bed with a purpose, resolute. She didn't need Robert Brady in her life. She would stand on her own two feet just as she always had.

Now, she would be attending the trial by herself. Not for Jocelyn. Not for Robert. But for Bill. She owed Bill this show of solidarity and, additionally, Bill's defense team had placed her on the list of character witnesses. She would likely be called to the stand.

Margaret's mind spun as she made her way down to the stables, barely taking in the day starting up around her, mired in the mess of it all. It was too early for Leonard to be in but she would begin grooming the horses using the activity to work it all out.

Margaret first walked into the farm office but immediately

stopped short. A huge cobalt blue glass bottle sat in the desk center; a bottle she did not recognize with paper weighted underneath. The desktop was empty otherwise of its usual contents which had been swept off, ending up strewn across the floor.

She made her way over and moved the bottle. She lifted up an official looking document with stamps from the local courthouse. Her eyes skimmed over it, picking up the gist. It spelled out a suit brought against her by Keith.

The brief summary under "O'Keefe vs. O'Keefe" detailed that Mr. Keith O'Keefe was suing Mrs. Margaret O'Keefe for his rights as tenant entirety of Needham Forest. She thumbed through the document which was in effect signed, sealed and, somehow, delivered.

She threw it down in disgust. It was the delivery aspect that incensed her the most. How dare Keith sneak into the farm office in the night? Alongside the outrage, a part of her wondered if she should be fearful of her estranged spouse and this skulking behavior.

In fact, was Keith still lurking about? She stepped out into the center bay of the barn and looked around. Leonard would be arriving shortly as Keith well knew; plus, he was a night owl, not a morning person. Margaret shook with rage more than fear. She went back into the office and collapsed into the chair Keith might have just recently sat in.

Leonard found her there in the same position a quarter of an hour later. He stopped at the door and said, "You alright, Miss Margaret?"

She pushed the paper forward for him to read. "This was on the desk. A judge has allowed for Keith's lawyer to open up an investigation into the rightful heirs of Needham Forest. And here it is."

Leonard pulled it close to his face, squinting at it. Then he looked up as if it had just occurred to him. "How did it get here?"

"I guess you could call it 'special delivery'." Her voice emphasized the last bit with dripping sarcasm.

"O'Keefe was here?" There was now grave concern in Leonard's wrinkled expression.

She nodded. "He must have snuck in last night."

"You want to call the sheriff? For trespassing?"

Margaret sat back in the chair, thoughtful. "No, not as yet."

Leonard placed the papers back down. "What judge in his right mind would entertain something so ridiculous in his court? How the dickens did he get this to happen?"

Margaret pointed to the signature on the last page. "This judge. Fritz. A buddy of Keith's from the club. It's remarkable he has hung on to his judgeship with his drinking and gambling ways."

Leonard shook his head. "Well, that explains it then. A drunk pal of his from the track. That's the only kind of judge who would do this."

Margaret sighed. "I imagine Keith concocted up this scheme after plying the fellow with more than a few rounds of Irish whiskey. Also, his shyster lawyer had a hand in it."

"Just goes to show how it pays to have friends in high places," Leonard said, shaking his head again.

She let out a huge sigh. "This means something else to deal with. Not to mention the money involved with more lawyer bills on my end. How am I ever going to get him out of my life?"

"Yeah, you need to be quit of that fellow once and for all. That's for sure. Can I do anything for you?"

"No, no... Oh yes, wait. There is something. Come on up with me to the house."

At the house, Cassie greeted them at the front door. "Mizz Margaret, you up right early today." Her gaze took in Margaret with some suspicion. "You ready for your breakfast and coffee? My biscuits just came out of the oven."

"Yes, to both. And for Leonard as well. In the drawing room, please. We have work to do," Margaret said, with a decisive tone.

She grabbed the plans and brought them to the low cocktail table which was generous enough to hold them. After she unrolled them and placed paperweights on each corner with Leonard's assistance, they took a pause as Cassie brought in a tray.

After coffees were poured, they sat companionably snacking on Cassie's ham biscuits, the house plans in front of them. When finished, Margaret wiped her hands on a napkin and stood up over the table.

She pointed to the area on the plan. "What I see here is an anomaly, Leonard." She went on to explain why it did not make sense. "And this plan here shows that my ancestor, Nathan, was very involved in woodwork. He would have been the one here during the war."

After Leonard studied it for a few minutes, she asked, "What do you think?"

He scratched his head. "I ain't one for architecture but I do see what you mean. This gap right here between the old house and the new one. So that means..." He stood up from the sofa and headed over towards the hall. She followed him.

"That means it's here somewhere," he said, with arms akimbo in front of the stairs.

They stood in the hallway, staring at the area in question. The old and gracious staircase of vintage dark pine wood was possibly concealing something. But how could Margaret figure it out?

Leonard finally spoke. "It's not like that black walnut tree.

We can't take a saw and cut into this thing. Not without a big repair job later."

Margaret made a sound. "God knows, I can't afford that level of repair, so no, we can't do that."

Leonard walked up to it and began tapping around the triangular section of paneling that enclosed the area under the stairs. "Nothing odd about it sounding hollow. That's as it should be."

He knelt with some effort and began to work his hands along the paneling. "Maybe, just maybe, they left a way to lift it somehow. Looks to be made up of several panels."

Margaret knelt down next to him, hoping against hope that Leonard would be able to feel something. His hands suddenly stopped moving and he looked at her.

"What?"

"Here...there's a catch along the bottom of this one in the middle." His fingers worked to lift it up but it didn't budge. He stopped and sat back on his heels, eyeing up the space. He spoke again. "Might have been the panel opened up like this at some point. But not anymore. It's been too long. I'm going to need my toolbox and it'll ding up the wood. That alright?"

"Yes, yes. I'll get it fixed, eventually." She suppressed a shudder at more expenses.

While Leonard left to get his tools, Margaret paced back and forth in the hallway. What would they find? If anything?

When Leonard returned, he held what looked to Margaret like a crowbar.

"I hate to damage this old paneling. I mean, it's probably considered an antique, right?"

Margaret nodded absentmindedly then said, "But if there's a bigger antique waiting behind it, it will all be worth it."

Leonard took his time working methodically as he wedged the little instrument around the lines of the board. Then he said,

"Okay, here goes." As he lifted it up, the board separated from its companions of many years with a slight groan. He pulled it off, setting it to one side. They peered into what was behind. Despite the daylight from the center hall, it was too dark.

"Dang it. I left my light at the barn."

"Let me get a candle." Margaret hustled into the kitchen where Oliver picked up on her excitement and playfully nipped at her heels. "Cassie! Can you get me a candle? And matches too, please?"

Cassie looked up with surprise from the bread she was kneading. "Yes'm. What's got you all in a dither like this?"

"You'll see."

As Leonard and Margaret waited for Cassie, they both tried to look deeper into the space through the vantage of the one narrow panel removed. It was clearly hollowed-out but that was all that could be discerned.

"Seems odd to leave space empty and unused like that when they built over the original house," Leonard mused.

Margaret stared at it, thoughtful. Then she said, "Well, I did read something at the historical society about every room being taxed in the early days. Even closets. Maybe it was some sort of cost saving move. Who knows?"

"Don't make much sense to me."

Cassie shuffled into the hall, candle and matchbox in hand. Her eyes got big when she saw what the board had revealed. "What's in there?"

"That's what hopefully we are about to find out, Cassie." Margaret took the items and struck a match. She held the flickering flame out into the emptiness. But it was just...vacant. A wave of disappointment hit hard. "Leonard, you look. I don't see anything."

She switched places and Leonard did the same as she had. Waving the candle as much as possible into the space. Finally, he pulled back out with a shaking head. "It's a queer thing, ain't it? Just dead space, nothing in there."

Margaret leaned against the wall and sighed. "I really thought I might get a break."

"What are you going to do now with it, Mizz Margaret? You going to open it all up?" Cassie asked.

"I don't know. I mean...I guess I could?"

Leonard nodded. "Yeah, it's supported already. Not like you need the paneling on."

"Might be a nice little place for your telephone, I'm thinking," Cassie added.

"Maybe. But for now, I'll just wait on it. Let it stay as is." She dusted herself off and Leonard followed suit. "Thank you. Both of you. I'm going to take a break now."

The other two watched Margaret as she made her way slowly up the stairs to her bedroom. She felt as if she had aged years in the past twelve hours and all she wanted to do was sleep. All of it could wait for now. Calling her lawyer about Keith and his preposterous plans, thinking about Robert and their now troubled relationship, dealing with the bills and Needham Forest's future. It could all just wait for a couple of hours or so.

CHAPTER TWENTY-TWO

"Judith, it's all a complete mess. Everything."

"Now, Margaret. Nothing can be all that bad." Her sister's voice was rich with compassion and concern on the other end.

It was late, very late. But Margaret found sleep impossible and she knew Judith would be up in the wee hours. She had hesitated to call, not wanting to dump all her troubles into Judith's lap. It wasn't fair to do that. Judith had her own life with her own concerns. But the dark and lonely night took a toll and Margaret found herself sitting at the phone table with just the ticking hall clock for company. She needed to hear another voice—a voice apart from her own; specifically, her sister's voice.

And just like that, Judith answered her call and was now saying, "Break it down bit by bit. In pieces. Let's see if we can figure this thing out."

Margaret took a deep inhale and then said, "Okay...here goes..."

She told Judith all the goings-on that had led her to this point of sleeplessness. She included the loss of funds from Bill and the strange and sad turn of events with Robert. She ended with Keith's absurd effort to steal Needham Forest.

Judith interrupted her. "Oh stop. Okay, that right there. Clearly, you can deal with that right away."

"I can? How?"

"Oh dear. You really have gone far afield, haven't you? It's simple, Mags. The courthouse will have the deed that states Daddy had full rights. Surely, it has to be there. This is some kind of smokescreen effort on Keith's part. Like pretending it doesn't exist. Of course it exists!"

"Wouldn't the lawyer have..."

"The lawyer is as crooked as they come. You said so yourself. So, no, he wouldn't have. It's up to you. Or your lawyer."

"Yes, but my lawyer will charge an arm and a leg for any minute of work so— You are right, Judith. I can do this. Thank you...I don't know what's wrong with me."

"I know, Mags. It's weird for me to be the clever one." She laughed out loud and Margaret found herself giving in to the same merriment. It did feel good to laugh.

After they ended the call, sleep finally came to Margaret along with a resolve to take the next step.

The next morning, Margaret was standing at the kitchen door of Needham Forest when Albert's pickup truck pulled around the rear to drop off Cassie. Margaret approached the driver's side window and leaned in. "Albert, could you take me to Rockville right now? I'll cover your gas money. It's really important."

Cassie interjected immediately from the passenger seat. "No need for that. Albert, you go on now and give Mizz Margaret this ride."

Albert gave a nod. "You ready now then?"

"Let me just grab my bag and I'll be right out." Margaret

also made a mental note to plus up Cassie's weekly envelope of wages to cover Albert's time and gas.

Cassie followed Margaret in through the kitchen and fussed. "You don't have any food or coffee in you! You gonna be working on fumes, Mizz Margaret."

Margaret waved a hand at her as she breezed her way through the kitchen and back out to Albert. Her stomach had been giving her issues of late. Maybe the stress of all that was going on made for poor digestion.

When they pulled into town, the courthouse loomed in the very center of the town. Of recent vintage, it had cost the city a fair penny but was viewed as emblematic of the town and what it wanted to represent. The architecture was dramatic, just on the edge of fanciful. Albert pulled up right in front of it and they made arrangements for Margaret's pick up.

In the foyer, Margaret approached a receptionist staffing a visitor desk. "Good morning, I would like to peruse the land deeds." As an afterthought, she added, "And wills too."

"That's up on the mezzanine."

While Margaret had been in the courthouse here and there over the years, she could not recall ever being on that level. "And where might I find that?"

"Take the staircase at the end of the hall and go up one flight."

After Margaret climbed up the stairs, she exited out into the main area. She let out an "oohh" at the mezzanine floor. The light from underneath made the glass floor tiles glow. As she moved into the space, her heels connected with a click on the glass of each tile. There was something magical about the sound and feel.

The mezzanine was filled with shelving stacks that held huge canvas-covered books labeled "Deeds". It overwhelmed

Margaret as she searched through for books that included "Index" in the title. After spotting one, she tugged on it to lift and found it much heavier than anticipated.

She carried the hefty book over to a nearby work table, setting it down with a thud. When she opened it, dust flew up and immediately tickled her nose. She tried to hold back a sneeze not wanting to ruin the perfect quiet of the place. But the sneeze came out anyway, loud and dramatic.

Margaret pored through several indexes but was not finding mention of her distant great-great uncle or her father. She was down to the last one and hit pay dirt with a listing for her father, Charles Magruder. She jotted down the liber and folio numbers and then searched anew through the stacks for it.

Finally located, she pulled it out with arms now fatigued from all the heavy lifting. The paper in the book was brittle and she turned the pages with care to avoid inadvertently ripping or tearing any of it. She found the right page and her finger ran down it until "Charles Magruder" popped out in elaborate cursive.

The deed was written in unique script, sometimes hard to decipher, on paper now old and faded. Margaret read and then reread it, eventually grasping the meaning. It was titled "An Indenture" which she assumed to be antiquated terminology for a contract. It stated that the property was handed over to her father for one dollar from his great aunts. At the end of the dense legalities spread out over several pages, the transfer of ownership to her father was declared:

We, the undersigned, Elizabeth and Moriah Magruder, daughters of Bartholomew Magruder, late of this world in the year of the lord nineteen

*hundred and one, do hereby acknowledge receipt of
one dollar in American money from Charles
Magruder for the transfer of ownership of our
family property known as Needham Forest.*

The two distant relatives had signed off to that effect in spidery and faint signatures at the very, very bottom of the last page of the indenture.

"Yes!" Margaret said aloud. This had to be the proof needed to contest Keith's ridiculous claim. Margaret looked back through it all, not finding a receipt for that one dollar but surely it would not be contained in a deed anyway. This indenture had to be enough, had to be what she needed to face down Keith at a court hearing. And face him down she would.

She remembered at the last second to head over to where indexes for old wills were held. Something tickled in her mind about that. She had never seen a will for Nathan's estate but that didn't mean there wasn't one. And if there was one, would it possibly include anything about the gold? Maybe not overtly but in a way that could provide a clue?

Again, she struggled with another unwieldy book and then ran her finger down all the "M" surnames that were cataloged for the time period. And there it was: Nathan Magruder. His will was dated several years before he had passed away.

She felt a prickle of excitement as she went over to the stacks to find the right book. Ignoring her now sore arm muscles, she lifted and then carried yet another heavy book to the table. After she turned the pages and found the right one, she eagerly read the words of her ancestor's wishes.

I, Nathan Magruder, being in sound mind but

weak in body, do hereby state that my estate shall pass down to my sisters, Elizabeth and Moriah, should they outlive me.

My house, Needham Forest and all its appurtenances and contents, along with the original land tract consisting of one hundred and twenty-two acres, shall be passed down. This includes the house and all its contents, seen and unseen, and all other attendant property.

Somewhat perplexed by the wording, Margaret reread it. She had not read a lot of wills in her time but the phrase, "seen and unseen", seemed unusual. Was it just standard legalese fare of that time period or an underlying message?

The will book made a decisive slap as Margaret closed it. She placed her hand on top of it and resolve came over her. She was ready for whatever came next.

Back at Needham Forest, Margaret settled onto the drawing room's sofa. The sun was beginning to set and radiated a nice, comforting glow about the room.

Cassie's footfall in the hall announced her approach. "Mizz Margaret, is Mr. Robert coming to eat with you tonight?"

She felt a pang at the thought that "Mr. Robert" would not be coming to dinner anytime soon, or ever again. Instead of making a paltry excuse, she said simply, "No, Cassie. It's just me for tonight."

"Alrighty. I'll get your plate ready."

For now, she would let Cassie think that all was fine, all was the same. But she knew the truth of the matter would soon be obvious. Robert, the person by her side of late, had vamoosed.

She lifted herself up from the sofa, a heavy weight of fatigue in her bones. She headed over to the credenza with the cocktail fixings. She opened the decanter that held the vodka but paused.

Her stomach felt funny and, despite how much she had been craving a stiff drink with the day she had, the thought of consuming one turned her off. It was so unlike her to deny herself this end-of-the-day pleasure. But she would pass on that particular kind of refreshment for the evening.

Instead, she reached for the small greenish bottle of Coca-Cola that had become her mainstay lately. Her father had sworn by Pepsi-Cola as a cure for all stomach ills. Margaret had read the name was trademarked to be a derivation of dyspepsia, a fancy term for indigestion. Sadly, the company had gone bankrupt a decade earlier so she had been substituting Coca-Cola.

When Albert took Cassie into town to pick up groceries, Margaret made sure it was on the weekly shopping list. Even though her father had used Coca-Cola just for headaches, the soda was taking the edge off her digestive unease. The only thing she could tolerate, in fact.

After she cracked open the beverage, she slumped back onto the sofa, taking in the still and quiet of the house around her. It felt very big and she felt very alone. The drink might have allayed that for a bit but really drinks were much more enjoyable when shared with someone. Robert's absence stung all over again.

Margaret could hear Oliver's nails clicking on the hardwood in the center hallway as he approached. She wondered if he sensed her melancholy. When he entered the room with his wagging tail, she patted the seat cushion next to her. He jumped up and then settled in with a sigh.

Margaret stroked his fur as she took small sips of the soda. As she tried to puzzle it all out, that phrase *seen and unseen* popped back into her thoughts. "Seen and unseen," she said aloud to Oliver. "Seen and unseen."

CHAPTER TWENTY-THREE

Margaret berated herself for a late start at leaving for the trial. She caught the last morning train from Rockville, followed by a taxi. When she finally arrived at the front of the courthouse, she was greeted by a scene of chaos that included a mixed crowd of reporters and bystanders and a buzz of electricity in the air. She should have realized the first day of a murder trial involving one of the District's most renowned lawyers would be bedlam.

Bill's defense team had let her know in advance she would be called up to the stand as a character witness at some point on the first day. She dressed with the utmost care to give herself the boost of extra confidence. Her cream-colored suit paired with a matching hat pinned atop her carefully coiffed hairdo. At the last minute, she added a brooch that her father had given her. It was a bright green emerald in the middle of a small spray of gold. She hoped it would give her the luck, along with the confidence, to say her part.

But what was her part? She could vouch for Bill as someone her father had trusted when he was a much younger man. And she could also vouch for him in her life currently as a valued business partner. She could do this.

Margaret hastened up the imposing staircase that provided the formal front of the courthouse. Intimidating in its size and austerity, the architecture was typical of the District in that concerted effort to posture the city as the most pivotal amongst all other cities in the country. She paused halfway up the stairs to catch her breath as others crowded around her, also making their way up.

Moving off to one side to avoid the throng, she nearly stumbled right into a cluster of men sitting near the top steps with what looked like piles of belongings next to them. She stopped short, taken aback at the bedraggled men. Despite their torn and dirty attire, their faces could be the faces of any businessmen she had encountered over the years in a boardroom or an office.

She had heard about this, what the papers were calling "hobos", homeless and wandering men down on their luck since the crash. But it was made all too real to see it close up. These were strange times indeed.

When she said, "Please excuse me, gentlemen," a couple of them shuffled over so that she could skirt around. As she walked through the main entrance, she wondered if she should have offered them some spare change but the moment had passed.

She waded through the crowded corridor, following the crowd who were all going to the same courtroom for the trial of Bill Miller. She hoped to find a seat by the time she got in there, not relishing the prospect of standing throughout the entire proceedings. Off to one side of the courtroom doors, she could see Bill's head above the rest, his height making him stand out. She scanned the small group he was with only seeing Jocelyn and a couple of men she assumed made up his defense team. There was no sign of the one she was hoping to see, Robert.

She worked through the crowd to make her way over to them. Bill's eyes lit up upon sighting her and he reached for her with outstretched hands. His clasp was dry but warm and he hung on tightly. His eyes were again the limpid pools of sorrow as they had been for so many months prior and since the incident with Dr. Michaels. It was clear right off that this was not the drugged-out version of Bill who Margaret had visited at Patapsco Manor.

"Margaret! It's a good day!"

He kept hold of her hands as she tried to control her reaction. "It is?"

"Yes, indeedy. Friday the thirteenth. I always win cases on this day. It's a lucky day. The day I was born, in fact. A Friday the thirteenth."

Margaret nodded dumbly while the others in the little group shifted uncomfortably. Was Bill now mixing in numerology on top of all the religious mumbo-jumbo? But, she thought, if it all worked out in his favor in the end, why not just go along with it?

One of the lawyers cleared his throat and said, "It's time now."

They headed through the courtroom doorway. As the rest of them walked to the front, Margaret held back, scanning the packed-out room. Bill made his way to the front table with his attorneys, while Jocelyn took a seat in the row behind them.

In the row across from Jocelyn, she spotted Robert and her breath caught. There was space to one side of him. Could it be that he had saved her a space? But...

She couldn't, she wouldn't. It was all too raw still, the memory of their last night together. Instead, she took an available spot in one of the rows towards the rear of the room.

As Margaret settled into the seat, she became aware that the room was filled with a droning chatter and a hopped-up energy. It seemed wrong that people would get excited about such an event but she supposed it was human nature to do so. Within a few minutes, the bailiff walked in and ordered, "All rise!" There was the shuffling of all in the room obeying his directive as the judge walked in and took his seat. It was followed by a complete hush coming over the space in direct contrast to the din from the moment before.

The proceedings began with the prosecutor, Ned Armstrong, standing up at the front. His face had the look of a weasel and his slicked back hair was almost greasy. Margaret felt immediate dislike based just on his appearance. His voice came out glass-cutter sharp and her dislike intensified as his opening statement detailed the events that had unfolded on the day in question.

His words were precise as he painted a picture of Bill as an evil monster. A killer intent on killing his prey no matter the result. He wrapped up his opening saying, "By the end of the trial, the government will show pure and simple that this was murder. Deliberate, premeditated and, most especially, malicious murder in cold blood."

Bill's defense lawyer, Joe Patterson, then bounded up. He began to regale the courtroom with an opposite version of the story. A story about a man who was deeply in love with his wife and who was driven crazy by the machinations of another man. This other man, a doctor, had manipulated her and wouldn't let her out his grasp. It was a compelling version but, as Margaret looked around, it was not clear which side public opinion was being swayed, one way or the other.

After the two sides had laid out their stances, the proceedings led to evidence being brought forward. The prosecutor went for high drama and started with the most sensational pieces: a hot pink brassiere of a large size in one hand and a shopping bag in the other with the name of the department store emblazoned on it but also splattered with crimson spots. There was a collective gasp from the courtroom when he held them up high into the air.

Margaret looked at Bill in the front row, shoulders hunched, back bowed, an air of defeat rapidly coming over him. He whispered something to Patterson. His attorney leapt up to interrupt the proceedings but, before he could say anything, Bill slumped over in the seat into a dead faint. Just as he had done a couple months earlier at the arraignment.

Margaret felt like she was watching a movie at the Tivoli. People rushed up from the sides but were batted aside to make space for Bill to lay out. Her stomach, already upset, began to clench even more. A man rushed down the center holding a bottle of what looked to be ammonia and a pad of smelling salts saying, "Clear the way, clear the way!"

Margaret couldn't help the sigh of relief that escaped from her mouth when Bill was revived and sitting up again. She had worried about how he was going to withstand all of this. There was, though, a worm of doubt in her mind. Was the faint real? Or could it possibly be an act?

After the excitement of Bill's fainting spell died down, the judge convened at the bench with the lawyers and then made the announcement that the court would recess for an early lunch and reconvene later that afternoon.

Margaret barely had a chance to stand up before Jocelyn was smack dab in front of her. "Oh, Margaret. There you are. You had me worried you left. I didn't see you anywhere."

Margaret said, "Well, here I am" but her gaze drifted back to the front of the courtroom where Robert stood with a cluster of other lawyers in deep and intense discussion.

"How about a cup of coffee? I'm so parched from all of this."

She stared at the woman. Jocelyn was back to her glib self. Margaret didn't know if she could stomach it—especially because her stomach was still off. Also, she couldn't help but think Jocelyn would be in the middle of a firestorm if they tried to walk freely amongst the reporters.

"Don't you need to be with Bill?"

"No, they want him to sit somewhere in a back room and go over a few things. I'm on my own for a bit."

Another part of Margaret also felt uneasy at being spotted in Jocelyn's company. It would not help her one bit with her clients to be associated with Jocelyn's kind of notoriety, pink brassiere and all. She posed it as a question. "But can you just walk out the front without being badgered by the press?"

"Oh, we'll slip out the back. I know a spot down the alley behind the building."

Margaret was taken aback at Jocelyn's savvy. She did need a breather, even if it wasn't the most ideal situation. And, in a way, it was all part of her support for Bill.

"Okay, then. Lead the way."

Jocelyn headed for the rear exit which opened into a back hall. They peered through but no one seemed particularly interested in them. Jocelyn beckoned Margaret with one hand and they high-stepped it to the door. It opened into the alley which they had to themselves.

They walked side by side in a stiff and uncomfortable silence. A block away, a small awning announced the Bitter Grounds Coffee Shop and they entered through an inconspicuous entrance.

Once seated, Jocelyn's gaze skirted nervously around the place. It wasn't until they had coffees in hand that Jocelyn spoke, breaking into the charged air between them. "So...it's going well, don't you think?" Jocelyn beamed a bright stare directly at Margaret.

"It is? Jocelyn, Bill fainted and it's only day one. I don't know that we can say it's going well."

"Margaret, you are already acting like we are at Bill's

funeral. For goodness' sake, can't you show a little bit of support?"

"I am, Jocelyn. I'm here to support Bill in any way possible. That's why I am testifying today on his behalf. As a character witness."

"Look, Margaret, if I've heard Bill say it once, I've heard it a hundred times. He always tells his clients, 'Tell the truth'. That's his motto and, as long as he does that, he should be just fine."

Jocelyn had really changed her tune since they had met in Ellicott City. Apparently, she was going to keep blinders on.

"But Jocelyn, what *is* the truth?" Margaret said, her tone almost shrill.

A mulish expression came across the other woman's face. "You of all people should know what the truth is! Don't play games with me."

Margaret stood up. She just couldn't do it. She couldn't deal with the ridiculous and foolish woman in front of her. And her stomach was feeling so odd. "I can't, please excuse me." She rushed to the facilities without casting a backwards glance.

Once in the toilet stall, she couldn't control the rush of bile. Her body had taken over and she couldn't stop it. After she retched it all out, tears streamed down her face from the horrible effort to get out whatever it was that needed getting out.

She splashed water over her face at the sink, grateful no one else was there to witness such an embarrassing act. She looked at her reflection and became worried. Her coloring was ashen and she felt almost feeble. Had she picked up an infection? She groaned at the thought of having to go to a doctor on top of everything else.

Margaret took in a deep gulp of air and stood tall, steadying herself. It would have to be mind over matter at this point. She needed to go back to the trial and testify for Bill.

The door to the washroom opened and Jocelyn stood there with a confused look. "Margaret, are you okay? You rushed off like that..."

"Yes. I think...I think I ate something bad yesterday. It's fine now, though. I'll be fine." Since she had not eaten much of anything yesterday, it was a lie but she needed to cover it up. It would never do to appear weak to Jocelyn or anyone else for that matter.

"Well, we need to get back to court," Jocelyn said, eyeing Margaret with some suspicion.

"Oh, okay. Well, let's go back now then."

The two women collected their belongings at the table and left the coffee shop, went back into the alley and up the block to the courthouse. As they walked, Jocelyn gave Margaret a side-eye stare but said nothing.

"What?" Margaret asked.

"Uh, well, it's none of my business at all."

"What do you mean?"

"Have you had your monthly on time?"

Margaret halted. "What are you implying, Jocelyn?"

"I'm not implying anything, Margaret. It appears though that you have a...sickness of some sort."

As they began to walk again, Margaret did not respond. Instead, her mind started going in circles. She was a woman almost forty years in age. Surely she was way past the time of having to worry about being pregnant. Way past... She banished the very thought. Jocelyn was just a silly person with inane ideas. It was not possible for Margaret to be with child. Just not possible.

CHAPTER TWENTY-FOUR

Margaret made her way to the same seat in the rear of the courtroom and settled in for the afternoon's proceedings. At the first pronouncement, her body gave a reflexive jolt.

"The defense would like to call Mrs. Margaret O'Keefe to the stand, your honor."

She felt the visceral moment of walking up to be sworn in surrounded by rustlings in the room. Once she turned around, the crowd was a sea of faces. She purposefully avoided looking at one face in particular in that sea.

Bill's defense lawyer kept it simple and merely allowed her to testify to Bill's stellar character. After his brief line of questioning, it was Ned Armstrong's turn to cross-examine if he chose to. Which he did. Margaret inwardly steeled herself as the weasel-like man approached the stand with a calculated expression.

"Mrs. O'Keefe, tell us again of this financial arrangement with Mr. Miller." His voice had a pointed inflection when he said "financial arrangement."

Margaret explained that, due to the economic turn, her horse farm had fallen in jeopardy and needed investors. Since

Bill had worked at the farm years earlier, he had an understanding of the farm and, of course, he knew horses.

Armstrong took a big audible sniff in through flared nostrils. "So, it would be fair to say that you have a vested interest in the outcome of Mr. Miller's trial. Because if he is indicted as a murderer, there will be no more money provided to your farm, is that right?"

"Objection!"

"Overruled."

Margaret could not believe how blunt the man was. She twisted his words on him. "My vested interest is in seeing a man I know and admire be treated fairly by this court."

"Is that really the case, Mrs. O'Keefe?"

"Yes. Yes, it is."

He turned on his heel while saying, "No further questions."

After Margaret left the stand, she sat with an anger rinsing through her. The weasel had painted her in a questionable light, suggesting she was only testifying for her own self interests. It was part of the reason, of course. But was that such a wrong thing?

As the trial continued, she was only able to pay attention to bits and pieces, barely concentrating on the testimonies that followed hers. The bigger part of her mind was still seething, still working through the accusation of the prosecutor against her character.

Her attention was diverted on hearing a familiar name called aloud: Mr. Robert Brady. It was Robert's turn. Margaret steadied herself as she watched the court official swear him in.

They had not talked since he had left her bed that night. Her heart was in torment at the very sight of him.

Once in the stand, Robert's eyes flitted around the room until landing on her. Then he turned his attention to the question being asked of him.

"Please tell the court your relationship to the accused and what you know of his character."

Robert relayed how long he had known Bill and then gave a resounding endorsement of his high moral fiber and conduct, not only as an officer of the court, but also as a gentleman. It was not unlike the testimonies of the others who had already been up on the stand, including Margaret's. The defense was making it perfectly clear to one and all that Bill Miller was an esteemed character, in and out of the courthouse.

But the tables turned once again as Ned Armstrong sprung up for his turn with Robert. "So, Mr. Brady, you have stated that you only know Mr. Miller in a professional capacity for..." he went over to his papers and moved them around before continuing, "...for about eight years or so, I think you said. Is that right?"

"Yes, that's right." Robert's tone was guarded.

"The thing is, though," the weasel paused and gazed around the room, "It appears you have a financial arrangement with Mr. Miller as well. Isn't that correct?"

Margaret felt stunned. What was Armstrong talking about? Robert did not respond and the weasel prompted him to do so. "Mr. Brady?"

Robert cleared his throat and then said, "Well, we have a very loose arrangement. I provide him with services on a retainer as needed. That is true."

"And what do those services entail exactly, Mr. Brady?"

Margaret was all ears along with the rest of the room.

"If Bill—Mr. Miller—has a case requiring some deeper research, I have assisted on an ad hoc basis. Here and there."

"Huh. Here and there, you say. Well, I think it is fair to say that you are beholden to Mr. Miller."

"Objection!"

The judge turned to the weasel. "Counselor, keep your opinions to yourself and reframe your questioning."

"Alright, your honor," Armstrong paused and looked out into the room and then said, "Does this arrangement with Bill Miller provide you with a source of income that you rely on, Mr. Brady?"

"No, it does not." Robert's voice was steely cold.

"Mr. Brady, surely that extra money comes in handy. Maybe even something you depend on. As a younger man in the profession—"

Robert cut in sharply and interrupted the prosecutor. "No, I do not depend on Mr. Miller financially."

"Well, Mr. Brady, some might beg to differ."

"Objection!" Joe Patterson stood up. "Pure conjecture, your honor."

The judge looked at Armstrong over half-rimmed spectacles. "Strike it from the record. Reframe your questioning, Mr. Armstrong."

Armstrong looked away from the stand and out into the room with a perplexed expression. The showmanship was obvious acting as though he was trying to make sense of Robert's explanation. He turned back to face Robert. "Let's put a dollar figure on it, Mr. Brady."

Robert said nothing. Armstrong repeated. "Mr. Brady?"

"What is your question?" Robert seemed to be hedging the answer for some reason and Margaret felt her nerves go all aflutter.

Armstrong gave an exaggerated sigh and then said, "Please give the court an approximate dollar figure of how much income you derive on a yearly basis from your retainer relationship with Mr. Miller."

During the pregnant pause it took for Robert to answer the relatively simple query, all was pin-drop quiet in the room.

"Four thousand dollars a year. Approximately."

Someone in the room let out a low whistle and murmuring could be heard all around the room.

"Well, well, well. Not an inconsiderable amount of money at all. Not at all..." Armstrong paused to let that sink in and then finally ended with, "No further questions, your honor."

Robert took his leave of the stand, throwing another look over to Margaret, an indecipherable one, amongst the loud whispering surrounding him. She looked down at the tiled floor beneath. Doubt had been cast on how he could possibly be considered an impartial witness to Bill's character. In fact, all the character witnesses including Margaret might now be viewed with a jaded eye. Greater than that, though, was the doubt cast in her own mind about Robert.

She was baffled that he had never mentioned this so-called "arrangement" with Bill to her. Why would he not have? It seemed a lie by omission especially given her own financial dealings with Bill as a silent partner. Now even...she had the sudden thought. Was Robert's "ad hoc" business with Bill the primary reason for her own partnership with Bill? Some kind of favor that Robert had set up behind the scenes? That made it all much more complicated...and it would take her a while to think it all through.

For the time being, she tried to set it all aside and concentrate on the rest of the day's proceedings. But, as the afternoon wore on, Margaret found herself drooping, her eyes partially closing. Along with her stomach distress, she had been so overwhelmingly tired of late. She shook herself when the bailiff told all to rise. The judge announced that the court would be recessed for the entire weekend and would resume first thing Monday morning.

The crowd began to shuffle out. When Margaret looked towards the front, she could see Bill being escorted out, Jocelyn right next to him, towards the back of the courtroom presumably to avoid the reporters. His brother-lawyers were again clustered talking amongst themselves, Robert included in their fold. Would he at least talk to her now?

Margaret stood, undecided about what to do. When it felt too awkward to stand there any longer and wait for Robert, she turned and left the courtroom. As she made her way back out to the city street, she longed for a familiar tap on her shoulder. But it didn't happen and she stopped looking back.

She felt the sting as she walked to the cab stand. The taxi ride to the train station was just a blur as she tried to process what had happened between her and Robert. How it had all suddenly gone so wrong?

On the train, Margaret slumped into a seat, feeling hollow. As the train picked up speed, she stared out the window barely taking in the city neighborhoods that whirled by. Instead, she became mired in how much she had deluded herself. How naïve she had been to think their relationship so harmonious and their personalities meshing so well with never any conflict or strife between them. That was foolish.

On her end, she just assumed her feelings and thoughts about the future didn't need to be spoken aloud. On his end... well, he had been covering up what needed to be said. It was a two-way street, though. She was as much at fault as Robert.

The scenery outside shifted as the city tapered off and it finally just became country. When the train eventually pulled into the Rockville train station, Margaret took in the familiar sight with its distinctive slate shingled roofline and red brick walls. She wiped salty tears off her cheeks. She was almost home.

Later, Margaret sat in her study behind her desk with the now familiar but still awful feeling roiling around in her stomach. Cassie walked in holding a plate. "Now, Mizz Margaret, you have to eat something. You just have to. I got this ready for you. Be real easy on your stomach."

Even though Margaret had not talked about it, Cassie knew something was wrong. She placed the steaming plate in front of Margaret. Margaret stared down at the toast points that were positioned around a cup that held a soft-boiled egg. Despite the ongoing nausea, she suddenly also felt an intense hunger in the mix.

Her stomach and intestines had become a foreign country. Thus far, she had navigated it by attempting to sidestep and stem off the worst, trying to establish an uneasy peace with her inner workings. Maybe the light meal would allow her to rally and keep in good stead for the night ahead. It was time to get back to all that paperwork that required her attention. She dug in with a silent prayer it wouldn't come back up.

After taking a couple of bites, though, Margaret knew right away that was not the case. She made a lunge for the washroom just in the nick of time. After she had finished eliminating those few bites, she grasped the sink with both hands and looked into the mirror. As she stared at herself, she also asked herself the question: could Jocelyn be right?

Cassie was lurking in the hall when she emerged. "Mizz Margaret, you need to go see Doc Pender first thing tomorrow. I'll get Albert to take you down there."

Margaret hesitated and almost demurred but she knew Cassie was right. "Alright, Cassie. I guess I should."

"That's right. Now you sit yourself down. Just rest easy... until tomorrow."

CHAPTER TWENTY-FIVE

The doctor's office was situated in an old frame house painted white, not too far from the historical society. Margaret couldn't even recall the last time she had needed to see Doc Pender. It had been a long time though. She did know that.

After Margaret was escorted into one of the three exam rooms and given a gown to change into, she sat on the exam table and waited impatiently. She was reminded all over again about why she did her best to stay away from the doctor's office. The eternal wait.

After a good twenty minutes, she heard rustling outside the door followed by Doc Pender's large form striding in. His florid face was heavily jowled and he took her in through smudged eyeglasses. "Well, Mrs. O'Keefe! To what do I owe the honor of you in our office today?"

Margaret gave a perfunctory smile and then explained her predicament. "Hello, doctor. So, I've been struggling with my digestion of late. I just can't seem to tolerate eating much and um, I've even been vomiting here and there."

"Hhmmm." The doctor had already begun examining her while she spoke. His eyes were magnified behind his glasses as he shone a light into her nostrils. He then began to palpate either side of her neck. "How long did you say this has been going on?"

"Uh, I think several weeks now. On and off maybe."

"Lay down on your back for me." He tapped around her abdomen next as he made conversation. "And how is Mr. O'Keefe faring these days? Such a delightful fellow."

"He's fine." Margaret saw absolutely no reason at all to go into the current state of affairs between her and "Mr. O'Keefe".

After he seemed satisfied by the physical examination, he prompted her to sit up by lifting one of her elbows. He propped his substantial girth against the exam table. "Everything seems perfectly fine. But I will go ahead and do this new-fangled test we have to see if perhaps you may be in the family way. Always have to consider that when we have an upset stomach."

"But doctor, I'm nearly forty—"

"Yes, yes. That's true. But that doesn't necessarily mean that if you and Mr. O'Keefe um...well, it doesn't necessarily mean you cannot become in the family way as it were."

"Well, okay. What does this test involve?"

"Very simple. The nurse will give you a cup to provide us with some urine before you leave."

"And then?"

"Well, in about a week, we'll see what happens to the rabbit."

"The rabbit?"

"Don't worry your pretty head about it, Mrs. O'Keefe. It's following the science."

Margaret held back biting out a sarcastic comment on how her pretty head could handle the science and a lot more than that. Instead, she just gave another perfunctory smile and nodded.

"Come back in a week for the results. But probably it's just a spot of indigestion that will resolve itself by then. Oh, and give my regards to Mr. O'Keefe. Always enjoy chatting with him." He gave her a solicitous pat on the shoulder and left the room.

Once Margaret had provided her "sample" in the office's washroom, she got dressed and waited outside for Albert to pick her up. She felt heartened that the doctor was on the right track, that it was just simple, everyday digestion she was suffering from. That had to be it.

As she sat on a bench in front of the doctor's office, she could see a walker with a dog by her side approaching. As the twosome picked their way along the brick-lined sidewalk, she recognized them as Lucinda and her lemon-colored beagle, Chauncey.

Margaret stood up as they were a few feet from her. "Hello Lucinda!" She looked down and added, "And Chauncey." She stooped to give him a pat.

"It's Margaret, right?" Lucinda asked.

"That's right."

Lucinda glanced at the doctor's building. "Everything okay?"

Margaret waved a hand, dismissing anything serious. "Yes, yes. Just a...just a checkup."

"Well, why don't you walk with us for a bit? Chauncey and I like to get our daily constitutional in."

Margaret looked at her watch. It would still be another half hour before Albert would pick her up and it was a nice, sunny day. "Alright. That's a good idea."

Now a threesome, they walked companionably through the oldest section of Rockville. Lucinda began a running commentary pointing at the various residences and describing their history and their inhabitants, former and present. When they eventually reached a small area fenced off in wrought iron,

Lucinda gestured towards it. "Why don't we have a quick sit here? Get a breather?"

As they entered through a gate, Margaret could see it was a little pocket park tucked into an empty lot of green space. They headed over to the one bench and Chauncey began to run from bush to bush with enthusiasm, sniffing at the corners of the little space.

Some fresh blooms could be spotted, daffodil stragglers and deep blue hyacinths peeking about in the corners. It was a heartening sight, spring with its chance to start all over again. Tucked into one side of the fence line, Margaret noticed a very ancient-looking gravestone. "Oh...so this is a cemetery? For a party of one?"

"Indeed."

Margaret took a closer look. The stone was thin in width, like slate, but the color was a tan hue. The etching was almost cursive, a throwback style of writing. Margaret read:

"'Here lies ANNA, born on the 3rd of June 1725 and departing from this life in the year of 1745. May God grant to her eternal rest.' Oh...how tragic." Margaret turned back to Lucinda and the bench. "She was just twenty."

Lucinda nodded. "Yes, I came upon it years ago and it was almost completely covered up. I made it my mission to find out more about Anna and why she was buried here by herself."

"Really? What did you find?"

"Well, after many years—of no small effort, mind you—I discovered she was the consort of a wealthy landowner in the area, Randall Earle."

Margaret frowned. "Consort? Does that mean..."

"No, no. It sounds like it means that, a soiled dove or a lady of the night. But it was actually the term they used for wives back in those days. It's a bit degrading, isn't it?"

"Yes, it really is."

"Don't get me started on the term 'relict'." Margaret raised her eyebrows and Lucinda elaborated. "They referred to widows as 'relicts'."

"I guess our gender has seldom gotten the credit we deserve."

"Yes, but, like I said, I made it a personal mission to give Anna her due. I researched for many years with no luck. But eventually an explanation rose to the surface. Genealogy is like that—a lot of the time."

"So, what did you find out?"

"It was a mystery wrapped up in another mystery. I wanted to find out why she died so young and also why she was by herself, not in any family plot or a community graveyard."

Margaret stayed silent, feeling tingles that something untoward was going to be revealed in this story.

"Her husband found her at the bank of the Potomac River where his plantation was situated. She had been attacked by a rabid fox and wandered away from the house. And it was at the river that she perished. But the details were all based on his say-so."

"You don't believe it?"

Lucinda shrugged. "That's one part of it; the other is why did he bury her here in town away from his farm or her family or his family? It's an oddity all around."

They sat in thought for a bit. Then Margaret asked, "Who takes care of the plot now?"

"I do. That's why Chauncey knows it so well."

"That's really nice of you."

"It's a debt, in a way."

"Really? It seems like you do so much already for the historical society."

"It's a debt for someone else. My daughter."

Margaret again stayed silent knowing that something even

bigger was going to be shared. She snuck a look at Lucinda's face, well creased through the years having experienced so many things. But, overall, carrying it well.

"She died, you see. Many, many moons ago."

Margaret murmured her condolences.

"When I discovered this gravestone, I just knew what I had to do."

Margaret was confused how this could possibly be connected to Lucinda's daughter. She looked over at the woman wondering if something was off balance with her.

"It's a bit strange but my daughter's death was...suspicious. She was married to a real ne'er do well. And well, she too died young. At the age of just twenty."

"Oh, I'm so sorry, Lucinda. So difficult."

Lucinda nodded absentmindedly at Margaret's comment. "But the main thing is that her name was also Anna. So, you see, it felt like I just had to do all this. It does help...a bit. Especially since her grave is a thousand miles away so I can't tend to it. And this does make for a nice and private spot, doesn't it?"

Margaret's woes and complaints seemed to shrivel and pale immediately in contrast to what the woman next to her had suffered all these years, the tremendous loss she had experienced. Margaret tried to say as much. "It makes my worries and troubles seem silly, Lucinda."

"Not at all, my dear. Life does go on no matter who is left behind. That's the real truth, Margaret. The truth we all eventually learn one way or the other. And speaking of that, did you figure out that problem that you had with your husband?"

Margaret looked straight ahead before answering. Had she figured out her problem with Keith? "Yes...and no...and maybe."

Lucinda gave a laugh that came out in a delightful tinkle. "Tell me the 'yes' part first."

Margaret explained how Keith had shown his hand with his

ridiculous law suit but that had led to her locating documents of proof in the courthouse. She finished by saying, "The 'no' part is whether that will be enough or if they will require a receipt of some sort for that one-dollar transaction. I guess that's also the 'maybe' part as well."

Lucinda nodded thoughtfully. "I think that should be enough but let's face it. So much of this kind of thing comes down to who is making the decision, doesn't it? In a way, it tends not to be about the truth of the matter but rather who is the most persuasive and convincing."

"Are you saying I need to figure out how to be the one that is most persuasive...and convincing?"

"Yes. I think that would be a good idea on your part."

The two women went quiet and watched Chauncey who continued to find interesting areas to examine in the small space. Margaret's dog, Oliver, was in the habit of doing the same and she often thought there was a lesson in that somehow. It also occurred to her that the same advice about the court case with Keith applied to Bill Miller and his trial too. The exercise to find the truth in the gray area when no black and white could be found.

CHAPTER TWENTY-SIX

Early Monday morning, Margaret found her way back into the city. It was a glorious spring day filled with the promises that the season always held. A glaring contrast to what her dear friend and mentor would be facing down again. The newspaper coverage predicted that Bill would be called up next on the stand.

Throughout the weekend, Margaret had debated returning for the second day of the trial. Her part—testimony on Bill's character—was done; yet, she felt the need to be there, to bear witness.

Overwhelmed, she made her way through the crowd and commotion outside the courthouse. It was more heightened than on the previous day, and even carnivalesque. The trial had become sensational in a way that intensified it, making it even more lurid and horrific.

Once all were seated and the clock struck nine, the defense called Bill Miller to the stand. Margaret winced at the very sight of him. The trial had already taken a heavier toll, evident on his visage with deep, dark under-eye shadows along with his slumped shoulders. After he was sworn in, he began rubbing his tie this way and that, a long-standing habit that Margaret had noted at other times. Some sort of comfort measure, she assumed.

The first question was put forth and Bill held it together through the follow-on "softballs" from his defense team. But Margaret readied herself because she knew the weasel would have no mercy during his cross-examination.

"No further questions for the witness, your honor." Bill's lawyer, Joe Patterson, made a sweeping vague gesture over to the prosecutor's side of the room.

The judge looked over at Mr. Armstrong above his half glasses. "Counselor?"

"Yes indeed, your honor." Armstrong sprang up and marched to the front, moving too close to Bill. An intimidation tactic that Bill himself had probably used countless times on witnesses. Bill leaned back but kept his expression in check.

"So, tell us, Mr. Miller. How was it that you found yourself on the corner of 11th and G Streets on February twenty-first of this year?"

"I was keeping track of my wife. I knew that she planned on shopping that day and that store is her favorite. I took a walk down from my office at lunch time to...uh...see her."

"Why exactly were you, as you put it, keeping track of her?"

"I...I needed to keep her away from that man." Bill's jaw thrust forward in a lock as if emphasizing that fact.

"And, by 'that man', do you mean the highly regarded Dr. Michaels? The psychiatrist known throughout the world for his achievements?"

"Objection!" Patterson barked out.

"Sustained. Stop over-reaching, counselor."

Armstrong nodded his acknowledgment and then went back to it. "So...when you did see Mrs. Miller at the front of the store, what happened?"

Bill let out a sigh. Margaret thought about how hard it must be to repeat the same story over and over again. In a low voice, he began to retell the event. He paused to mop his brow at one point but the prosecutor pushed him. "And then?"

"Well, I heard him say 'I'm going to shoot the bastard's gray head off' and I pulled my gun out and shot him first."

"Now, how was it you happened to have a gun on you, Mr. Miller?"

"I have a permit to carry and, lately, I was worried about the threats from Dr. Michaels."

"Threats?"

"Yes, Jocelyn had warned me. Told me the man carried a gun on him around town. I wasn't taking any chances."

"Alright. Back to the shooting. It wasn't just one shot was it, Mr. Miller? It was two, one to the heart and one to the brain. Two very well-placed shots. As though a perfectly planned execution."

Bill cried, "I was out of my head. The man wouldn't let go of my wife. I had to stop it!"

"Had to, Mr. Miller? Or wanted to?"

Bill was coming apart at the seams. Tears now streamed down the deep lines on his cheeks and he did not wipe them off.

"Objection!" Again, Patterson tried to stop the vein of questioning that was so demoralizing to his client.

"Redirect, counselor," the judge said.

"Alright then." Armstrong turned and walked away from the stand. Then he swiveled back to Bill. "Did you have one gun —or two?"

Confusion came over Bill's face. "One. The one I shot him with."

"Hmm. Mr. Miller, did you plant a second gun in the manila envelope on Dr. Michaels' seat?"

"I did not."

"Are you sure?"

"Yes. I had one gun."

"I would like to present this gun for state's evidence, your honor." Armstrong announced, holding up a nickel-plated revolver for the court to see. "Now, Mr. Miller, isn't this the second gun you brought with you and planted it at the scene?"

Bill pulled out a plaid handkerchief and began sobbing loudly into it.

"Your honor, please," Armstrong gestured to Bill with a look of disgust.

"Mr. Miller, please answer the prosecutor's question."

Bill sniffed and pulled himself together. His voice came out thick and raspy. "I did not have a second gun and I did not plant that one on the car seat."

Margaret was dismayed at how overwrought Bill was on the stand, a puddle of emotion. Her mind went back to the conversation with Robert about the gun as she tried to remember the specifics. Robert had seen the gun in the envelope as best she could recall. Was this the same gun that Bill saw on the seat?

She had not been able to talk to Robert about any of it. All she had was a glimpse of the back of his head many rows in front of hers and she felt a swift surge of anger. It was ridiculous they had not spoken since that night at Needham Forest in her bedroom. She was going to confront him whether he liked it or not when the court recessed.

Once the weasel's relentless questioning finally ended, Bill was assisted down from the stand on wobbly legs, emotionally spent. The next witnesses called up were the doctor's surviving immediate family members, a son and a daughter. The daughter took the stand first and was all angry eyes blazing in Jocelyn's direction.

"Can you please tell the court how many guns your father owned?"

"One."

"And do you know the whereabouts of that gun at the present time?"

"It is in the same place it has always been. In his nightstand drawer at his house."

"Did you worry about your father, Miss Michaels?"

"I told him to stay away from that woman. That it would bring no good to him." Her voice cracked as she finished and said, "And I was right."

Michaels' son was young, still a teenager. He repeated the same testimony that his sister had. Their father owned one gun. After he was slain, it was found in his nightstand drawer where it was always kept. It did wrench Margaret's heart to see him on the stand and to know that he had lost his only living parent in this way. It would take him a lifetime to recover from it, if he even could.

As the day continued with other witnesses and more conflicting testimonies, Margaret tried to digest the two sides of this story argued in court, boiling down to a he said/he said situation. Bill had a throng of fans every day outside of the courthouse, well-wishers who felt he had been grievously wronged by Dr. Michaels. That didn't make murder right, though.

She reflected on what Lucinda had said about the truth and how it came down to which side had more weight, not more truth. She could see it unfolding in that manner in this very courtroom. What aspects would hold the most weight for the jury? Would their decision come down to a popularity contest between the two men, Bill Miller or the deceased Donald Michaels?

After the court recessed, Margaret stood tall and marched

up against the traffic of others exiting the room. As was the usual pattern, the cluster of the brother-lawyers stood around at the front chatting amongst each other.

"Robert, could I speak to you please?" The small group of lawyers all went quiet as they turned and stared at Margaret and her interruption.

Robert murmured something to the group and walked over to her. His eyes avoided hers as he asked, "Margaret, how are you?"

She could hear her voice answer in a shrewish tone but she couldn't control it. "We need to have a conversation."

"I don't think that's wise, Margaret."

Her eyes shot daggers at him. How dare he? Did he really want her to announce to the courtroom and his lawyer pals how he had flung her aside like a used dishrag?

After a brief and silent beat, Robert grabbed one of Margaret's elbows, steering her out of the courtroom's back exit. He brought them into a back corridor of the building where there was no one else around. It was just the two of them.

He leaned against the deep marble sill of the old window. His body was backlit from the sun filling the opening. As he looked directly at her, she could see pain radiating from his eyes. Then he spoke. "What do you want me to say, Margaret?"

"I want to talk about this. I mean, why have you cut me out of your life? There has to be a way we can work through this."

He rubbed a hand over his jawline as if it hurt him to do so. "I...I don't know. This trial is— I need to get through this and then...maybe we can."

"Can what?"

"We can maybe meet after the trial and I can explain better, I guess. I blame myself for letting this get ahead of us. For not facing that— I just don't think..."

Margaret was baffled that the usual precision of Robert's

words was failing him. It seemed all his lawyerly skills had flown out the window behind him. "Robert, please. You're not really making sense."

"Okay. You're right." He paused, collecting himself and then he took her hands in his. "Margaret, it's not going to work between us. It's over."

She wrenched her hands out of his. She could barely catch her breath after his statement, much less take in the fact that his affections towards her had changed so dramatically. It seemed to come out of nowhere so suddenly. Maybe she hadn't been paying attention, even though she thought she had been. Now, stunned silent, no words of response came to her.

Finally, Margaret turned on heel and headed down the back corridor, barely able to see in front of her through the blur of tears. As she found her way out of the building, Robert didn't stop her or come after her. She knew now there would be no more conversation, no matter what happened with the trial, during or after. Robert had made his mind up about their relationship without her having any say in the matter really. It was over, as he had said.

CHAPTER TWENTY-SEVEN

The third day of the trial with Jocelyn testifying had the feel of an unavoidable collision, a collision that Margaret couldn't hold back from viewing. Questions swirled around her mind about Robert; not only about the abrupt end to their relationship but also the revelation that Bill kept him on retainer. If she were a different kind of woman, she would have stayed away because of the break-up. But that wasn't enough to keep her away from the trial. If Robert thought that, he had deeply underestimated her.

Margaret watched as Jocelyn was sworn in and got situated behind the witness stand. Her wren-like persona from the sanatorium was back in play with matronly-colored attire covering her bosom. There was minimal hint of the bold and brassy usually on display, ironic given all now knew how Jocelyn's bosom and the pink brassiere featured in all this business, as unsavory as that was. Even though her physical attributes were now downplayed, it was difficult for most eyes in the room not to imagine otherwise.

Margaret could only assume that Bill's defense team had prepped her to the nth degree in regards to what was fitting for a woman in her situation. Although they must be on tenterhooks given that Jocelyn could be a wild card, the goal was for her to be an asset rather than a hindrance for Bill's defense team.

As Jocelyn faced the courtroom and presented herself in a subdued, demure manner, her eyes were wide and showed how fearful she was of the process. Margaret wondered who she was more afraid for: Bill or herself?

Joe Patterson began his directive right away. "Mrs. Miller, tell the court what happened on the twenty-first of February of this year in front of Woodward & Lothrop, in your own words."

As Jocelyn began to speak, her lower lip quivered and her voice came out in a halting patter. "Well...I was returning an item at the department store that day and had arranged with Donald—Dr. Michaels—to provide me with a ride afterwards." She gulped.

The attorney said, "Go on, please."

"When I entered his car, Bill—my husband—came out of nowhere and said, 'Jocelyn, get out of that car'. Donald pulled my arm to stay in the car and Bill pulled my other arm and leg to get out. I felt like they were tearing me in two!"

Jocelyn's metaphor carried some rich irony in Margaret's mind. Jocelyn was the one who had instigated the tug-of-war game between the two men. It was her doing, not theirs.

"And then?" Patterson prompted again.

Jocelyn let out an audible sigh. "Then, Donald yelled out, 'I'll shoot the gray-haired bastard.' Oops—can I use that word in court?" She looked over at the judge who immediately gave a dismissive wave of his hand. Jocelyn continued. "Anyway, then he reached for his gun."

"Please clarify that, Mrs. Miller. Who reached for his gun?"

"Donald. Dr. Michaels."

"Where was that gun?"

"On the seat in a manila envelope just like always. I did

warn Bill about it. About the fact that Donald always carried a gun around town that is."

"So, after he reached for the gun, what happened?"

"Bill leaned in front of me and—" Collecting herself, she continued. "And then he shot Donald. I moved out of the car to the sidewalk and a crowd had formed. Bill told all of them that Donald was going to shoot him so he had to shoot him first. And he was right. I believe that too." She pulled out a white lace hankie and began to sob into it.

"No further questions, your honor."

"Prosecutor, your witness," the judge said.

This was the cross-examination all were waiting to hear. Mr. Armstrong leapt up with a charged air towards the stand. Jocelyn visibly shrank back and Margaret could see panic illuminated in her eyes. He began by clearing his throat in an attention-getting manner.

"Now, Mrs. Miller, you say that you warned the defendant, your husband." He pivoted and pointed to Bill. "That is your husband right there. Is it not?" When Jocelyn nodded, he continued, "...about your lover's habit of toting a gun around town."

"Objection! Prejudicial intent."

The judge paused in thought then spoke. "I'll let it stand. The relationship has already been established as such."

Armstrong nodded and then continued. "I'll repeat the question. Mrs. Miller, did you warn your husband about Dr. Michaels' tendency to carry a gun around town?"

Jocelyn visibly swallowed and then nodded.

"Answer with a yes or no please, Mrs. Miller."

Her voice came out in a squeak. "Yes. Yes, I did."

"Wasn't that like setting bait in the trap then?"

Patterson jumped to his feet as he bellowed, "Objection! Leading the witness."

The judge turned in the direction of Armstrong. "This better be going someplace, counselor."

"It is, judge. Bear with me. Mrs. Miller, was it setting bait?"

Jocelyn sniffed. "I have no idea what you mean."

"Did you tell Mr. Miller where you were going that afternoon? To Woodward & Lothrop Department Store to exchange a pink brassiere that was a size too small?"

Jocelyn looked down to the side and mumbled, "I don't think so."

"Then how do you think Mr. Miller knew where you were exactly? At that precise location and time?"

Jocelyn went wide eyed and gave a shrug.

"Please answer the question, Mrs. Miller."

She stuttered out a response. "I really...really couldn't say."

"Huh. You couldn't say for instance that you told your husband the exact whereabouts of you and Dr. Michaels so that he could maybe take a shot at him?"

Jocelyn yelled out, "No, of course not! I would never!"

Patterson rose up declaring, "Objection! Leading the witness, your honor!"

From Margaret's seat in the courtroom, she could see Bill's face at an angle and it was a study in pain and misery.

The judge weighed in, saying, "What's your point, counselor?"

"Well, it just seems a little too well planned for this to be a coincidence, does it not?"

"Move on, Mr. Armstrong."

"Alright. Let's get back to this gun you say you always saw in the envelope. We've heard contrasting testimony from two people who knew Dr. Michaels very well—his children. They say he had one gun and it was always where he kept it. In his bedside table. Still was after his murder. So how is it that you say you always saw it on him?"

"I did. What more can I say about it? It was always in an envelope on the seat."

"But did you actually see a gun in the envelope? Or just the envelope?"

Jocelyn looked like a deer caught in a lamp light and went silent. Finally, she said, "I saw the gun."

But there was a subtle shift in the courtroom vibrations, doubt thrown and splattered into the room.

"Are you sure about that answer, Mrs. Miller?"

She nodded and then added, "Yes. I'm sure."

"Well, can you recount about how many times you were in the car or with him when you saw it?"

"How many times... Well, I guess it was about...um...maybe fifty? Maybe a little more."

There was a buzz immediately in the room, a buzz of astonishment at how many times Jocelyn had been with her lover. Again, the screw of public opinion turned.

"Huh...fifty. Or more. How about that?" He let out a big sigh. "And you said earlier you were about done with him though? That you wanted the relationship to be over."

"Yes. Yes, I did want to end things but he wasn't letting me."

"And you made that clear to your husband?"

"Yes, we cried about it together. I was...I was saucy and ugly to him and felt just awful about it." All could see how Jocelyn snuck a look over to Bill. He was bent forward with his forehead supported by both hands, the proceedings getting to be all too much once again.

"Did you come up with any possible solutions to this problem?"

"No. We just... Um, we just were trying to carry on."

"So, 'carry on' meant meeting Dr. Michaels again in front of Woodward & Lothrop that day? When you could have just as easily taken a taxi to return your...brassiere?" He threw a sneer at her.

She lurched back. There was no avoiding a fall right into yet another snare set by the wily prosecutor.

Jocelyn began to sob into the hankie again. Armstrong's derision was plain to all with no attempt to rein it in as he pressed her. "Answer the question, Mrs. Miller!"

She stuttered out the answer. "I met him that day...but I did intend to break it off. I did..."

He looked away and out into the room with pure disgust on his face and announced, "No further questions."

The undercurrent of buzz continued as Jocelyn stepped away from the stand. Margaret sat back not knowing which way the tide had just turned for Bill. There were too many holes in Bill's side of the story, too many avenues left open as to what had really happened. The prosecutor had spun a clever maelstrom of questions. Was the shooting a premeditated event? Did Jocelyn and Bill possibly even coordinate it?

Yet, Armstrong hadn't proven any of it, rather he had revealed suspicions not facts as far as Margaret could discern. That seemingly would be reasonable doubt. Bill couldn't be prosecuted for being probably guilty, could he? It all left Margaret with one overarching question, however: had Jocelyn and Bill orchestrated this thing together?

Margaret snuck off before the recess and meandered through the city's financial district, well away from the court doings and its players. The walk did her some good and her digestion seemed to be less in a rumble. She readied herself for what the afternoon would bring in the courtroom and walked back into the building with others doing the same.

Once all were situated, Joe Patterson stood up and announced a surprise witness. There was the usual clamor at the announcement of such a twist. The judge summoned both sides and there was a brief discussion at the bench.

Margaret could see the judge nodding finally, indicating a green light for whomever this witness was. The defense attorney announced, "Defense recalls Mr. Robert Brady, Esquire, to the stand, your honor."

Margaret leaned back taking this new wrinkle in. Robert had already been up on the stand the very first day offering testimony about Bill's character and the like. However, he had mentioned a possible scenario arising with him as a surprise witness. But she felt a nerve prickle that something was not quite right.

She stared at Robert's tall form as he walked forward to the stand. A form she had been so intimate with and was now cut off from completely. She thought he had been hers. She had been wrong.

When he turned to be sworn in, the sight of him pained her. She could barely take in his handsome face and the way his hair was brushed off to one side. She had asked him once how he had perfected his coif. He swore by a product from England called Brylcreem and claimed its gimmick on the package "a little dab'll do ya" was his secret. They had laughed about it.

Now, she took note of a deeply troubled expression on his face, an expression he could not mask. She couldn't flatter herself that it was about her and their relationship. That meant it was about what he was testifying to.

The first question from the defense was lobbed his way. "Mr. Brady, please tell us about your acquaintanceship with the deceased, Dr. Michaels."

Robert looked out into the room. "I knew Dr. Michaels purely in a professional capacity. We were involved in the same cases together on several occasions. In other words, his testimonies were a part of my cases or other cases from my firm at times."

"So that said, was there ever an occasion where the two of you spoke outside the courtroom?

"Yes."

"Tell us about that."

"Well, sometimes we would need to go through points of the cases we were involved in. We would talk outside of the courtroom or in my office and also one time in his car."

"And did you see a gun at any of those times?"

"Yes." The room took on a low hum with this revelation.

"Where exactly?"

"On three occasions. He carried it around in a manila envelope and I saw it once in my office, once in his car and, the last time, in his office."

"So, in your estimation it is reasonable to assume that there was a gun in Dr. Michaels' car on the day in question?"

"Objection, your honor!"

"Overruled. Answer the question, Mr. Brady."

"I would say yes. It seemed he made a habit of carrying it on him at all times."

"Now, is this about what the gun looked like?" He held up the gun that was in the evidence as Dr. Michaels' piece.

"As best as I can tell, yes. But I'm not a gun aficionado."

"Thank you, Mr. Brady. No further questions."

"Prosecutor? Cross-examination?"

"Indeed, your honor." The weasel man rose up at the opportunity. "Now, Mr. Brady. When you say you saw the gun three times, let's be clear for the court here. Did you only see the envelope?"

There was a pause on Robert's part. Margaret's brain scrambled back to when he had told her about the gun. Her memory was that he had just seen the envelope, not the actual gun. Also, he had only seen it once. Unless he had purposely left out the other two times in talking to her. But what reason would he have to do that? Again, her nerves prickled.

"I saw the envelope and the gun was in the envelope." Robert had chosen his words carefully but it left it open.

"Mr. Brady, did you see the actual gun or did you assume it was in the envelope?"

"I saw the gun."

A whirr of murmurs tore through the room. This was a huge boon for Bill's side. In fact, Margaret didn't need to be a legal genius to understand that this was the golden seal on the defense's case. Robert, a brother-lawyer with a rock-solid reputation, had just tipped the whole thing over to their side. But at what cost to himself?

The prosecutor pressed it one more time. "With your own eyes, you saw the gun?"

"Yes, I saw the gun."

Margaret's eyes bored a hole into Robert as he walked back to his seat. Had he lied? He had never told her specifically about seeing the gun when they talked about it. She gathered her bag and excused herself to those she needed to move past. She hurried out from the courtroom, gutted by the possibility that Robert might have just perjured himself. She couldn't stay there another second.

CHAPTER TWENTY-EIGHT

The following day at Needham Forest, Margaret roamed through the house, unable to focus on any particular task.

Finally, without much enthusiasm, she began to sort through the pile of mail that Cassie had placed in the silver-plated tray on the hall table. She discovered most of the pile consisted of bills, until she stopped at the one with the official looking bold type in black. It stood out from the rest and, rightly so, as it was a notification from the Montgomery County Courthouse.

She took it to her desk where she sat down heavily. After slitting it open with her mother-of-pearl letter opener, she read the decree that set a date for the hearing over Keith's allegations. It was to occur in two days' time. "That was quick," she said aloud.

Margaret gazed up and out into the room. She now had to contend with Keith and his silly machinations. With her finances rapidly dwindling, she could represent herself. Her divorce lawyer hadn't been worth a plug nickel to date anyway. Nor did she think it necessary to procure a lawyer to present the proof she herself had hunted down. She could do it. She would have to.

Bill's situation would have to go on without her. In a way, it was just the excuse she needed to avoid the ongoing drama of the Millers' plight and, if she was being perfectly honest, to avoid being in the same room with Robert.

After prepping over the brief two-day period allotted for the court date, Margaret was as ready as she could be. Arranging yet another ride from Albert to Rockville at an early hour, she purposely allowed plenty of time before court was to convene. As she sat in the passenger's seat of Albert's truck, she took in the sun still rising to one side of them. She tapped down any worries that Keith could possibly become a victor in this charade and also tapped down the uncomfortable fluttering in her lower regions that seemed to rule her life day in and day out.

After Albert pulled the truck to the curb to let her out, she walked up the court steps, mentally preparing herself for whatever was to come from the day. She was directed to the assigned courtroom and walked down the marble tiled floor with her heels clicking in the otherwise empty space. The sleepy little county seat was such a contrast from the courthouse in the nation's capital where she had been spending her days. Despite the circumstances, it gave her some breathing room—of a kind.

The spectator's area was largely empty, apart from a few stragglers, the types that entertained themselves by sitting in the rows, day after day. Margaret herself found a wide-open aisle to position herself and sat to wait, glad to have gotten there so early to collect her thoughts.

Eventually, more people filed in and, soon enough, Keith sauntered in behind his lawyer and took a seat across from her side. She kept her gaze straight ahead not wanting any kind of nuance to occur between the two of them to throw her off her game.

When the bailiff announced, "All rise", the small group stood as the judge assigned to the court made his way out to the bench. But Margaret did a double take at the sight. It wasn't a 'he' judge—it was a 'she' judge.

The bailiff added, "The court today will be presided over by Judge Baxter due to Judge Fritz being indisposed."

Margaret sat up a little straighter as she eyed up the severe woman in the black-robed garb of a judge. A woman? This was certainly a surprise. She didn't even know that Montgomery County had any female judges.

When they were all directed to take a seat, she snuck a peek at Keith at this change in the proceedings, "Fritzy" out of commission and replaced by a woman judge. The look of a sulky schoolboy came over his face as he shrunk into himself probably knowing favor might not tip to his side now. In fact, the judge might even lean towards a sensitivity of her own gender's struggles.

Margaret knew Keith's look too well. He'd had the very same ridiculous expression when caught red-handed in the farm office stealing a stash of money, money taken from her Aunt Blanche's hidden coffers. It had been the final straw for Margaret, the realization that she had been saddled with such an immature man.

They sat through a couple of traffic cases and then, within short order, O'Keefe vs. O'Keefe was called out. Keith's lawyer approached the front of the room to present the plaintiff's side.

"Your honor, my client has brought up the charge that his wife's supposed inheritance was not received in a legally binding and appropriate manner. There was clearly not a transfer to rightful heirs. In addition, given all the years my client lived and worked on the estate, he is fully entitled to rightful ownership along with his wife."

He paused to catch his breath and then continued to lay out further details. "Now, he is in a delicate situation due to his wife suing for divorce which cuts him out of this rightful ownership. The case today is to reinstate his rights as half owner of the estate called Needham Forest."

Margaret watched the judge carefully to see how she was processing the lawyer's words. All she could discern was just the slightest raise of eyebrows above her heavy black rimmed glasses. Keith's lawyer wound down by saying "...so we ask that the court review the facts and authorize Mr. O'Keefe in the land deeds by drawing up a current indenture."

"Alright, counselor. Defendant's turn," the judge said.

Margaret rose up from her seat and made her way down the aisle to the front. "Good morning, your honor."

"Are you the counsel?"

"No, I am Margaret O'Keefe, representing myself."

"Proceed."

"The allegation of the plaintiff—my estranged husband, Keith O'Keefe—is patently false." Margaret held out the paperwork from the courthouse that she had ferreted out. "Here, I have the proof that my father, Charles Magruder, received the entirety of Needham Forest in this indenture, dated September 1, 1901. Also, I have the will that designates my ownership and inheritance of the estate upon my father's passing. Indeed, my father stipulated that it was solely mine, not to be under the ownership of any marital partner I may have."

She paused, realizing her voice was shaking slightly. Pulling herself tall, she continued. "In addition, Mr. O'Keefe has been— for lack of a better word—stalking me. He has found me out in public locations and he has also come to my residence uninvited. I have a list here of the times and places where he has sought me out."

The judge motioned for the bailiff to hand her Margaret's stack of documents. The room went silent as she took a considerable amount of time to read through it. Finally, the judge looked up into the courtroom and its players. Then, she turned her fearsome gaze directly to Keith who stood next to his lawyer.

"Sir, I am appalled that you decided to waste the time and energy of this court. This is clearly a case of sour grapes. You want your wife's money. It's obvious. But, here in our great state of Maryland, like in many other states, inherited property is regarded as separate property. You have no control over Mrs. O'Keefe's inherited farm, nor, quite frankly, based on this nonsense, should you."

She waved at the bailiff who handed her the court write-up. "This case is dismissed." She began to sign what she had been handed.

Margaret cleared her throat knowing that this was her only chance. "Judge, could I ask the court for...something else?"

She looked up at Margaret sternly. "What is it?"

Margaret knew she was pressing her luck but was going to try. "Mr. O'Keefe—the plaintiff—has withheld signing the final papers for the dissolution of our marriage. I do not know if this was because his lawyer felt it could be held up due to this case. But the bottom line is that I have been stalled for months now. Also..." She cleared her throat and then continued, "I find his behavior to be a possible endangerment to my person."

The judge stared at Margaret with a critical eye. "This is highly irregular, Mrs. O'Keefe." She paused for a moment and then said, "But the court will allow it. Do you have those papers on you as well?"

"I do." Margaret gladly handed the packet of divorce paperwork over to the bailiff who then took it to the judge.

The judge took the briefest of glances at it then spoke again. "Mr. O'Keefe, the court orders you to sign this paperwork right now. Bailiff, please take this over to him."

"And we will be preparing an injunction against you being within fifty feet of Mrs. O'Keefe so you will no longer be able to harass her. Am I making myself clear?"

Keith's lawyer nudged him. He nodded.

"Answer me with your voice for the court record."

"Yes, I understand." Keith's voice was his most smooth, most unctuous. Margaret knew that inflection of his voice. She had heard it far too often when he had not gotten his own way. But he did as directed and signed the paperwork handed to him.

"Now, this case is dismissed. Once and for all. And I don't want to see any of you again."

"Thank you, your honor," Margaret said as the bailiff handed her the signed divorce papers.

The judge banged her gavel and said, "Next case!"

Before Margaret turned away from the judge's view, she thought she saw the slightest of winks. A wink meant only to be perceptible to Margaret. Margaret restrained herself from breaking out in a wide and triumphant grin.

She walked out behind Keith and his lawyer. Once they were all out in the hallway, Keith stopped, looking back her way. His lawyer saw what he was doing and pulled his arm hard. Margaret continued on not saying a word. She sincerely hoped Keith would mind the judge and not pop up in her life randomly anymore. But if or when he did, that injunction, once recorded, would offer some protection.

Once outside of the courthouse, the sun was beaming and she breathed a big sigh of relief into the beautiful day. She walked down the street straightaway to her divorce attorney's small, one-story frame building in the block where lawyers kept offices, not too far away from the historical society.

She strode into the small, cramped front area where a receptionist sat looking pretty. She looked up at Margaret's blustery entry. Margaret skipped any niceties and went straight to the point. "I need to see Mr. Collins right away."

"Oh, Mrs. O'Keefe. You don't have an appointment today and he's rather busy."

"I am done with this nonsense." She walked right to the back of the building with the receptionist calling after her the entire way.

The attorney, Fred Collins, sat at his desk with his feet propped up, not looking very busy at all. Margaret pushed the paper into his hands. "I got Keith's signature on this. You need to file it right away. I've paid more than enough for this to happen."

He sat up immediately and repositioned himself in his chair. His face took on a hangdog expression. "Times are tough, Mrs. O'Keefe. I could only spare my staff so many times to track him down. He's an elusive devil."

"That he is. But I have now taken care of it myself and all you need to do is finalize it. Yes?"

"Uh, let me see..." He pulled spectacles out of his pocket and scanned the document. "Well, yes, it does seem to be in order now."

"So, I'll expect to receive the final divorce decree from you. And no other bill. Are we understanding each other?"

He nodded but then added. "Well, there will be a filing charge of course."

"No, there will not be. Because I have done the work here."

They had a stare-off. His beady eyes finally looked off to the side and she knew she had him. With reluctance, he said, "I'll call when the decree is ready. You can pick it up."

"Fair enough. I'll look forward to it."

She flounced out of the office building, well pleased with the day and its accomplishments.

Later at Needham Forest, she sat in her drawing room, Oliver curled in a ball at her feet, recapping it in her mind. Just to herself. Robert was not there to share it with. Or anybody else. Except Judith. She could call Judith.

With a steaming cup of chamomile tea beside her, she dialed out to New York City. The tea was to keep her digestive tract settled so that she would not have to abruptly end the call. Judith picked up after a few rings out into the ether.

"Oh Mags! How are you? Fill me in on all the latest. Did you find the proof?"

Margaret immediately took comfort in hearing her sister's voice and began to relay all that had happened. She stopped to take a breath and then got to the last bit. "So, I could swear the judge winked at me—unless it was an eye tic—after it was all done. Then, with papers in hand, I stormed down to that waste of a lawyer's office and told him in no uncertain terms that he would process it all and get me my decree."

"Well, that is a day of fine work. I admire your chutzpah."

"Chutzpah?"

"Oh, a Yiddish expression. I spend so much time in the Lower East Side markets. I've picked up a lot of their idioms and such. It means moxie. Which you have a lot of, of course."

"Thank you for saying so, Judith. Although..."

"Although?"

"It feels like a hollow victory. In a way."

"Why do you call it that, Mags?"

"Well, it just feels a bit flat, I guess."

"But you needed to get rid of him once and for all. Keith, I mean. As far as Robert goes...I don't know what to tell you over that. Could you have misunderstood the whole gun thing?"

Margaret thought about that. There had always been so much drama and chaos whirling around them, with Bill and his issues. Then for her, there had been the problem of Keith... and who knew the things Robert kept to himself. She answered. "Maybe. Maybe I did misunderstand...maybe that's the case."

PART 3

CHAPTER TWENTY-NINE

"Margaret, where have you been? Bill has been asking for you." Jocelyn's tone on the other end of the phone was plaintive. Wheedling even.

"He has?" Margaret hadn't mustered up the energy to go back to the trial and sit through any more of it. It would play out whether she was there or not.

"Well, of course he has. He values your friendship so very much."

Margaret wondered, not for the first time, whether Jocelyn really understood the nature of the arrangement between her and Bill. Of course, he was a friend from old, but he also was providing the financial backing needed to keep Needham Forest afloat. Margaret's support of him and her vested interest in seeing him exonerated was all tangled up in that. At the end of the day, would the scales tip more to the financial rather than the friendship aspect?

Jocelyn continued to chat. "Tomorrow will be the closing arguments and they are saying there could be a very quick verdict to end all of this mess."

"Really? Why?"

"Well, mostly due to Robert's surprise testimony. You were there for that, weren't you?"

Indeed, Margaret had been there. That was exactly what was keeping her away now. Robert's testimony had thrown her off course. She had thought he was somebody that maybe he wasn't. It was too painful to be in the same room with him.

The situation had been turned upside down. She didn't know what to believe anymore. Was the defense's side all fabrication? Bill's story? Jocelyn's story? And Robert's? Was Bill being duplicitous about his killing of Michaels? Was Robert lying about seeing the gun? And Jocelyn? Could she be believed about anything?

"Yes, I was there," Margaret answered simply.

"So, you'll come tomorrow then? We'll celebrate afterwards." Jocelyn's voice vibrated with an odd excitement.

Margaret felt immediately aghast at the idea of a "celebration". Something was so very wrong with that word choice. But, she did feel compelled to see this through on several different levels. "Alright, Jocelyn. I'll be there."

Margaret placed the receiver down, sighing heavily. She wished she could call Robert and just talk things over with him. But she wouldn't. She couldn't. She still had her pride. If he didn't want her in his life, that was his choice and she would make the best of it. She stood up, firming her shoulders, to face the rest of her day.

She headed down towards the stables for a chat with Leonard and a visit with the horses, putting off the inevitable wrestling match with more bills. On her way, she passed by a bundle of straw which led to the wry thought of how helpful it would be if she, like Rumpelstiltskin in the age-old fairytale, could figure out how to spin gold out of straw.

Her stroll came to a stop and her head swiveled at the noise of a vehicle on Needham Forest's drive. A black town car, slow and steady but purposeful, made its way towards the front of the house. The car had the unmistakable look of a government vehicle and Margaret swore under her breath as she walked back to face the inevitable music.

At Needham Forest's entrance steps, Margaret took what she hoped was a confident stance while the man in the car turned off his engine. When he emerged from the driver's seat, he stood up, tall with a black homburg hat on his head and a matching black suit. Margaret marveled at the hat. She hadn't seen one in years but maybe it was making a come-back. Or maybe this was an odd man.

"Mrs. O'Keefe?"

"Yes. And you are?"

He walked towards her with an outstretched hand. "Mr. Goodman. Internal Revenue Service."

Margaret inwardly gulped. "Ah. And what can I do for you today?"

His face cracked into what served as a smile. "Perhaps I could come inside and we could discuss."

Margaret was conflicted about inviting the man in but there was no denying it anymore. She had to face it head-on. This was quite possibly the tipping point of Needham Forest's demise. She and the man stood in a staring contest until Margaret finally relented, gesturing towards the front door and saying, "Alright. Won't you come in?"

He followed her but paused halfway up the stairs. "What flower is that there? That smell is so unusual..." Margaret looked back to see him staring at her purple wisteria which had just begun blooming at the edge of the house.

"It is indeed. Wisteria it's called. Some find the fragrance overpowering." Margaret knew some found it even sickly sweet but she herself adored it.

"I quite like it."

Margaret gave a curt smile and headed inside, thinking it strange for a man to notice a perfumed flower. Cassie stood in the hallway when they walked in, wringing her hands and eyes big at the sight of the visitor. Margaret knew it was that hat more than anything else that struck a chord.

"Cassie, could you please bring some coffee for our visitor and me?"

Cassie bobbed her head but her eyes showed her suspicion.

Margaret and Mr. Goodman entered the drawing room and stood while the man gazed around before commenting, "You have a fine house here, Mrs. O'Keefe."

When she thanked him, he asked a few questions about Needham Forest that seemed more about making conversation than quizzing Margaret on her finances. She answered briefly and then gestured towards the sofa and said, "Please. Have a seat."

Only once seated did the man take off the remarkable homburg, placing it off to the empty seat next to him. His hair underneath the hat was also black, a thick and oily mane. He then reached down into a very worn and tattered leather satchel and pulled out a large file folder.

He cleared his throat in a phlegmy fashion. "Well, Mrs. O'Keefe. I am sure it comes as no surprise that I am here."

Just as Margaret gave a curt nod in way of response, Cassie made a loud noise butting the drawing room door open with the coffee tray. There was silence as she set up the coffee cups and poured.

"Thank you, Cassie. You were saying, Mr. Goodman?" Margaret lifted the steaming cup to her lips with a bit of a tremble in her hand.

"In brief, I regret to inform you that there is a government lien against your property now." He then provided a long-winded explanation of what exactly the lien meant in financial terms and other particulars leading to the eventual and obvious ramifications.

It's like a death, Margaret thought. *Like being informed about a death.* After he finished speaking, she placed her coffee cup down carefully. "How much time do I have before...before you—"

He cut in. "It's a process. A process that works its way through our court system. So it will take some time, if you are unable to pay us now in full." He looked up with a question in his expression.

After a sharp intake of breath, she answered. "Yes, well. I am certainly going to try to do that."

He slurped his coffee down in one jarring sip and stood up. "I won't keep you any longer." He reached down and tapped some paperwork with a forefinger. "This is for you to peruse. It lays out the process as I just explained it and what will happen next in a more condensed version."

Margaret started to stand up but he stopped her. "No need, Mrs. O'Keefe. I'll find my way out."

She stayed put hearing the old door creak to a close behind the ominous man. A minute later, Cassie came back into the room.

"Who was that fella in the black hat? Why he got a black hat on like that on a spring day? Something ain't right there..."

Margaret looked up at Cassie. "Huh? Black hat. Oh right. It does set an unnecessary tone, doesn't it? Mr. Goodman, he said his name was."

Cassie shook her head. "Nothing good about him. I could see that right aways. Uh-huh."

"Yes. He was different. And it was so strange. He liked the wisteria out front. Speaking of which, it's in bloom right now. I'll bring some in to fill the hall vase."

"I'll do it, Mizz Margaret. I know how much you love that bush."

"Thank you, Cassie."

When Cassie left the room, Margaret found herself staring at the ring on the table left behind by the man's coffee. Bill Miller being exonerated was her last hope at this point. She had to put aside all her mixed-up feelings about it. She had to go down to the city and stand by him. And if he was set free, she needed to talk to him about saving Needham Forest from this latest and ultimate calamity.

She stood up all of a sudden, her stomach roiling with the cup of coffee she had just drunk with Mr. Goodman. With delicate steps, she made her way to the staircase. She felt and heard the creak of the first riser and, just like always, it brought comfort. But as she continued the climb, she took in all the family portraits along the wall, her heart getting heavy at the thought of letting them all down. It might all be taken away from her. All of it.

Her limited understanding was that she could stay put like a squatter for some time until the process wound through the courts. She had no idea how long that would go on, but she would hang on, shameful or not, until the bitter end. Until she was maybe even physically removed from these hallowed walls.

CHAPTER THIRTY

The next morning, the circus-like atmosphere in front of the courthouse had become even more so. The last day of the trial was the final opportunity to soak up the scandalous excitement of a story that had captivated the city and beyond for some time.

Inside, the judge banged the gavel a couple times to get some sort of order out of the situation. All Margaret could see from her vantage point were the backs of the players that held her interest; Bill, Jocelyn, and Robert.

After the judge's invitation to proceed, Mr. Armstrong stood up and moved with purpose to the front with his usual air of complete confidence. The weasel, as Margaret thought of him, began his closing arguments, his last chance to win his case.

"Good morning, folks. Well, here we are. Our opportunity to consider once and for all what really happened that day last February." He paused for dramatic effect and walked back and then forth in front of the judge's bench.

When he looked back up, he focused out into the room with his intense gaze. "Throughout the course of this trial, we have heard smatterings of the truth from the two people who have survived this very jagged and twisted love triangle. Just smatterings mixed in with a lot of untruths."

"But let's cut through all that and lay out the bare facts. Mr. Miller knew his wife was having an affair with Dr. Michaels. He also knew where she was going to be on February twenty-first. He went there with a gun. He walked to the car that his wife and Dr. Michaels were in and shot the man dead with bullets from that gun."

Armstrong unrolled his points mainly by cherry picking from witness testimony that supported the government's case. Margaret tuned in, especially when he cited something that must have occurred during a day she was absent.

"We've heard Dr. Watson Eldridge, chief of St. Elizabeth's, testify that he spoke plainly on several occasions with Mrs. Miller. She told him several key things. She told him that religious scruples in her household meant that her husband would never allow a divorce. She told him that Mr. Miller threatened to kill her and Dr. Michaels."

He paused and shifted to face the jury, before saying, "Then we heard Mrs. Miller deny all of it. So, folks, this is what we call a case of 'who is telling the truth.'"

Margaret considered these details. He was clever, as befitting the nickname she had given him, and she understood his strategy. He knew there was too much reasonable doubt so all he could do was throw the most controversial pieces at the jury to shake them up.

"When this is the case, it is your job as a jurist—" here, he paused and looked at one jury member in the eye, "—to sift through the preponderance of evidence we do have, circumstantial though it might be."

He walked away from the jury and pivoted on one foot, then spoke again. "When Mrs. Miller denied she had conversations with one of the heads of St. Elizabeth's, we ask ourselves, is this truth or a lie? When Mrs. Miller says she was 'saucy and ugly' to her husband in conversation about ending the affair, is that a truth or a lie?

"Now, we do have a few things that we can see with our own eyes." He reached over to the box by the side of the bench and pulled out the gray package and its crimson-stained items. He held them up and circled around with them. "There is no denying with this evidence there was a crime committed. Here is the stain from blood splatter on Mrs. Miller's things."

There was a silence in the court as he lifted the items for all to gaze at again. He turned and placed them back. Next, he pulled out the two guns that had been entered as evidence and placed them in open view on the table. "The guns I have here are another game of 'what's the truth', are they not?"

He picked up one and held it aloft. "This one is the weapon that Mr. Miller used to murder Dr. Michaels. There is no disagreement on that."

He placed it down and picked up the other one, the nickel-plated revolver. "But this other one... What is the true story about this other one? We had an eyewitness on the street right there on the scene at the exact time of the crime testify to you all that he saw Mr. Miller holding a manila envelope and leaning into Dr. Michael's vehicle with it. We also heard a brother-lawyer of Mr. Miller's say he saw the same gun a couple of times in a manila envelope. Who do we believe about the gun? What's the truth? What's the lie?

"Look, did Dr. Michaels make poor choices in his life by having an affair, not only with a married woman, but with a patient? Yes. Yes, he did. But did that mean he had to be gunned down in the street for it?

"The fact is, folks, this was a murder in cold blood. It

245

happened. There is no denying that fact. It is now up to the jury to decide if it was done in self-defense as Mr. Miller alleges or if it was planned out and done purposefully. The prosecution rests its case, your honor."

As the weasel took his seat, Margaret reflected on all that he said. She didn't envy the jury the job in front of them. As she gazed over at them, she could see faces that seemed conflicted and troubled. Their task was daunting. She herself, even knowing the players, could not say with any certainty at all where the real truth lay.

Bill's defense lawyer strode up to the front of the room with alacrity. "Your honor, ladies and gentlemen of the jury, I present to you a case of an honorable man being tried for a horrible tragedy. When I say tragedy, I mean the rash moment where he was forced to defend himself with the only option available to him."

Patterson began to walk to and fro. "The defense has shown the stellar record of Mr. Bill Miller. We have heard testimonies from numerous colleagues and professionals who have never known Mr. Miller to be anything other than forthright, honest, distinguished and respected."

"Now, an unblemished record such as that is put on trial due to a witch's brew that was stirred up in a cauldron to boiling point. Then it got completely out of hand and that boiling brew spilled over the day Jocelyn Miller, Mr. Miller's treasured bride, went shopping one afternoon."

He let out a huge sigh, a bit exaggerated. "We all know now what happened as a result of that decision. But what is important to remember is that Mr. Miller had been pushed to the last possible edge of sanity. His wife, by this point, had become known around town as 'Dr. Michael's girl' with no apparent end in sight to the situation. In fact, he was pushed into temporary insanity, a fugue state even. So yes, he was carrying a gun to the scene in a possibly irrational state of mind."

"On the other hand, because he had that gun on him, he was able to shoot Dr. Michaels in an action of self-defense. The same man who had a habit of always having a gun by his side and who also had threatened to shoot Bill Miller's, and I quote, 'old gray head off'."

"Mistakes were made by all parties in this travesty including many on Mr. Miller's part. But the defense argues that the one mistake Mr. Miller did not make was having a gun on him to defend himself and his lawfully wedded wife when he went to get her away from her lover's clutches."

Margaret looked over at the faces of the jurymen and women. She wondered if the defense's argument would win them over as predicted by all the pundits. Patterson finished his soliloquy with, "The defense rests."

The judge set out the rules of the game to the jury and they were excused to go and decide a verdict. The court was recessed and Jocelyn hustled back making a beeline for Margaret.

"Oh, thank goodness you are here. I'll be sitting on pins and needles until we get called back. Sit with me?"

Margaret thought too late she should have snuck out to avoid Jocelyn and to avoid sitting with her. She could only nod and agree to it as any other response would be churlish.

"Where shall we go?"

"Well, we need to be close by. So, there is an anteroom they have on offer with some refreshments."

"Uh, who else will be there?"

Jocelyn looked at her curiously. "It's just me. As far as I know. I mean, maybe Bill's lawyer will come in to talk to me at some point."

"Alright then."

They made their way to the small chamber and the wait began. After preparing cups of coffee, they made desultory conversation, both focused too hard on other things.

Margaret stared at the coffee mug her hands were wrapped around. Despite it being springtime, there was a slight chill in the air. Or she was coming down with something else? A sigh escaped from her.

It gave Jocelyn the prompt she needed. "Did your stomach troubles ever settle? I was worried things had taken a turn when you were gone after that."

Margaret waved a hand of dismissal. "Yes. All better. So strange how these things can come on so quickly."

"It is..." Jocelyn started to tell a rambling story about her own woes in that department. Margaret let her mind drift. After this business wrapped up, she could concentrate on plans for the summer and fall seasons at the farm. She even began to feel the flicker of enthusiasm at the prospect. It would be good to get her mind on the farm. Back where it needed to be. Put all of this behind her. All of it.

They both startled when the door swung open and one of Bill's defense team stood in the opening. "The verdict is in!" he announced with some triumph. His manner made it clear he took it as a potential win for their side.

"But it's so quick?" Jocelyn's face was a big question mark.

"Yes, only an hour and fourteen minutes. This is a great sign, ladies. Come on!"

Jocelyn and Margaret bustled out to the courtroom. The room was buzzing in a bigger way than it had over the entire period of the trial. The judge made his way to his bench and the bailiff handed him the paperwork.

He looked over to the jury. "Has the jury reached a verdict?"

The presiding juror stood and answered. "Yes, we have, your honor."

The judge opened the envelope, read it and then handed it over to the clerk of the court.

"Will the defendant please rise?" Margaret took in Bill's tall figure, gaunter than ever, in his suit. She could glimpse his profile from her seat. He was expressionless. It had been a long siege, now almost over.

The clerk announced the verdict to one and all in the courtroom. "The defendant, Mr. William Ingleside Miller, is found not guilty on all counts."

Immediate reactions were heard throughout the courtroom from whispers to loud gasps. Margaret thought she even heard a low moaning. Even though the most sensational trial of possibly the century had come to its end, the verdict would be the talk of the town for the days to come. This was just the beginning of that talk. The judge banged his gavel to stop the clamor enough so that he could pronounce, "The defendant is free to go on his way."

Bill's expression remained the same as he spoke up, simply saying, "Thank you, your honor."

He worked his way around his defense team, shaking all their hands, but then moved apart from them to scurry his way over to Jocelyn. He grabbed her and they exchanged a big, slobbery kiss. Then they quickly exited the courtroom arm in arm to begin the next chapter of their lives, whatever that was to be. The rest of the room's crowd streamed behind them in chatty, excitable groups, led by the gaggle of the reporters who had been fixtures during the trial.

Margaret stayed in her seat digesting all of it while all the people filed out. An immediate anticlimactic feeling came over her. It was done.

When she finally worked her way up and out of the

courthouse, there was a crowd out in front with the bevy of reporters and the teams of lawyers. Bill and Jocelyn were in the very middle, being peppered with questions left and right. The news reporters were now all recognizable to Margaret: they'd become part of the scenery on the days she had been present.

The periphery of the crowd seemed to all be well-wishers based on their shouted comments. No naysayers. Like a play, this was the final curtain call, what was left of a "closing night."

She was sure Robert was buried inside the cluster but she made no efforts to pin her eyes on him. There was no reason to anymore. They would probably all go now to "celebrate" as Jocelyn had mentioned. But Margaret would not be doing that. There was something deeply troubling about it. Something she needed to detach herself from, needed to move on from.

She walked across from Indiana Avenue into a plaza. She soon found herself studying the statue of Chief Justice John Marshall, one of the most revered men of justice.

There were stone benches on either side. Margaret sat, needing a moment. She felt breathless again. Maybe the residual effects of all the hubbub, the stress of it. She stared at the pinpricks of light scattered off the statue's bronze and fell into a reverie about whether justice had just been served—or not —in Bill Miller's case. So caught up in her thoughts, she startled when he sat down next to her and said her name.

She looked over at Robert. His eyes were smudged with dark circles underneath, revealing his fatigue and the weight of the trial. She didn't say anything as she turned to look back at the statue. The wings of hope began to fan just a bit as she wondered why he sought her out.

Robert cleared his throat. "So, Bill has been exonerated."

She acknowledged the obvious with a nod.

"That's good. Good all around. You'll be able to—"

She turned to him sharply. "The outcome needed to be the

truth, Robert. No matter what that would mean for Needham Forest and me."

He reared back as if struck. "What are you implying?"

"Robert, you testified you saw the gun. But you didn't. You just saw the envelope. How could you do that? How could you lie?"

"I saw the outline of it, Margaret. I saw the outline of the gun in the envelope. It was obviously the gun. He was trying to twist it that Bill...that Bill..." his voice was anguished.

"But what if it wasn't a gun, Robert? What if it was...I don't know...a spare part for the car or...or anything? How could you say that when you really didn't see it for sure?" Her voice came out shrill but she couldn't stop herself.

Robert shook his head. "Margaret, Bill could not take a fall like this. Don't you understand? I couldn't let that happen. But now..."

"Now?" she prodded.

"I don't know anymore. I really don't know anymore."

They stared at each other. The glimmer of hope was still in play. Maybe they could talk it all out and she could understand. She waited for what he would say next.

"It doesn't matter," he finally said. He stood up and said, "Well, look. Could I give you a ride back to the farm?"

She looked up at him with dismay. Why would he ever offer to do that? Did he think he could cut her off so coldly and then return to her life as before? In her bed even? She had no idea what was going on in his mind, nor did she want to decipher it anymore.

"That's not a good idea."

"Okay." He inhaled and then said, "I guess this is goodbye then."

She nodded again. "I guess it is." The hope was dashed as quickly as it had started. It was false hope.

He tipped his fedora and walked away. She watched to see if he would turn back around. Turn around and come back to her to make everything alright again. But he didn't. Soon, he became a speck, swallowed up by the city's streets. Margaret sat for a bit longer, not quite ready to stand up again.

CHAPTER THIRTY-ONE

As Margaret walked up to the doctor's office for her follow-up visit, she tried to let go of all the angst over Robert. Maybe the qualities she saw in him—qualities in direct contrast to Keith's—were not based in reality. Maybe it had all been her doing—putting him on a pedestal and conjuring him up to be something he wasn't. She shook her head and pulled the door to the office open.

Inside, Margaret went through the same rigamarole of waiting in the lobby followed by waiting in the exam room. She became irritated with herself that she had even made the appointment. Despite the upheaval in the courtroom, her digestion had been far better of late. In fact, the problem had almost solved itself. She looked down at her watch deciding that if the doctor did not enter in the next five minutes she would leave.

No sooner had she looked up when there was a rap at the door, followed by the bustling entrance of Doc Pender, his presence immediately filling up the small space. He propped himself alongside the exam table and gave her a big smile, his eyes twinkling underneath his half spectacles.

"Congratulations, Mrs. O'Keefe. The rabbit died," he declared in his loud, booming tenor.

A part of her wondered if he sang in a church choir. It was the part of her that wanted a diversion from the wrongness of those two sentences. The Mrs. O'Keefe part. And the rabbit dying part.

"It did?" she finally managed to sputter out.

"Indeed. You can expect your bundle of joy come late autumn, I suspect." The doctor lifted his watch fob out from a pocket on his white jacket. "Now, you'll have to excuse me but Martha can set you up with your next appointment and some vitamins I recommend to all my new mothers."

"But Doc, aren't I...I mean my age. Is this wrong?"

He patted her hand. "You'll be perfectly okay, Mrs. O'Keefe. Why, I had one mother in here recently who was forty-nine when her little one was born. Mother Nature doesn't make mistakes. Just take those vitamins and all will be well."

He began to leave the room but Margaret stopped him. "Wait—"

He turned with a quizzical expression clearly thinking he had covered all the ground that needed covering.

"Does the rabbit actually die?"

He smiled. "Mrs. O'Keefe, let us handle the science. And make sure you give Mr. O'Keefe the heartiest of congratulations from me. That rascal."

Margaret stared at the door that closed after the doctor. What was it exactly that he liked so much about Keith? And *rascal*? She shook her head and stood up in a daze.

Margaret left the office and it began to hit her all at once. She was pregnant with Robert's baby and, now, unmarried. What was she going to do? It was so unlike her not to know what to do, to not know the clear path, to not know what decision to make. What was happening to her?

Back at the farm, Margaret made quick work of changing into barn clothes and heading down to the stables, keeping mind-numbing thoughts at bay. She stopped at Midnight's stall and took comfort in stroking his forehead. He made small braying noises and gently nipped at her for more attention.

"Everything okay out here, Miss Margaret?" Leonard stood in silhouette at the open entrance to the barn.

She waved a hand. "Yes, I'm fine. Just talking to Midnight for a spell."

He stood for a beat and then said, "Well, come git me if you need anything."

Margaret watched his departing back and couldn't stop the big sigh that came out. She wished she could lay it all in Leonard's lap, or anybody else's lap. All these problems to figure out...

She gave Midnight one last pat and moved on through the rest of the barn checking on the other horses. Eventually, she found herself outside and began to wander through the fields, her mind running in circles.

As Margaret traversed the paths throughout the farm, she attempted to work out each angle of the situation she found herself in. If she did nothing, people might assume it was Keith's child. Keith would know different though since they hadn't been in the same bed for over a year. And he was a potential powder keg. He might bring it up in a fit of vengeance and publicly call her out for being pregnant with another man's child. Technically, she was not pregnant out of wedlock because the divorce had just been finalized. So, she could say otherwise. But what an unholy mess that would be.

Then there was Robert. Was telling him the right avenue? The moral right avenue even? But where would that leave them? He had made his thoughts about marrying out of his religion crystal clear. But he may feel strong-armed into doing the honorable duty of marrying her. She didn't want to be with someone who didn't want to be with her.

Plus, would she ever be able to reconcile Robert's actions surrounding Bill's trial? She was still incredulous about what he had stated on the stand and how he'd justified doing so.

Then the big question: did she want to have a child? If it was just her and no one else involved, was it something she could even take on? Emotional issues notwithstanding, with her current state of finances, she just didn't know. There were, of course, friends of friends who might know someone that would take care of it but...she couldn't go there. The very thought made her go ice cold.

Margaret stopped at the crest of a hill, taking in her surroundings and sighting the black walnut tree nearby. She went over and stood by it. As she touched the bark, she recalled the day she and Leonard had dug around in it and how hopeful she had been. It felt like a lifetime had gone by since then. If only she could find mythical gold bars, the weight of all these problems would be lifted. Even...even the weight of this surprise baby in her life...

After a time, she headed back to the house with a weariness she did not know was possible. She had not resolved a thing. What was the way out?

Inside the phone was ringing as she walked through the door. She sat heavily at the phone table and picked up the receiver.

"Hello, my dove." Keith's silkiest tone came through the line, jarring her.

She sat up straighter. "Keith, it was made clear. The injunction and all that. There is no contact between us anymore —except through lawyers."

"Of course, I know all that. I can't help but call with my concerns..."

She let out a snort. "Concerns about what?"

"Well, there have been reports out of Rockville that you are visiting Doc Pender. More than once."

Margaret stiffened. Had someone at Doc Pender's office told Keith her news? Surely that would violate every patient-doctor confidence but...Rockville was a small town.

"Not that it's anybody's business at all but it was just a checkup. I'm fine."

"Really? Are you sure about that, Margaret?" She could almost see his raised and groomed eyebrows through the phone line.

Margaret paused and felt a frisson of fear. Her child would need a legal father on his or her birth certificate along with a legal surname. It would have to be O'Keefe. There was no other way around it. She had to play this right.

"Yes. But, you know, if Doc Pender finds anything wrong, I'll...uh...I'll keep you informed." He went silent and she felt a quiver of worry that Keith was not buying what she was selling.

Finally, he spoke. "I think you should do that, Margaret. I do indeed."

Margaret cut him off curtly and ended the call. She hung up the phone, with the conversation leaving a bad taste in her mouth. Or maybe it was some residual nausea. She sat like that for a long time, feeling heavy sadness at the choices she had to make and not knowing if Keith was about to complicate her life even further. Was it a veiled threat...or was Keith just on a fishing expedition? There was no way to know.

CHAPTER THIRTY-TWO

A suffocation of a kind came over Margaret as she sat at her desk with head in hands. A head that felt like it was exploding. All of it was now a crushing weight on top of her. The man in the black hat, the baby news, Keith's phone call, the leftover sick feeling...

A crash in the center hall diverted her attention. "What in the world..." She rose up in an abrupt motion and banged her knee hard against the side of the desk. "Ouch!" she screeched.

She reached the hall at the same time that Cassie came bustling out from the kitchen, dishrag in hand. They both stared at the broken glass vase and the pool of water with the wisteria blooms in the center of it all.

"Did you bump into it by accident, Mizz Margaret?"

"No, I was sitting in the study. How ever did it happen, I wonder?"

Cassie shrugged. "Dunno. I'll clean it up."

"Alright. Thank you." Margaret's gaze stayed rooted as the strong scent of the wisteria wafted upwards.

"Mizzus?"

Margaret looked up to see Cassie's concern. "I'm fine. Just

wondering how it— Well, anyway, I'm going to change and then go down to the stables, if you need me for anything, I mean."

"Alright, Mizz Margaret." Margaret could feel Cassie's eyes on her, wondering why she was acting so strange. Margaret started towards the stairs but paused at the sound of Cassie whispering.

"What did you just say, Cassie?"

"Mizzus?"

"Were you— Did you just say something?"

The other woman shook her head. "No."

"Huh, I thought I heard somebody whispering."

"What did they say?"

"I don't know. I guess I'm just all in a state. It's fine." Now she was hearing things on top of everything else. She let out a huge breath and looked around the hallway, not hearing it again but getting another curious stare from Cassie.

She began climbing the stairs and suddenly it happened. With a flash of recognition, Margaret knew what had been tickling at her all the past months. The distinctive thud on the very first riser. A creaking thud that never occurred on any of the others. She stopped and looked at Cassie.

"Did you hear that?"

"What?"

"That noise. It's always just this one spot. Have you noticed it before?"

"Well, is that the whisper you talking 'bout? I done wondered about that myself all these years. Just always figured it's an old house talking to us like old things do."

Margaret went stock still at what Cassie had just said. "Old houses talking... My God, Cassie, it was right here talking to me every day!"

"Now, Mizz Margaret, why don't you come on back to the

drawing room? I'll get a cloth for your head and set you up on your sofa. You ain't making much sense right now."

"No, no. I'm making perfect sense." Margaret walked off the stairs to where Cassie stood.

"You feeling alright?"

Margaret couldn't hold back the laugh that slipped out at Cassie's concern. "Yes, I'm fine. Just trying to figure out why that thud is there."

"Oh, alrighty then."

Margaret went over to the now exposed area underneath the staircase with Cassie close at her heels. Leonard had cleaned it up and it remained wide open. She stared at it. Since it had been exposed, she hadn't given it much more thought than maybe making it a place for the phone table or installing bookshelves for a reading nook.

She stooped inside of the space for a closer view to examine the underpinnings. She couldn't make out anything that stood out or looked different about the bottom stair step from the ones above it. She crouched her way back out into the hall with Cassie looking at her as if she had grown two heads. "What is it, Mizz Margaret?"

"Cassie, I need you to walk up the stairs for me."

"Huh?" Cassie's confusion over the request was on her face.

"Just— It's just something I need to figure out. Could you..." Margaret pointed to the staircase.

"Alright, Mizzus. If you say so."

"Okay, I'm going into the space underneath to see what happens. Try to make it as slow a footfall as possible. I'll yell out when I'm ready."

"Yes'm."

Margaret scrunched herself again into the space and then yelled, "Okay!"

She watched and waited for Cassie to walk up. Indeed, it

right away led to that noise on the bottom step. When Cassie rose higher, the other steps gave more of a squeak along with some give. She stuck her head out and said, "Do it again please, Cassie. Just keep doing it back and forth for a bit."

She heard Cassie let out a mutter followed by her movements back on the staircase. Margaret watched carefully each time Cassie's weight hit the bottom step. Why didn't the bottom step have the play like the other ones? She pushed her way in for a better view. It appeared there was extra wood to the bottom step, making it look thicker than the others.

Margaret exited out of the space and felt a little breathless. That had been happening too much of late and now she knew the cause, of course. She never really understood all the attendant physical issues that came with a pregnancy. But she was finding out.

"Alright, Cassie. We need back up. Have you seen Leonard around?"

"He said he'd be by at noon for lunch."

"Ask him to come into the study when he arrives, please."

"Alrighty, Mizz Margaret."

Margaret paced back and forth in her study, torn between excitement and exasperation that she couldn't just hack into the staircase right away. A short but anxiety-filled time later, there was a knock at the half-opened door and Leonard poked his head in.

"What's all the fuss about?"

Margaret leapt up and began leading Leonard back into the hall. "Oh Leonard, I think I'm onto it now. I really do."

At the bottom of the staircase, she said, "This is it. It's got to be." Leonard threw her a quizzical look. She trod on the stair step in question and it made its obligatory and customary noise. Once a couple of stairs up, she turned back to go down making the noise again when stepping on the bottom riser.

Cassie had joined them in the hallway and watched Margaret with a frown on her face. Leonard, too, had a perplexed expression.

"I'm not going crazy. Watch." Margaret knelt down and tapped with her knuckles. "Hear that? It's different from the others." She knocked on the stair right above to prove her point. "And I had Cassie walk up and down it and I could see all kinds of give and play from underneath for the others, but not this one. Underneath the staircase, I mean." She knew her words were running away from her but she couldn't stop the bubbling over of excitement.

Leonard scratched the side of his head. "So...you want me to..." He left it dangling clearly not sure of where Margaret was going with it.

"I want you to pry off this top riser."

"Hmmm. You sure about this?"

"As sure as anything. Look, if nothing else, I wonder why it makes the noise it has always made. It's done so for...well, as long as I can remember."

"Alrighty then. Let me just grab my tool bag from the truck out back. Hang on."

Margaret paced back and forth until he came back holding a canvas satchel.

"Okay, let's see what we can do." Leonard lowered himself down near the riser with a wince and became preoccupied with running his hand over the wood. "Huh."

"Huh?"

"There's a weird ridge underneath. Did you feel that?"

Margaret leaned in. "No, where?"

Leonard took her hand and placed it there. She felt her fingers ease into a ridge as if they were meant to be there. She felt the fluttering of anticipation in her stomach mixed with the other kind of fluttering that had been happening. The quickening, it was called. She would take both.

"What is it?"

Leonard's gaze moved up the staircase with one eye in a squint. "The other risers don't have it."

He moved his hands across the entire first step riser. "Well, it's nailed down at either end for starters. Lemme take those out." He pulled out a flat wedge from the bag and then began to work at the nails.

Margaret impatiently waited while he meticulously applied some effort and said, "It's been set in its place all these years. Takes some doing."

Once he finally got the nails out, Leonard crouched down further, peering eye-level to the stair riser. "Huh. I see mortise and tenon right here. And it's not on the one above."

"Well, what could that mean?"

"It's got me thinking that this piece is locked in somehow. Like one of those old-timey wood block puzzles maybe."

"So…" Margaret's utterance was left hanging in the air as they all three stared at the riser.

Finally, Leonard spoke. "Let's all put our fingers under that ridge line and on the count of three pull forward."

With Margaret on one end, Leonard on the other and Cassie in the middle, Leonard said, "Alrighty, big tug. Here goes…one…two…three."

As they worked in concert pulling at the same time, the old wood gave a loud groan followed by the splintering sound of something stuck pried loose. Leonard exerted more pressure and it finally popped and moved back like the bread bin lid in the kitchen. Whatever had been holding tight was released.

He landed on his bottom behind them with an audible thud as Margaret let out a loud gasp and Cassie yelled out, "Lawdy!"

All three loomed over it as a smell like old leather wafted

into the air. Different from the horse saddle leather scent that Leonard had hanging about him. This was an ancient smell.

They stared at the sight in front of their eyes, dumbstruck by the burnished but undeniably gold bars lined up precisely row by row. Margaret had walked right over them time and time again, completely oblivious of the hidden cache underneath her step.

Leonard gave a low whistle, breaking into their shock at the open stair drawer. "Well, if that don't beat all," he said, then added, "You found them."

CHAPTER THIRTY-THREE

Margaret sat behind her desk, sweaty and dusty, with feet propped up and a huge grin. She had done it. She had found the treasure.

With Cassie's and Leonard's help, they had lifted the gold bars one by one out of the drawer and laid them out on the hallway floor. Each one had a heft of a couple of pounds or so. The sight of them all spread out on the hall floor was a strange but welcome one, with a final tally of twenty gold bars.

They placed them all into a leather carryall which now sat heavy at her feet. She would not be letting it out of her sight. While the amount didn't make her a millionairess, a cursory tally in her head of the fluctuating but rising price of gold during the economic downturn, meant that she was well able to take care of Needham Forest's financial woes. When Leonard finished some work down with the horses, they would drive it down to her bank for safe keeping. The irony was that it had already been kept safe for almost seventy years—and walked over every day.

Earlier, as they were liberating the gold from its "home" of many years, Cassie had spotted something tucked along the side edge. "There's something else in there, Mizzus." Margaret had looked in to see a black velvet jewelry bag and a rolled-up but flattened document tied in twine.

She was now ready to open them up after taking a quick break with coffee and a roll. She first reached for the jewelry bag. The ties were stiff with age and almost falling apart. She untied them and carefully shook the bag into her palm. The glint of a diamond in her open palm sparkled back at her. She picked it up with her other hand and studied it. It was a good size, by her estimation, a couple of carats, with a simple, elegant setting that looked to be white gold. It was curious. Maybe an engagement gone wrong?

She moved to the document and worked at the twine. Finally, she resigned herself to cutting it carefully to free the document. As it unfurled, she placed it out open on the desktop.

It was dated 14 February 1873. She moved her eyes to the bottom to see the signature and, as she suspected, it was signed "Nathan". Her two times great uncle. As she began to read the body of the letter, she felt pinpricks of nerves, not knowing what the read would leave her with afterwards.

Dear Sisters,

The War Between the States ended and the victor was not the one we wanted but such are the vagaries of life.

Herein lie gold bars that were intended in part to save the Cause. After the unfortunate event of the Surrender at Appomattox, they were never delivered to the capital of the Confederacy as originally intended.

In fact, messages were crossed and the hiding place was unknown to this Confederate. While not directly privy to the secret plans of Colonel Gordon, I (like others in the community) knew a nearby skirmish possibly involved the gold from a heist that occurred at Monocacy Junction some ten miles north of this location.

The skirmish on the edges of Needham Forest land was an unlucky one and prevented a band of soldiers from getting the gold where it needed to be—in Jeff Davis's hands. It resulted in Captain Bennett and others taken as prisoners of war. At the time of their capture, no mention of the gold was heard.

I discovered the gold purely by accident. The black walnut tree in the south field of our property was struck by lightning a year or so after the war ended. As I traversed the fields on horseback one day, the scar of the lightning strike on the tree caught my eye. Upon examination, the edge of a canvas satchel was exposed. I can only surmise the band of soldiers saw a tree hole and stashed the gold into the interior of the tree right before the skirmish in a rush to hide it. Maybe they intended to return but fortunes intervened. By the point of my discovery, the gold was of no use to the Confederacy. I retained it and kept it guarded in the hope that the Southern cause will rise again at some point.

As I am fond of working with wood, I fashioned this hidden drawer after seeing one similar in a grand house in Paris during my travels to Europe. It has been my safe-keeping box since that time known only to me. Indeed, it also holds the diamond ring that was intended to be for my precious Kristobel. But that was not to be as you well know.

Sisters, you now know the existence of this gold. My intention was always to inform you of its existence when my death is imminent. It is for your use now. Gold will always be the safest haven for currency. Do with it as you see fit.

With brotherly love and affection,
Nathan

Margaret let the letter fall from her hands. A thousand thoughts crowded into her head. The sisters had never found the gold. He had never told them as he intended to. Or presumably told anyone else. She vaguely remembered hearing that he had been cut down unexpectedly with the same kind of heart attack that took her father, an instantaneous extinguishing of life.

Nathan, like most others, probably assumed he had plenty of time to get his affairs in order and set up future financial well-being for the farm. While his maiden sisters were specified in the will that Margaret read at the courthouse, he had not let them in on the specifics of his treasure trove. Now the underlying message and unusual phrasing in the line, "the house and all its contents seen and unseen", made sense.

So, the sisters never knew they were sitting on money that would have made their lives far, far easier. By the time Charles, her father, made inroads with them, the place was on its last legs, decrepit and nearly lost to the family by neglect.

The mystery lady in Nathan's life, Kristobel, and the diamond ring were a sad note with no explanation. Thwarted relationships seemed to be part of the family legacy. Aunt Blanche and her tragic life came to mind with that cad, Blackwell Swann, who had hurt her so terribly. With a sudden squeeze on her heart, Margaret realized she herself was possibly repeating this family pattern.

The biggest issue was how the gold bars had ended up in Nathan's possession after being stolen in a train robbery by the rebels. Nathan should have returned the gold to the government upon its discovery. But that didn't happen.

All these years later, there were still so many in her area who upheld the Confederacy and its actions. Margaret wanted no part of that legacy and all the injustice associated with it.

In theory, the gold was stolen goods even though stolen

seventy years earlier. On the other hand, she did not think that keeping the treasure for the purposes of saving Needham Forest aligned her with the wrong side. Not at all.

Margaret stood up on that thought and dusted herself off. She wasn't going to dwell on anything negative. Her world could get back on track with the gold. She wanted to seize that and make it happen.

Leonard gave the open door a tap and stuck his head in. "How you doing, Miss Margaret?"

She beckoned him to come in. "Ah Leonard, what a day it's been."

"Indeedy." He gestured to the document and the jewelry bag on the desk. "That clear things up?"

"Here. Read it and see what you think."

He sat down and pulled the document closer. After several minutes, he placed it down and said, "Well, that's really something."

"Leonard, what should he have done with the gold?"

He pointed to the letter. "He didn't do right by keeping it at that time, for sure. But he did think it would be taking care of his sisters."

"But that didn't happen. They never knew about it."

"Well..." Leonard paused with a furrowed brow. "Now, it could be like giving it to them if it's put to a good purpose here at the farm. Don't you think?"

"Yes. I do think that. I just needed somebody else to think so too. Thank you, Leonard."

He nodded. "Yes, indeed. Now let's get them into safe keeping. You got a safe deposit box at your bank already set up, right?"

"That's right. Yes. Let's get it done."

Much later, after Leonard had driven her into town and she had placed the gold in her safe deposit box at the Farmers Bank and Trust Company of Montgomery County, she sat down next to the hall phone and placed the call out to New York City. Her sister's voice came through the line, strong and clear.

"Mags! Finally! You have kept me hanging, my dear. Last we talked, all was in a complete upheaval. I do hope I have not heard from you because things have been resolving, not getting worse."

"Well..." Margaret began to tell her sister all of it. During the telling, Judith let out exclamations of astonishment on all that occurred. But Margaret saved the two biggest news items until the end.

"So, you remember how I opened up the staircase but it was a red herring?"

"Yes, of course."

"It turns out it wasn't a red herring."

"What does that mean, Margaret?" Her sister's voice sharpened on the other end.

"I found it, Judith. I found the gold that Bill Miller said Daddy talked about."

Judith emitted the biggest gasp yet. "Oh, my lord. That's... that's..."

Margaret chuckled. It was very unlike Judith to be speechless. "I know. It's pretty amazing. So, no worries for the farm now. And, of course, I will sort out your take. There is also something else..."

"Something else? What could possibly top that?"

Margaret hesitated. The moment was finally here to tell someone about the event to occur in the fall. Judith would be the first person she told. It was a moment of gravitas. She took a deep breath and then told her sister that she would soon be an aunt.

After the lengthy conversation with Judith that was punctuated with so many questions, emotions and thoughts, the sisters ended their call. It was heartening to Margaret that Judith was excited for her and in no way negative about the baby despite the personal complications. Judith expressed complete confidence in Margaret's ability to raise her child and it buoyed her spirits even more.

After ending the call, Margaret settled herself into bed. All of her worries had gone poof in a way she could have never conjured up. Now the Millers' affairs did not impact her one way or the other. Needham Forest was rescued and, this time, she would make sure it would stick and never be at risk again. As she drifted off, the slightest whiff of cigar smoke came into her senses. A smile came over her face as she fell into the best night of sleep she had in months.

CHAPTER THIRTY-FOUR

Margaret's eyes popped open and took in her surroundings. It was her bedroom but there was something different. In the fogginess of coming out of slumber, she could not quite figure it out. Then it came to her. She felt...she felt normal again. A palpable sense of relief came over her. Pregnancy upsets were on hold—at least for the time being.

She sat up and moved her arms into a big and luxurious stretch. She couldn't stop the big smile coming over her face as she basked in the deep-rooted satisfaction of her financial woes being lifted. Finding the gold treasure was making her giddy.

She would also take full advantage of feeling well, especially on this particular day. The horses were running on the track at Pimlico for the Preakness Stakes, one of the biggest races in the nation. She would be there in a viewing box.

Once out of bed, she began to ready herself for the day's event. The Preakness was known for high-style glamour and Margaret was now up for that challenge. As she pondered the selections in her closet, she looked for one that would be billowy enough to hide her recent but slight weight gain. She finally pulled out a smart suit in blue.

She held it next to the hat on her dressing bench with an appraising eye. There was a special emphasis at the Preakness on headwear. Ladies in attendance outdid themselves in that department and Margaret would not be a slouch. Her hat had been carefully crafted to include a long, flowing peacock feather procured from a neighbor who bred the birds. Horrible creatures, loud and messy, but their colorful and exotic plumage offered a nice selection to choose from. She was satisfied her outfit choice picked up on the particular blue shade of the peacock feather.

Once dressed, she headed downstairs carrying the hat carefully. Cassie greeted her at the bottom of the staircase. "Good morning, Mizz Margaret. Don't you look a picture this morning? And you don't have that peaked look about you anymore." She added a big smile to go with her observation.

"Good morning to you, Cassie. You're right. I am feeling quite well this morning."

"How about a nice cooked breakfast before you head over to the races?"

Margaret felt rumbles of hunger at the very mention of food. "Yes! That would be wonderful."

Cassie cast a quick glance over Margaret's belly. Cassie most likely had her suspicions but Margaret was not quite ready to have a discussion yet. Soon, she would do it. Soon.

After savoring a huge breakfast of eggs, bacon and pancakes, Margaret sat back in her seat with hands wrapped around a second cup of coffee. She could hardly believe how well she felt.

She moved into the drawing room with coffee in hand. On the cocktail table sat the latest copy of *Time Magazine*. She leaned over the table and opened to the centerfold. She had put it off long enough, reading the article about the trial.

She perused the words that laid out the high points of the trial that had kept the city spell-bound by its twists and turns making national news along the way. The article, titled "Lawyer Freed in Death of Rival", was a scintillating summation of the trial's finale.

The end tally had been twenty-four persons testifying on Bill's behalf, a group that included four judges, three federal prosecutors and fourteen citizens in the legal profession or public life. One of those, of course, was herself. The "not guilty" verdict had come in swiftly from the jury with Bill being exonerated. Really, it boiled down to entertainment trumping justice, the defense being favored to win.

She studied the photographs of Bill, Jocelyn and the jurors and tried to extract the truth out of the black and white images as if that were even possible. She read and then reread the words sprinkled with colorful and somewhat apt descriptions. Bill Miller came off as the possessive husband of a wife that he did not want to share. Jocelyn Miller came off as a wayward, immoral hussy who steered the whole thing off course and caused the mess it became. But yet still...they won.

The last line of the article had this to say about the two survivors, the couple comprised of Bill and Jocelyn: "...whether their life is a heaven or hell is their own secret." Margaret folded the magazine, pondering those words especially. Wasn't that the truth of any marriage?

Bill Miller had contacted her a few days prior. He was still on board with investing in the farm. She had let him down easy, telling him that he should focus on his practice instead, then maybe give her a call. She knew he was overrun with clients after the trial, people lined up for his services after his exoneration.

Her feelings about Bill were all over the place, a sort of twisted loyalty left over from her father's legacy. Also, she would have never known the existence of the gold if he hadn't so casually mentioned it.

She stood up and stretched, immediately feeling the baby move. She placed her hands on her belly at the wonder of it and smiled. Maybe the baby was trying to tell her something. Although what that was, she didn't yet know but looked forward to finding out.

Back in the center hall, Margaret collected her belongings casting a parting glance towards the stairway with its underpinnings still exposed. There was no creak or whisper left to be heard. She lifted up a silent prayer of gratitude for the much-needed salvation it had provided. She picked up the key that lay on the silver-plated tray on the hall table and walked outside.

It was parked right in front. Her new car, a Roamer Roadster, was the same model she had urged Robert to purchase for himself. But hers was a different color, a camel tan rather than gunmetal gray. She was justly proud of the purchase. No more cadging rides off Albert or Leonard. She now had her own set of wheels and it revived her confidence to be officially back on the road again in more ways than one.

She had already begun to pay down all the various outstanding credit lines and settled with all the creditors, managing the fresh influx of funds wisely. There was plenty left over to invest prudently in more horses and to expand the operation in the interest of sure-fire returns. Even after gifting very special bonuses to Leonard, Cassie and Albert and wiring Judith her fair portion, she had some disposable cash to make some purchases apart from the business. Like her new roadster.

Margaret got behind the wheel and fired up the engine. The weather was perfect to take the drive across the Maryland countryside to Baltimore City. Enough of a breeze but not too much and plenty of sunshine.

After the first half hour headed northeast, she merged onto the macadam highway that traversed the central part of the state. The roadster kicked up dust, a result of a dry spring season, but soon settled into a calming lull. As Margaret gazed out the windshield into the landscape, she was reminded with a pang of loss of her drive to Ellicott City with Robert a couple of months earlier. It would take a lot more time to forget him.

On the edge of the city proper, she headed south on Park Heights Avenue. She soon reached the turn onto Belvedere Avenue where traffic had already begun to back up in the city neighborhood of densely stacked brick rowhouses on the racetrack's borders. Pimlico had been around for years and was known as "Old Hilltop" due to a slight rise in the infield where many congregated to watch the event. It could be a bit of a madhouse out there. Fortunately, Margaret had snagged a ticket for a box seat where she could rub elbows with the horse crowd from around the state and beyond. The day was an opportunity "to see and to be seen" now that Needham Forest was back in the game.

After navigating the busy parking area, Margaret strolled towards the gate feeling excitement all around. She was more than ready for a little fun herself. She merged with the rest of the colorful crowd, rainbow-like even, with the pageantry of hats, outfits and other regalia, into the massive entry hall. Decorations festooned the hall with a heavy use of the colors of the state flower, the Black-eyed Susan, yellow petals daubed black in the middle.

An acquaintance from the foxhunt club approached Margaret right away. They began to compliment each other on their hats and finery. Soon, she was surrounded by others from her neck of the woods, including an older gentleman who walked over with a drink in each hand and handed Margaret one. "The house drink. It's called a Hilltop Honey."

Margaret hesitated slightly before taking it and giving in to the slightest sip. She sent up a silent prayer that her stomach would cooperate with the taste of it. The flavors of bourbon, honey and lemon glided over her taste buds recalling drinks from years past at the races. What Margaret really desired was a nice, cold bottle of Coca-Cola with condensation dripping off its green glass. Instead, she said, "Delicious."

Soon, the master of ceremonies announced to all gathered that it was time to get to their seats or the infield. The group around Margaret dispersed and the crowd began to file away into their chosen places.

Right before she veered out of the hall, there was a loud bellowing of hellos. Along with others, Margaret looked over to see Bill and Jocelyn pausing at the hall opening. They apparently intended to make a grand entrance. Like everyone else, they were decked out in Preakness finery. Bill looked distinguished in a powder blue seersucker suit that offset his snowy mane of hair. Jocelyn was back to her usual form-fitting attire. She had also chosen blue as her color, donning a teal number that accentuated every curve. Her hat matched with blue feathers pluming off the back.

Magnet-like, they attracted a crowd. It appeared that the murder trial had not tarnished their standing. Instead, they seemed more popular than ever amongst the horsey set. Margaret held back, almost with a feeling of revulsion. She couldn't face them yet.

As she moved on ahead to find her box seat, she again was stopped by an outcry of greeting for another couple. This time, it was Laney Davis, a popular horse farm owner from Northern Virginia, with none other than Keith O'Keefe on her arm. Margaret remembered that one of Laney's horses was a top contender in the showcase purse of the day, the Preakness. She had long suspected that Laney was known in a more intimate manner to Keith. How he had managed to stay in Laney's good graces with all his money woes was a mystery to Margaret.

She now couldn't help but note with irritation Keith's dapper appearance. His misfortunes and bad choices had not changed that up. He took relish in his attire, choosing only the finest fabrics and tailors. He wore a similar seersucker suit to Bill's but in a shade paler. Laney, by contrast, was garbed in a red dress, brazen in its statement. Her blonde tresses hung long accenting the color of the dress.

Margaret kept her head down and finally found her seat in the jam-packed box. All the boxes at the event were that way, with not one empty spot to be had. She settled in with race card in hand and soon found herself chatting with those around her. The box's occupants fell into an easy and familiar languor.

When the first races took off, some around her stood up in anticipation or excitement while others just continued on with the social engagement that was all part of the mix. Margaret herself stayed seated but became aware of a sensation. Someone was watching her. She discreetly looked around the box. In the opposite direction from her seat, she locked her gaze with Robert Brady as he stared at her with intensity. She looked away first but not before clocking the group he was with.

It appeared to be lawyers and their wives from his firm. He himself had a woman by his side. Margaret snuck another peek at her. The willowy blonde, delicate-featured and the exact antithesis of Margaret, was also younger by a lot of years.

A pulse of jealousy zipped through her along with a cascade of other emotions. She put it aside quickly. It did no good to expend energy on those feelings. She tried to concentrate on the next race being called out. But there was now a pall over the event and the day.

Margaret suddenly felt a rough clap on her back as Keith leaned into her with boozy breath. "Hello there, Mrs. O'Keefe."

She reared her head back from the alcohol fumes emanating off his person. She twisted herself away from his hand on her back and stood up, ignoring his presence as he was so clearly ignoring the judge's order. Already three sheets to the wind, she knew from experience Keith would soon be getting louder and sloppier. But that wasn't her problem anymore.

She placed a false grin on her face and murmured to the woman next to her, "Please excuse me. I'm heading to the powder room." She skirted around Keith and worked her way out of her row and through the crowded box. She needed a breather.

CHAPTER THIRTY-FIVE

With most in their seats readying for the Preakness, Margaret experienced some much-needed personal space in the almost empty hall. As she made her way to the facilities, her heels made a satisfying click along the concrete floor. In the powder room, Margaret found a vacant stall and sat, an oasis amongst all the goings-on.

When she emerged from the stall, she discovered another person in the anteroom. Jocelyn was primping herself at one of the oval mirrors, applying powder. They caught each other's eyes in the reflection and Jocelyn said, "Margaret! Why didn't you come over and say hello? Bill's been looking all over for you—"

"Jocelyn, do you ever think of Dr. Michaels?" Margaret said aloud, immediately unsure if she had meant to keep that question internal or not.

Jocelyn paused with a comb in hand mid-stroke. Her stare at Margaret in the mirror was an enigmatic one. Then she answered the question. "No. I really don't. Even though..."

"Even though?"

She let out a sniff. "Even though he consumed my thoughts for every waking moment for all that time." Jocelyn lifted the comb and worked it back through her blonde curls.

It chilled Margaret through her core that the Dr. Donald Michaels chapter of Jocelyn's life was put aside, even forgotten, so very quickly. Bill and Jocelyn had apparently fallen back into their old ways without really missing a step. With a sudden flash of insight, Margaret knew she needed to extricate herself from this woman—permanently. Which sadly also meant extricating herself from Bill as well.

As Jocelyn placed her comb back into a small purse snapping it sharply, she said, "Well, Margaret. You'll come over to our box now?"

Margaret took in the bright and artificial smile pasted on the other woman's face. Between the Millers, Keith and Robert with his new woman, she couldn't wait for the day to be over with. But she gave Jocelyn a nod.

As they worked their way into the Millers' box and approached Bill, Jocelyn said, "Oh Buddy, another drink? Is that your third?"

"Who's counting, Mom? This is a celebration! Little Margaret, it looks like you need some liquid refreshment!"

Margaret felt the pull of days of old at the affectionate nickname. She smiled at him. "I'm fine for now, Bill."

"Sit with us for a spell." He patted an empty seat next to his. Margaret sat with reluctance while Jocelyn moved to his other side.

As Bill cleared his throat, there was an awkwardness between them. Then he spoke. "I can't tell you how glad I am to put all the nonsense from this past winter behind us. And get back to business. We'll meet soon to discuss where things are with the farm since my, uh, since my absence."

Margaret simply nodded. For the moment, it was best to play along.

He leaned towards her in a confidential manner and said, "You know, in the end, it all worked out the way it needed to, right?"

She closed her eyes briefly before looking back at him. "Of course, Bill. It all worked out in the end." She didn't think that but it did neither of them any good to say otherwise.

After some idle chit-chat about the horses on the race cards, Margaret said, "Well, I need to get back to my seat. The Preakness is soon to start."

Bill accepted that excuse without too much protestation. As they all knew, the races before and the ones after the Preakness were just window dressing.

Finally, back at her seat, Margaret tried to enjoy the excitement of the main draw of the day, the race of the two-year-old horses that had been cosseted, nurtured and groomed at horse farms around the nation. Most were placing sure bets on the two top contenders for the win, Twenty Grand and Mate, Laney Davis's horse.

Just before the start, the announcer called all to come to a stand for the singing of the state anthem, "Maryland, My Maryland". Jostling and rustling in their box began as all stood and sang along. Within short order after the song's end, the shot was fired and the race was on.

All stood to get the best view possible. Margaret could barely see through the opening due to taller people crowding her view. Once the race was over within a couple of minutes, there was much shouting and back slapping after the winner was loudly declared to be Mate. Laney Davis had a winner.

In the intermission before the final round of races, many began to make their way out of the box to get a closer view of the winner's circle. Margaret stood with the others. As she merged into the exit, she came face to face with Robert—and his date.

"Margaret..." his voice was strained.

Margaret gave a grim smile and said, "Hello, Robert."

As they continued to exit, Margaret was much too aware of the familiar smell of his cologne mixed with the stilted air between them. Once in the big hall, Margaret moved apart from him and the blonde on his arm as the crowd made their way to the winner's circle. She watched his form move deeper into the crowd, away from her.

By the time Margaret got closer, a line had already formed to congratulate the proud owner. The wreath of yellow lacquered in black had been placed over the horse in keeping with the tradition. Laney's red dress made a striking contrast with the wreath. Keith, mercifully, was nowhere to be seen.

Laney oozed with excitement to all her well-wishers and Margaret was no exception. "Hello Margaret!" she bellowed out.

After a few minutes of congratulatory sentiments, Margaret stood aside. Others behind her impatiently waited for their turn with Laney and her winning horse.

She returned to her box after getting an icy cold soda and settled in for the last of the day's races. A more relaxed pace took over and, in fact, some in the box had already departed. She watched to see if Robert and his colleagues would return to the box. It made her wistful when they didn't, but, at the same time, she wouldn't have to engage.

As the event drew to its finish, Margaret experienced an uncontrollable wave of fatigue. She knew it was a part of the process inside of her—the baby growing process. But she didn't want to embarrass herself by falling asleep in the box, especially if Robert's eyes were still around somewhere. She decided to bring her day to a close and gathered her belongings.

As she worked her way out of her seat, she felt the immediate relief of being out of the cramped space. Along her way to the parking field, she passed a few revelers partaking of libations in private little groups. But the event was by and large reaching its end.

At her car, she started to get into the driver's seat but paused. Her attention was caught by two approaching figures. As they neared, it was apparent that it was Keith, so inebriated that he could barely stand. The other figure was Robert, holding Keith up as he staggered across the parking field.

They came to a stop when they were in front of her. "He was getting out of hand in there," Robert said.

"Where are you putting him?"

"Laney Davis said to put him in her coupe." Robert gazed around and then said, "There it is."

Margaret grabbed Keith's other arm and helped Robert steer Keith over to a jaunty beige coupe. Robert lifted him under his arms and dumped him unceremoniously in the rear seat. "There you go, O'Keefe." His voice was bitter.

"It's kind of you to drag him out here, Robert."

"Yes, well..." his voice trailed off.

They both looked over at Keith. His eyes immediately closed with snorting noises coming out of his mouth. "Seems like old times," Margaret said.

"How so?"

"I guess I'm reminded of when we were working on Aunt Blanche's house and he came in stumbling drunk that day. You had to help him into a car then too. I was so embarrassed..."

"Are you embarrassed now?"

"Not in the least. He's none of my concern now."

The sun had almost set but Robert studied Margaret in the available light with a discerning gaze. "You look... There's something different about you."

She waved a hand. "I'm just tired. That's why I came out. Didn't want to embarrass myself by falling asleep at the races." She let out a fake and brittle laugh.

"Margaret, I feel like there is a lot unsettled between us, a lot we need to talk about."

"I tried. Remember?"

"Yes but..."

"But?"

"Things are different now. I've figured out a few things, I mean."

"Yes. I have too."

"For starters, I never stopped by to help you with the blueprints. To help you with what you found. Did you—"

She cut him off. "That was done. Leonard helped me."

"Oh well...what did you—"

She again stopped him. "Nothing. A blind alley." She had not told anyone about the gold. It was nobody's business. Nobody at all. Except for Judith of course.

"Oh, I'm sorry. I know you were hoping for that to come through."

A charged silence filled the space between them. There were any number of things to reveal to Robert but she didn't feel obligated to tell any of them.

Robert cut through it and said, "Look, could we talk?"

"Robert, you made your sentiments perfectly clear to me at the courthouse that day. Remember?"

"That was a mistake. The trial really... Well, it was all a mistake."

"That's one way to describe it, I guess."

He inhaled sharply and looked off into the field back towards the lights of the track. He turned back to her with resolve on his face. "Can you give me a ride back to the District?"

"What?"

"I'm without a ride. They left...earlier. I was hoping to..."

"To?"

"To find you."

Margaret's tiredness was overtaken instead with anticipation. Anticipation at why Robert wanted to find her.

She tossed him the keys. "You can drive."

CHAPTER THIRTY-SIX

As they drove away from Pimlico, lights from other cars passing by briefly illuminated the interior allowing Margaret a view of Robert's profile. A loaded silence filled the space until he spoke up. "I like your car."

He glanced her way with a smile, and, without being able to stop it, she smiled right back. "Yes. Yours is so nice, I decided I wanted one too."

They went back to a brief silence and Margaret had no doubt Robert was wondering how she was able to make such a purchase. But he didn't ask and she wasn't telling. At least... not yet.

Instead, he changed the subject and said, "I know of a diner a few blocks south that's probably still open. How about we pull in and have a chat?"

Margaret paused before answering. But there was no reason to have an internal debate about this. She wanted to know what he had to say before she spoke her piece. "Yes. That's fine."

Within several blocks, Robert pulled over into a parking lot off Park Heights Avenue with a cheeky neon sign for the High Stakes Diner. Inside, there were just a few stragglers, the dinner rush long over. Fans whirled along the ceiling, hitting them with a cool breeze. A waitress gestured towards an open booth.

As they took their seats across from each other, the tight quarters felt intimate to Margaret. The man in front of her didn't seem like the one who had so abruptly cut off their relationship. It felt like that stranger was gone and her Robert was back.

Once they had coffees and slices of pie in front of them, Robert began. "I had a vocation."

She stared at him with some confusion. "A what?"

He let out a whoosh of breath. "A vocation. In a lot of Catholic families, one son is sort of chosen to be sent into the priesthood. Sometimes they step up and decide on their own but most times they are told they are that person, that son."

"Wait, a priest?" She couldn't stop the giggle that escaped. "But Robert, I mean…"

He nodded. "I know. Not a good fit."

She held back from saying that a virile man such as himself would never last in such a situation. She had a feeling that even this bit of information about Robert was really just the tip of the iceberg. "So, you rebelled, I take it. And got married instead."

A cloud of deep sadness crossed over his face. "Yes, at a great cost. You met my sister briefly. I don't know if you picked up on the fact that my religion is deeply entwined with being a family member."

"Okay, I understand it a little, I guess. But how does it…"

"Tie into us?"

"Yes."

"Well, I rejected the priesthood, then I got married to a Catholic gal but it had to be annulled and the third possible strike would be marrying a non-Catholic, a divorcee to boot. To be blunt."

Margaret looked up at him and said sharply, "Who said

288

anything about marriage? I never asked for that." Her anger at him casting her aside had abated but had not gone away.

"I know that, Margaret, but for me, that was the natural progression."

"I see. So, the pressure of that... I mean, obviously I haven't met your family, your parents... How could I have done, until the divorce from Keith was final?" Margaret knew she was rambling but let the thoughts spill over. "I understand that. But I guess I didn't take into account that even after the divorce, the politics of this would be tricky. Maybe insurmountable."

"It's not on you, Margaret. It's on me. The logical side of me knows this is ridiculous. It's just family ties run deep."

Margaret gazed down at the table. Now that she knew more, did it change anything?

Robert continued talking. "And then this whole affair with Jocelyn and Bill."

She looked up at him with a direct stare. "You mean the gun?"

"It goes beyond the gun. It's...it's watching their relationship play out like it has. I'll be honest, it has made me even more jaded about marriage."

She took a sip of the piping hot coffee and then said, "Well, then. Here we are at another impasse."

"Is that what this is?" He gave her the crooked grin that always melted her heart.

"I mean, it's not for me. I've been clear about that."

"What about the trial and all that with the gun?"

"You know, now that the dust has settled, I have to wonder if your testimony changed anything up."

He looked at her, curious. "How so?"

"I think it was a popularity contest when all is said and done. Look at Bill now—people lined up at his door." She shook her head ruefully. "Who am I to say what you did was right or wrong?"

"Really? Because it seemed like you did have a lot to say about it."

She paused. "I guess I was grabbing onto anything I could to be angry at you about. For cutting me off, Robert. It was an easy outlet. But the proverbial smoking gun is between you and your God. That's not really my business, is it?"

"No, no, it's not. But what is your business is...you and me."

"What?"

He reached across the table and, with the lightest of touches, moved a wisp of hair back behind her ear. She felt a tingle of vibration at his touch. "I've made mistakes, I'm not going to deny it. But I want us together, Margaret. Whatever it takes. I'm in."

She sat back, gauging the man in front of her with a critical eye. After everything that had happened, it was hard to process. Could she just let it all go, forget about it and trust him?

EPILOGUE

Margaret breathed in the thick and sweet scents of summer as she drove south from Needham Forest into the District. As the traffic built up and became heavier, she handily guided her roadster around the potholes of the District's city streets over to the western side of town. It had been too long since her last visit to the family cemetery plot. There was a lot to catch them up on, especially her father and her Aunt Blanche.

Soon, the pillars that marked the entrance to Oak Hill Cemetery in Georgetown loomed into view. She pulled alongside the roadway that bordered the area where Magruder family members were buried. It was a storied section of the cemetery that included notable folks in the city's history and, strangely, also housed the graves of a small number of female Confederate spies. But, more importantly, it was a fine and private place for her aunt, her parents and other Magruders to rest in peace.

Margaret set the parking brake and headed into the plot with flowers picked up enroute. Having the place to herself didn't make her nervous. She liked it that way.

She brushed aside a few leaves before placing bouquets

beneath the standing stones. She stood back, thinking about all that had recently happened in her life. The trial, finding the gold, almost losing Robert but, especially, the soon-to-arrive new Magruder family member.

Margaret stared at her father's name on the marker. She placed a hand on top of the stone along with a fervent wish that she was doing him proud. Then she moved the few steps over to her aunt's gravestone which said "Here lie Blanche Magruder and her beloved daughter, Arabella. Rest in Peace".

Margaret spoke aloud, breaking into the peaceful silence. "If it's a girl, she will be named Marie. After you, Aunt Blanche. Your middle name. Just as I have your name as my middle name."

The slightest whiff of lilac drifted into the air surrounding Margaret. Or was it wisteria? Or was it all in her imagination?

She heard a car pull up behind hers alongside the berm and recognized its sound right away. In their most recent phone conversation, ones that they had fallen back into on a regular basis, Margaret mentioned she was planning a visit to the cemetery. Robert said he wanted to meet her there and they could go out for lunch afterwards.

Margaret looked up and watched him get out and lean against his car. He struck a match for a smoke and then stayed put, giving her the space he knew she needed. She gave him a wave before turning her gaze back to the stones. She placed her hand on her belly, now a noticeably sized bump, getting too hard to hide. But there was no need to hide it anymore. It was finally time to tell Robert a few things, and she was confident that it would all be perfectly okay.

THE END

ALSO BY MARY KENDALL

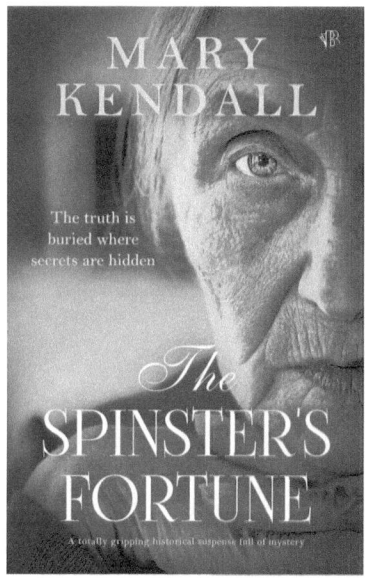

The Spinster's Fortune

In this gripping historical mystery, two women from the same family must face the truth in order to set themselves free.

BUY NOW

AUTHOR'S NOTE

In conducting genealogical research, I discovered my grandfather's involvement in a brother-attorney's trial for murder in the mid twentieth century. This scandalous love triangle murder in cold blood rocked Washington D.C. society for the better half of a year. As I delved deeper, details from the case such as "the pink brassiere" captured my imagination. I felt compelled to explore the machinations of this so-called middle-aged love triangle and the mystery of why it happened. I used fiction as the medium to do so.

As with any fictional account of a real-life event, it took artistic license to make it gel as a story. Thus, dates are changed to fit into the framework of Margaret and Robert's timeline (1930s era) which had already been established in its precursor, *The Spinster's Fortune*. There are other aspects of the timeline that differ, all in the interest of making the story work as a novel.

The real-life event ended up in a *Time Life* article with its own particular spin. If the reader is interested, it can be found in the archives of the Time Life organization at https://time.com/vault/issue/1944-03-06/page/23

I owe a debt of gratitude to those that assisted me along the

295

path of this story: my publisher, Bloodhound Books and their wonderful team including Tara Lyons, Clare Law and Hannah Deuce; my fabulous beta readers who always keep me in check, Nigel Lavin and Dart Clancy; and especially the grandfather I never met who, again, gave me the nugget of a story to write.

I also thank you, dear reader, for picking up this novel and giving it a chance.

A NOTE FROM THE PUBLISHER

Thank you for reading this book. If you enjoyed it please do consider leaving a review on Amazon to help others find it too.

We hate typos. All of our books have been rigorously edited and proofread, but sometimes mistakes do slip through. If you have spotted a typo, please do let us know and we can get it amended within hours.

info@bloodhoundbooks.com

www.ingramcontent.com/pod-product-compliance
Lightning Source LLC
Chambersburg PA
CBHW050552190726
48283CB00007B/2104